HEADLESS

The Ghost and the Mask, Book One

Headless

TRISTRAM LOWE

Mortimer & Ambrose

HEADLESS

The Ghost and the Mask, Book One

Copyright © 2016, 2020 Tristram Lowe

This is a work of fiction. Names, characters, places, and incidents either
are the product of the author's imagination or are used fictitiously. Any
resemblance to actual persons, living or dead, events, or locales is
entirely coincidental.

First Mortimer & Ambrose paperback: November 2016
Fifth printing (first series edition): November 2020

Cover design by MiblArt
Mask detail on cover by Michelle Tolo
Section separator art by achmadepp

ISBN: 978-1-946398-00-0

For Julia,
who keeps my head attached
and facing the right direction

CONTENTS

I
Sayaka

A noise came from the bedroom. It sounded like a thud and then something rolling. The closet door had probably fallen open again.

Sayaka lay on the couch entangled in a blanket. She did not want to get up, not in the slightest. Her boyfriend's golf clubs were in the closet, and the heavy bag would often lean against the door and push it open. A golf ball had likely tumbled out. Katsu hadn't even liked golf. He had only played because his boss did.

She heard another noise, softer this time, like boxes shifting. It was probably just her boyfriend's stuff being jostled when the golf bag fell. She extracted herself from the couch to investigate.

Sayaka hadn't opened the bedroom closet since Katsu's death a month before. All of his clothes were in there, and his stacks upon stacks of playing cards, which he had collected for years. There wasn't much room in the closet for anything else. Three suitcases and a dozen shoeboxes were filled and piled against the wall. He had bought them from every tourist spot and game store he had ever visited. He hadn't been able to leave a souvenir shop without at least three packs. Sayaka had often been frustrated with him spending so much money on cards when he had rarely taken her to dinner. "Cards are cheap!" he would say. "Dinner is much more expensive."

"Not when you buy ten packs!" she would counter. And sometimes he had spent up to 2000 yen on one pack. But he hadn't listened. At times she had believed his hobby was more important to him than her.

Sayaka kept her own clothes in a separate wardrobe. After Katsu had moved in, she removed her photo albums and her two boxes of old *Doraemon* comics and just let him have the whole closet.

Katsu's death had sent her into a terrible depression. She had found out about it initially from the news on her little black and white television in the kitchen. "Another man's body was found this morning at the train station here in Kofu," the reporter said. "And like the others found in recent months, it was only the body. This man also had no head."

Katsu had not come home the previous night. Often, he had to work late and would catch the last train from Matsumoto, where he was employed at a company that made high precision plastic products for light industrial use. He was in sales. It wasn't rare for him to not come home. His boss would always work late, and to Katsu, it was not only disrespectful but unthinkable to leave work before the boss. Some nights, when he missed the last train, he would stay with a friend. But he would always call.

She had known that the reporter was talking about Katsu. She felt it in her gut. She didn't answer her phone for two days. Finally the police came to the door. The body had been identified by fingerprints. The police questioned her extensively while she sat numbly answering. They wanted to know where she had been, what their relationship was like, and why she hadn't filed a missing persons report. In the end, they accepted that she was simply overwhelmed with loss and couldn't possibly be the killer.

Sayaka had returned to her job after a week leave of absence and now went through her days like a zombie. She declined all of her co-workers' offers to go to their local *izakaya* for drinks after work. Their weak attempts to console her with alcohol and mindless camaraderie made her want to be alone all the more.

Her apartment was empty, dusty, and quiet. The blinds hadn't been opened in weeks.

Her TV hadn't been turned on since its dreadful announcement of her boyfriend's death. It sat on the dumb waiter, dried ramen draped over the edge of the screen from when she had flung her bowl at it days later, recalling the broadcast. She wanted silence but couldn't find it. Even when it was quiet, the words replayed in her mind.

This man also had no head.

The neighbor's TV would sound through the wall some days. It didn't matter what it was playing. In between lines of cooking shows and anime episodes, she would hear it.

This man also had no head.

She would put pillows over her ears to try to block it out. She wanted to put a pillow over her mouth to smother herself.

If only that would work.

Sometimes, she sat in the dark quietly weeping. Three times, she had dropped to her knees to pray, but no words would come. So she would collapse to the floor, her long black straight hair pooling on the hardwood, mingling with the dust. Eventually she would fall asleep.

But she did not dream of Katsu.

She dreamt of samurai.

Her father had told her time and again that they were descendants of samurai from western Honshu. Sayaka's skin was far paler than normal. He claimed that was proof of their nobility.

When she was a girl, this had meant something to her. Now they were useless words, memories of a man she never saw anymore.

In her dream, her skin was white as chalk.

She stood in a vast garden surrounded by castle walls. She wore the finest kimono of pale purple with peonies adorning the wide sleeves. Bellflowers were intricately patterned across her chest, while irises blooming by a running stream encircled the hem.

Cherry blossoms fell all around her and blanketed the ground like pale pink snow. In her hand, she held a slender *naginata*, its long black handle ending in a short curved blade resting among the blossoms and dripping blood.

In front of her lay a dead crane.

She looked down at it with remorse, scanning its slender body and long neck. There was no wound that she could see. But it was clearly dead.

Had she killed it?

She looked up and saw people lining a balcony. She did not know them. Their faces were grave, dire and judgmental. They looked down at her with anger, with disappointment and disgust.

The flowers slipped from her kimono like leaves drifting from a tree, and the fabric's purple hue began to darken. It became deeper and deeper until it was nearly black. She fell to her knees, dropping her bloody weapon, and cradled the crane in her arms, but it dissolved into worms and ash. It fell through her fingers, repelling the cherry blossoms, which retreated from it like feathers in a sudden gust of wind.

She looked up and saw streams of light burning through the castle walls like fire through paper, burning through the people, who seemed oblivious to it. Playing cards fell through the gaps in the walls. Queens and aces, kings and jacks, clubs, diamonds, spades and hearts of all numbers fell to the ground where the cherry blossoms had just been. But now they landed in ash and dirt, and were eaten by the worms.

Sayaka hated that she didn't dream of Katsu, only of his damned cards. She resented her father for filling her head with the nonsense about samurai. It took up the dreamscape that her dead lover should be occupying.

It was Sunday, the day they used to walk together in Maizuru Castle Park, the day they would get crepes with ice cream and lay on the grass, the only day of the week they had time to be intimate. They would lie in bed afterward, dreaming of a house together on an island somewhere. They would have a farm, and maybe children.

She knew that just picking up his golf clubs would make her cry, but she had to do it eventually. She had been sleeping on the couch since it happened. She had avoided the bedroom altogether, but she knew she had to deal with it now. He was gone.

She had to accept that.

Opening the bedroom door, she discovered she was right. The closet door was wide open and Katsu's olive green golf bag was prostrate on the floor, its clubs splayed out and pointing accusations at her. A battered golf ball had rolled most of the way across the hardwood and stopped just where she now stood.

Steeling herself to the task in front of her, she picked up the golf ball and took one stiff step toward the closet.

She stopped abruptly. Someone was in there.

A large figure was hunched over in the closet. The shock of it made her breath catch. Someone had broken in. But worse than that, this intruder appeared to be in full samurai armor. It was like a figure from her dream had come to life. He barely fit inside the closet; hanging clothes were draped against the complex pieces of the *yoroi* carapace. A sheathed katana protruded from his left hip like a huge black tongue. His menacing *kabuto* helmet—a leering many-toothed dragon face adorned its front with ears like reptilian wings and twisting horns spiking upward—had been removed and placed next to the golf bag. His focus was intent on the contents of a shoebox. He sifted through the playing cards within, admiring each pack.

Fear froze Sayaka for a moment, but she quickly felt violated and angry. Her boyfriend was dead, and now someone was looting through his cards! She no longer cared that this intruder was in armor. *The freak must have climbed through the window.* She noticed it was wide open.

Without thinking, she shouted at the armored stranger and hurled the golf ball at him. "Stop it! Leave those alone! They're not yours!"

The samurai in the closet lurched upward, banging his head on the shelf above him, and turned to face Sayaka, a gruesome scowl of hatred embossed on his face. It was otherworldly, too pronounced to be real. It was a face of pure fury glaring at her. A pack of cards fell from his large, gauntleted hands.

The face was gray and bloodless. The teeth that showed through its scowl were an awful yellow with thick grime in the gaps. The eyes were wet, almost teary, but the pupils were a dead and lifeless black; no human soul resided there.

The black hair was matted and unkempt. So often had she told Katsu to brush his hair. It had always looked a wreck, but he had never cared.

Katsu?

The cheeks were hanging; the skin looked like burlap; the eyes were empty, but it was Katsu's face. It was unmistakably his face twisted into that angry, unfamiliar grimace. But it was most definitely not his body. The body that wore her lover's head was much larger than Katsu's. He had always been on the scrawny side. And besides, his body had been cremated three weeks ago.

Sayaka stood, unable to move. Her love had come back to her. But this reincarnation of him was unforgivably wrong. Her guts begged to cry out, but nothing came. Her lips did not even move, save a tiny, almost imperceptible quiver.

Then, in one swift and graceful movement, the katana's blade flashed from its scabbard and severed the air on either side of Sayaka's neck. In the same movement, the samurai with Katsu's face shook the drops of blood from the blade and re-sheathed it silently.

At first, it felt only like a cool breeze had passed just beneath her ears, then a tickle in her throat like the start of a cold. Then she was dizzy and the room spun around her until she was staring up at what looked like her own clothes still on her body, jeans and a lime green t-shirt. A fountain of red pulsed from her empty neck. Then her body collapsed. And her eyes went dark.

2

An Assignment

Akio sat at his desk looking over the front page of the *Dainichi Daily*, which had just come off the press. "FIFTH HEADLESS BODY FOUND" read the top headline. Underneath was the subtitle "With The Fourth Head!"

He pushed against his desk so his chair rolled back and he spun out of it. He walked three cubicles over and dropped the newspaper on a computer keyboard belonging to a smartly dressed woman with black hair, cropped short.

"They found a head," he stated matter-of-factly and leaned against her desk, not looking at her directly. He imagined this is what somebody cool would do.

"I know, Akio. I wrote the article." She pushed the paper away, slid her black, full-rimmed glasses up slightly on her nose and continued typing.

"That's wild." Akio turned his head to look at her over his shoulder.

Her hair caught the fluorescent light like a polished idol. Worship was not out of the question. Words sped across her reflection in the computer screen, an unstoppable plague spreading too fast to outrun. Her thin lips were pressed tightly into an expression that might have been endearing in a focused child, but was unnerving in this fierce, pertinacious and incomparable woman.

Masami Sato.

She had been Akio's obsession since he started working at the newspaper. It wasn't that she was a love interest—he was sure he would find himself ineffective if that situation ever presented itself—but because she was such an anomaly to all the other Japanese women he knew. The black fire in her eyes and her sharp cheekbones had grabbed his attention, but it was her deadly seriousness that wouldn't let him go. She had the grace and demeanor of a samurai sword. She was beautiful but dire, and would surely cut him if he crossed her. She was one of very few women that had been admitted into the very insular and very male press clubs. She had an indefatigable work ethic, and her skill with words was poetic and precise. It wasn't that there weren't other hard-working women in the office, it wasn't that the other women didn't focus and meet their deadlines—though none of them were in a press club—but they would smile, at least sometimes. They would giggle with co-workers when the boss wasn't around. They would come in a little hungover some days. They were actually people. Not robotic goddesses of doom.

To catch Masami smiling was a nearly impossible feat. It was something Akio worked at though—a life goal, one could say. It was like trying to not only catch a glimpse of the legendary, earthshaking catfish, Namazu, swimming along the shoreline, but of Namazu doing a full, twisting, double backflip with a perfect, splashless rip entry into the water. It was a little more than unheard of.

She worked long hours and hard. This was also not unusual for any typical Japanese employee, but she was relentless. Often that "hard work" by others really consisted of just wasting time interspersed with binge work when the boss was looking. Not for Masami. She was the real deal, in spades. And it paid off. Her articles were excellent, well praised, and often landed the front page. She demanded higher pay than Akio did by far, despite the salary gap which was all too common between men and women.

"The head of the fourth victim was found with the body of the fourth victim's girlfriend," Akio said, turning away again and folding his arms. "That is insane."

"I'm glad you find my articles so unhinged." Her fingers flew across the keyboard, as if they were working independently of the rest of her, a crack team on a highly time-sensitive mission with no extraction plan. She still had not looked at Akio.

"Unhinged!" Akio spun around to smile broadly at Masami. "See, I would never think to use a word like that! That's why you make the big bucks!" His admiration was genuine. "But I don't think your articles are *unhinged*. Not the writing anyway. It's just this whole crazy story. What do you think is really happening out there? I mean Kofu isn't that far from Tokyo. Someone's out there slicing heads off! And obviously there's some kind of connection. I mean, the guy and his girlfriend? And now the guy's head? It's so completely nuts."

"Whoever's doing it certainly is." Masami seemed uninterested and typed even faster. The sound of her fingers attacking the computer keyboard filled the room for a long moment.

Akio remained by her desk as she typed. He felt stuck there. He had had a goal in mind when he walked over. It wasn't just to pester her like it often was. He had a mission of his own, however ill thought-out. He knew he had to say something or go back to his own desk. But he had stood there too long for either option to make sense. Clearly he was hanging around for a reason. If he left, it would feel like he failed by not even trying. If he spoke up now, it would be obvious that he was petrified by what he wanted to say and had to build up the courage. He couldn't win.

What's new?

It wouldn't be the first time. He decided to just get it over with. He took a deep breath to steady himself and then tried to turn it into a casual yawn when it felt too apparent that he was attempting to calm his nerves. He gazed away from Masami's desk, trying to appear as disinterested as possible, and said, "I heard a rumor that you were heading out that way soon to try to catch some more leads."

Time slowed as he waited for a reply. Had he been casual enough? Had he made it sound like he couldn't care less? He stared across the room feeling each second of his life drain away. The third story view of Chiyoda Ward in the heart of Tokyo returned his gaze doubtfully from one wall of windows. Skyscrapers loomed above, their glass reflecting the newspaper's building back at him.

Her typing suddenly stopped.

"I know what you're going to ask, so don't bother."

The typing resumed.

"Oh come on!" Akio turned toward Masami again. He caved. He couldn't help it, his tactics thwarted. He would simply revert to begging like usual. "We'd make a great team! I could hold down the head-chopping maniac while you interview him!"

"Not going to happen." Masami's tone cut like a katana.

"But I know Judo. I could protect you."

Masami sneered and rolled her eyes. "Powell is coming with me. Tanaka's already approved it."

"The American?" Th at stung. "What right does he have to go along?"

"Only that he's our best photographer, Akio. Leave it alone." Masami powered down her computer and stood. "I'm going to lunch. Don't follow me."

Akio lay on his bed in his minuscule apartment. Th e white wall next to him was covered in newspaper photographs. Many of the photos were Powell's. He was good. *Really good.* He knew how to capture that perfect moment. Akio knew his own work wasn't quite up to par, but if he only had a chance to capture a bigger story, then the editor might take notice. He always got stuck shooting grade school plays and public gardens.

This Kofu assignment was exactly what he needed. A serial killer was out there collecting heads. And apparently he was tormenting the victim's loved ones with them. He couldn't think of anything more disturbing. But he also couldn't think of a better opportunity for him to gain some recognition as a photographer.

This was a big story. Really big. It wasn't just current news; it was popular culture. And it was scary as hell. It was something people would not be able to ignore. It fulfilled their desire for knowledge, praise, fear, and entertainment all in one go. It would soon overtake every online social network feed in Japan. It would be unstoppable. And his name could be under the photos that accompanied the articles.

But how?

Scanning the wall, he gazed over some photos he had taken that were tacked up next to the news clippings. Masami, with her usual sneer of disdain, filled the frame of one. "Go obsess over someone who cares," she had said after he had taken that shot.

"I'm not obsessing, Miss High & Mighty," he had retorted. "It's a party. I'm trying to catch you having fun, but that's like trying to catch a fish in a tree."

Next to that was a shot of the group at last year's *bonenkai*, the end of the year party. There was Powell, standing out like a strawberry in an ink well, white-as-a-ghost pale, with shocking red hair, surrounded on all sides by black hair and black eyes. His own green eyes were trained on Keiko, the cute, petite, young woman in accounting.

Wait a minute. Akio had seen this picture so many times, but he had never really paid attention to Powell. His focus had always been on Masami. She was in the picture as well, leaning over to Uzuki, another co-worker, as if telling a secret. It almost looked like she was having a good time. Akio had stared at that photo many times, trying to decipher what that secret might be. *What are Masami's secrets?* But Powell, he hadn't noticed.

Now it all made sense. Powell frequently made trips to accounting, supposedly to double check his hours or ask questions about his retirement plan. Everyone in the office thought he was just paranoid about money, just a greedy American. But that wasn't it! It was Keiko! Something was going on between those two.

And it was perfect. The light that had gone on in Akio's head just got brighter.

The next morning, Masami stormed over to Akio's desk, her razor cheekbones white with anger. "What the hell kind of trick did you pull?"

Akio looked up, putting on his most innocent face. "Trick? Whatever are you referring to?"

He tried hard to hide a smile. And equally hard to not run.

"You know damn well what I'm referring to! How did you get on the Kofu assignment with me?" Her eyes were like black daggers searing his retinas. "What happened to Powell?"

"I'm on the Kofu assignment?" He feigned ignorance. "Wow, I don't know."

"Knock it off, Akio. I know you know about it. I just came from Tanaka's office. What made Powell suddenly request a holiday and why in hell did he recommend you to replace him?"

Akio's smile slipped out, along with a nearly inaudible giggle. This unnerved Masami so much that her bottom lip quivered. She stamped back to her desk, fuming.

The grin spread across Akio's face like floodwaters through a burst dam.

Victory is mine.

3
Kofu

"You know, I don't mind driving." Akio grinned over at Masami from the passenger side of her black Honda Logo. The sun was low in the sky and in their eyes. They were rarely off work early enough to see the sunset, but Tanaka had shooed them out the door early.

"I don't want you dragging in Kofu tomorrow," he had said. Most likely it was because he wanted to cut their hours down a bit to help compensate for the trip expenses.

Masami ignored Akio's comment. She was silent for a long while, but something was clearly bothering her. Then again, it always looked like something was bothering her. Akio was pretty sure that this time, he was at the heart of the matter. Eventually she spoke.

"Funny how Powell suddenly decided to ask Keiko on a weekend getaway to Chichi Island. And at the last second," she said sarcastically. "Don't your parents own an inn there?"

"I don't know what you're talking about," Akio answered quickly —too quickly to not be full of it. *Damn it. I'm made.* He turned away to gaze out the window, hoping it would cover his lie and stifle the smile that threatened to spasm across his face.

"Whatever," hissed Masami. "Your deviousness may have gotten you on this assignment, but that doesn't mean we have to get along.

Just keep to yourself and do your job. We are investigating a dangerous serial killer. Any wrong steps and we could become victims." She gave him a dire look as she momentarily took her eyes off the road. "But if you do anything to sabotage this, I'll cut your head off myself."

The rest of the ninety-minute ride was mostly silent, with Masami ignoring Akio's feeble attempts at light conversation. He tried hard to limit his sarcasm, but he was restless and couldn't help himself. He began having conversations with the silence as if she were responding.

"It's nice getting away from the office, isn't it? Yeah, I prefer working in the field. You too? Cool . . . did you hear about how Ota got punched by that crooked politician? What was his name? Yeah, I don't remember either . . . It's been getting a little warmer at night lately. No, I know. Summer is almost here. Time to start carrying a sweat rag around. Oh yeah, that's true; you don't sweat. I forgot. Must be nice."

When she remained vigilant and quiet, he finally gave up. He really did want her to like him but couldn't seem to stop himself from being annoying.

The drone of the expressway was the only music as they headed west on the Chuo Expressway. At times they could see Mount Fuji in the distance, its symmetrical cone looming over the smaller hills in front of it. The snow was disappearing from its cap as the weather turned warm. But it was soon lost behind retaining walls and those same hills it dominated as buildings gave way to lush green slopes of trees.

They passed an idyllic peach orchard on their left, bathed in pink flowers that would soon be replaced with delectable fruit. A breeze passed through the trees, tickling the leaves and making the flower petals flutter like a million butterflies stretching their wings. Akio sighed at the beauty and wondered if Masami felt the same lift in her spirits. When he glanced her way, however, she was only staring forward at the road, seemingly oblivious. Her eyes were distant. It suddenly occurred to him that she wasn't wearing glasses. He had never seen her without them. He thought it should make her more vulnerable, her eyes not shielded behind glass, but somehow it seemed to make *him* feel more vulnerable. Her evil robot stare was uncapped and that much more deadly.

He leaned back, his head against the window, and tried to relax. He was equally thrilled and terrified. He had won his way onto this assignment with the impenetrable Masami Sato. Working with her, and on this story, could be a huge boost for his career. But there were very clear reasons to be scared witless too. He wasn't sure which was worse—the head-chopping killer or Masami. Either one could destroy him.

The last leg of their journey was wordless and calm. Alternating thoughts of glory and bloody doom filled Akio's head. He wondered what Masami was thinking. Probably about a way to send him back to Tokyo.

Akio was socially awkward. He didn't really have any close friends. Sometimes he just couldn't shut up, even though he knew he should. He talked when he was nervous. And he was nearly always nervous. He'd probably be annoyed traveling with himself too.

He tried to sleep but was wide awake. He just watched the scenery slip by and stifled any urge he had to talk. It wasn't easy.

Finally they exited the rolling green hills as the last of the sunlight drained from the sky, and entered the wide basin that cradled Kofu. Just to the south, Mount Fuji peeked out from behind gray-orange clouds to watch their approach.

But Akio didn't see it. His eyes were on the buildings appearing at the edge of the road—the small houses and the round, white love hotel with the English word "LOVE" mounted on the roof in big capital letters. He resisted looking at Masami and making a wisecrack suggestion that they stop there. Th en the view thickened with apartments, convenience stores, car dealerships, and a used clothing store. *Why would anyone want to wear used clothes? Yuck.*

The entire time, Masami's gaze was dead ahead.

Akio didn't sleep well. He awoke in the hotel room with the patterned yellow bedspread twisted around his mid-section and legs. The sun glowed through white curtains, and he rolled away from the window. His reflection stared back at him from the TV screen next to the bed. He looked terrible.

He put on the complimentary slippers and shuffled to the bathroom, which was small but functional. The blurred imagery of disturbing dreams still swirled in his head. After a shower, he dressed, put the slippers back on, and headed down to the lobby.

It was a very clean lobby. The tiled floor reflected the sunlight into Akio's still sleepy eyes. A beige couch and a couple of chairs sat across from the front desk. Two guest computers flanked a printer on a counter in front of the wide windows. These were evidently there for those travelers who hadn't brought their laptops. Akio and Masami both had, and thankfully there was Wi-Fi in the room. He couldn't bear the thought of having to upload his photos to the lobby computers and then emailing them to himself as backups.

There were some framed photos on the wall—one of Mount Fuji, two of the nearby Shosenkyo Gorge featuring a tall, natural granite spire and a streaming waterfall, respectively, and another of a statue of the samurai warlord, Takeda Shingen, gleaming greenish gray under a bright sun. A miniature version of the same statue sat on the highly polished registration counter next to a trickling fountain resembling a wavy ladder of stones.

Akio headed for the complimentary breakfast: miso soup, rice balls, some muffins. He went for a tea to start.

As the hot water poured from the spout, Masami exited the elevator. She was smartly dressed, shoes on, and adorned with the usual scowl. She saw Akio.

"I need something more substantial," she said, glancing at the rice balls. "There's a Jonathan's diner around the corner." She strode out the door, not waiting for a reply.

Am I supposed to go with her? Akio didn't know. *Why doesn't she just say? Dammit.* He abandoned his tea and began to follow her. But then he realized he still had his slippers on. *Dammit!* He pounded the elevator button and went back to his room to retrieve his shoes.

At the diner, Masami was already half way through her first cup of coffee. She didn't look up when he walked in, but there was a menu placed across from her on the table. So Akio assumed she had been expecting him to show. *Or did she just put her menu there?* It was fronted to where a person across from her would sit. So he assumed she must have ordered already and given her menu back. *Hmm . . . so she was either insightful, knowing I would follow, or hopeful that I would. I'll never figure her out.*

He sat and smiled at her. "Good morning!" he said in a chipper tone.

She looked at him and said nothing. She was red-eyed and distant. It was clear she hadn't slept any better than he had. He wondered if her dreams had been as bad as his.

Akio was weary but eager to get started. He had the youthful enthusiasm of a college student who was excited to begin a vacation despite having partied too much the night before. But there hadn't been any partying or even drinking—only nightmares of headless victims searching blindly for their missing braincases.

He passed over the American-looking offerings on the menu and ordered a combo that included a small omelet with heavy ketchup, some rice, miso soup, salted and dried mackerel, and a small bowl of slimy okra. He asked for green tea to replace the one he had abandoned at the hotel. Masami had ordered eggs, bacon, and sausage with a side of french fries. She refilled her coffee twice before the food came.

"We make a good team, you and I," Akio trilled. "I think this is the start of something really special."

"Special in that it will only happen once," Masami hammered back, pushing away the bowl of okra that had been dropped too close to her plate. "Don't start drooling."

"Drooling?" Akio feigned aghast. "It's not like I'm attracted to you or anything. I just thought it would be nice to work with an award-winning writer, that's all."

She gave him an icy stare but didn't respond, his compliment falling dead on the table. Of course he was attracted to her, in a kind of masochistic way. He had just gotten defensive and tried to make her feel bad. He had reflexively tried to make her feel guilty for seeing his true feelings. But he was terrible at hiding those. And she knew his games too well. It wasn't the first time.

"Do you want some?" Akio said pointing to his rejected bowl of okra.

Another cold stare, then back to her coffee.

Akio scooped his hand around the bowl, lifted it to his mouth and started slurping up the snot-like mixture with his chopsticks.

"So when are we meeting with the cops?" Akio asked, a mouth full of slimy green.

"We're not."

"Hmm?" He stopped mid-chew, perplexed.

Masami let out a small, irritated sigh. She was clearly reluctant to tell him anything at all, but evidently realized she had to. He was in this with her, whether she liked it or not. She answered quickly. "I spoke with them on the phone. They don't want us here. Don't want us *messing with their investigation*. So, no, we are not meeting the police." She paused and then added, "Not yet anyway. Not until we get on their good side."

"So where are we going?"

"To the crime scene, of course."

Akio was confused—not that it took much. "But if they don't want us here, won't going behind their backs get us on their bad side?"

Masami looked at him like he was some far inferior species. "Not if we get them some good information," she replied tersely.

Just before 7:30 a.m., they arrived at the apartment complex where the woman, Sayaka Inawa, had been murdered. It was one of two four-story white buildings with ice blue roofs that sat on a flat square of ground next to a winding irrigation channel. The buildings were boxy structures with tiny balconies, built in the 1960s for quick tenancy and with little aesthetic insight. Staircases accessed the upper floors at three intervals in each building.

A breeze caught Masami's hair and flung it over the bridge of her nose. She plucked it back, and Akio thought he almost caught a smile under that grim beauty she carried like a blade. He smiled back at her anyway and felt the morning sun begin to warm the air. He thought about what a nice day it would be if they hadn't been there to ask people about a serial killer.

A stone-faced man in a black suit and tie hurried past them. Masami turned on her reporter guise and asked him quickly, "Do you know anything about the woman who was murdered here three days ago? Can you talk to us for a minute?"

"I don't know anything. I'm late for work," was his only terse offering. He walked away even quicker than he had come, legs jerking forward as if he wanted to run but didn't know how.

They decided to knock on some doors in the building to see if they could find out anything from the neighbors. Most people were unwilling to talk, if they came to the door at all. The last apartment they tried was directly across the stairwell from the victim's door, which had two pieces of police tape tacked across it. An old woman answered and beckoned them inside as if they were favorite relatives who had made a surprise visit.

She was a small, stocky woman with a beatific smile. Her gray hair was tightly tied in a bun, as if in an attempt to pull the wrinkles from her face. Over tan trousers, she wore a pale blue blouse that gave a pleasant but worn impression, much like the woman herself. She insisted they sit, and offered tea, which they accepted graciously.

Her apartment was cluttered but lovingly arranged. Souvenirs and postcards from around the world were placed conspicuously on the many shelves. A thick smell of jasmine pervaded the air.

Masami quickly got past the pleasantries and began her polite interrogation of the woman, who had introduced herself as Junko.

"I was home on the day it happened," Junko began.

"Did you see or hear anything?" Masami asked, her eyes fixed intently on the elderly woman.

"Yes, I did. I didn't see anything, but I did hear shouting from next door." Junko squinted, and her face pinched tighter as if it helped her to recall. "I knew the girl lived alone, poor thing. She had lost her sweetheart so recently. He was such a nice young man, always polite when I saw him on the stairwell. He would help me with my groceries when he was home. Four flights is a long way up for my old bones, though I manage fine. I go up them twice a day just for the exercise."

She smiled at them both, and Akio couldn't help but smile back.

"But you'll excuse me, this isn't about my daily walking." She paused for a sip of tea. "When I heard the shouting, I wondered who she could be shouting at, assuming that she was probably by herself and just expressing grief. There had been some crashes and clamors before—since young Katsu had died, that is. But this time seemed different. Something felt wrong, if you know what I mean. It was more than the usual fit. I thought I should check on her. I went over and banged on her door. I called out, 'Is everything all right?' But all I heard back was a thump and some scurrying about. Then there was nothing."

"What did you do then?" Masami asked.

"Well," the woman cocked her head, thinking. "I didn't do anything at first. I figured whatever happened was none of my business, and poor Sayaka was probably just being emotional. I went back to my apartment. But something still didn't feel right, so I eventually called the police and told them they might want to look into it."

"And did they?" Masami asked, most likely just to keep the woman talking.

"Yes, they did. They sent a couple handsome, uniformed men over. They talked to me briefly and then knocked on Miss Inawa's door just like I had. And they got the same response too. Nothing. So they got the manager to come up and let them in. That was when they found her. Poor girl. She was so young, and had gone through so much tragedy already."

"It is truly awful," Masami agreed.

"The last few days have been busy, busy around here. Not a moment's peace."

"We're sorry to have added to the interruptions," Masami said.

"No, dear," Junko replied. "You're doing your job, and I'm happy to help."

Masami asked a few general questions about the neighborhood, and if there were any suspicious tenants, odd people or unusual activity in the area. She asked if Sayaka Inawa had had any visitors in the past few weeks, and if the young woman had behaved strangely at all, considering she was already dealing with loss.

The answer to all of these questions was, "No, not that I've noticed." The woman seemed to have nothing else to offer.

When Masami stood, Akio did too. They thanked the woman for her time and hospitality, and moved toward the front door.

"One last question," Masami said before Junko opened the door for them. "Were you afraid? I'm sure you'd heard of the previous murders."

"No, dear," said Junko, her wrinkled smile brightening the entryway. "The good spirits watch over me."

They exited the apartment to look again at the police tape across the landing. It read, "Crime Scene – Do Not Cross." The door was shut. It appeared that no one was working the scene at the moment. It was still too early in the day.

Akio followed Masami back down the four flights of stairs to the building manager's apartment. He greeted them indifferently and seemed unimpressed by their press IDs. "The police haven't closed the crime scene yet," he said. "I'm sure they'll come back later today."

"They'd better," Masami said. "That's what they told us. We spoke with the detective last night. We were supposed to meet up with them here, but I guess we're a bit early."

Akio clenched his jaw to prevent the shock from spasming across his face. *She's lying through her teeth.*

"Do you mind if we head on in now?" she asked.

The manager drew in a slow breath and seemed torn between talking to them and getting back to whatever game show was playing on the television in the other room.

"They said to not let anyone in," he finally grumbled.

"I know, they always say that. But this is your place, right? Don't you call the shots here? It's not illegal to let someone into your own place."

"That's true." It was unclear if the man was actually the owner or simply the manager, but Masami's insinuation seemed to make him feel like he owned the building regardless. He half smiled but then cocked his head toward the television as if trying to listen to it and Masami at the same time. The television appeared to be winning as laughter burst from the TV audience and he grinned in response.

"Look, I can make this easier," Masami said. She pulled out a 5,000-yen note and held it toward the man. "We have a very busy day, and we want to get this wrapped up. Who knows when the police will actually get here so they can approve what you could've approved this whole time."

The television held less interest as the manager looked at the banknote. It wasn't a lot of money, but it could afford him basic groceries for a week, a nice meal out alone, or a couple years' subscription to *Shonen Jump*, a stack of which lay on a low table nearby. "Okay," he finally said. "I'll take you up." He snatched the yen from her hand and led them up the stairwell.

Akio's head was spinning. Masami had just blatantly lied and then bribed the manager. *Who is this woman?* He thought he didn't know her before. Now she was even more an enigma.

They arrived back on the fourth floor. The manager unlocked the door and excused himself for a cigarette, letting them know he wouldn't be far. They ducked under the tape.

The door opened on a tiny entryway, one side lined with small shelves sectioned into squares containing mostly shoes, but also a few hats, gloves, scarves and a tattered stack of manga novels. Several umbrellas stood in a bucket next to the shelves. Slippers were set on a woven green mat on the floor. It was a lived-in place, a place someone had dug in and called home.

Removing their shoes, they stepped over the slippers and entered the apartment. The air was stale and heavy with loss. They scanned the front room. Akio half expected a ghost to jump out from behind a door to tell them to go away, that they shouldn't be there. But none appeared, and the two of them crowded in past the tiny entryway.

"Well, here she is," Akio said. "The master at work." He said it in amazement, but not without admiration. "No wonder your stories are better than everyone else's. Here I thought I was the rebellious one."

"We don't have time to be denied entry by the police right now," she said. "We'll connect with them later. Right now, just don't touch anything."

"Aye aye, captain."

To their left was a sink just outside of two doors, both of which were open and showed a toilet and a bathtub respectively. To their right was a small kitchen, the counters cluttered with emptied Styrofoam ramen bowls and half-empty boxes of sweets. A small television sat on a cheap metal-framed dumbwaiter in the corner. Dried noodles hung across the edge of it and part of the screen, as if someone had thrown them there.

Past the kitchen, but also adjoining it, was the living area. A short couch covered with tousled blankets and a pillow sat against the far wall. A low table displayed more empty ramen take-out bowls. Two yellow evidence markers sat among them like little numbered sandwich boards, one atop a ringed stain, and one just next to it.

Across from the living area, the door to the bedroom stood open. A numbered yellow tag was near the doorknob. Akio knew from Masami's article that the bedroom was where the murder had happened.

She started in that direction, but Akio stepped in her way. "Maybe I should check it out for you first." He didn't really want to, but it was the right thing to do. He had to show he was a man.

"Get out of the way," she snapped and shoved him aside. After a moment surveying the scene within, she stepped into the room.

"Masami!" breathed Akio in a whispered shout. "What are you . . . ?"

"Shush," she snapped back. "I want to take a closer look."

"You wanna add yourself to the suspect list with your footprints in there?" Akio stepped closer and looked into the room.

"I think they'll be looking for those ones," she said, indicating obvious imprints in the middle of a large, dark stain marring the wood floor, another yellow marker next to it, this one with a metric ruler printed on it. The stain was in an oblong shape, like an impossible Rorschach test, a thousand satellites of which had spattered the walls, bed and floor around it. More yellow tags. A numbered marker sat next to the stain, and another was in the stain itself next to a tiny round blank spot. Yet another was nearby where there was a gap in the floor spatter. Akio's eyes followed the narrow hardwood floor slats back to an overturned golf bag, aimed at him like a huge mouth with long crooked teeth—a monster coming out of the closet. Playing cards were strewn about the floor. Shoeboxes had been turned over and their guts emptied, fifty-two cards at a time. Little yellow numbered standees accompanied it all.

Masami stood by the window, which she had pushed open. She was peering out of it and down the wall.

There was a pungent smell that hung in the room—death and some other faint odor. A wisp of sulfur stench, like a recently lit match, lightly played on Akio's nostrils. He had seen murder scenes before, a couple of times, and he didn't think he'd ever get used to it. The hate that could cause such an act made his stomach turn. *How can someone hate anyone enough to take their life?* He'd been angry before, plenty. There were people he thought he had wanted to hurt. People that had hurt him. But killing them was out of the question. Often, after he'd reflect on those feelings, he would just end up blaming himself. *Maybe I deserved it somehow.*

But then he would hear his grandma's voice.

You deserve good things, A-chan. And right now, you deserve mochi. And she would give him a treat of *mochi*, filled with sweet red bean paste. It always made him smile.

She had also said something else whenever something awful like this had happened in the news. *One cannot hate others unless one hates oneself first. And the reverse. One cannot love another unless one loves oneself first. So don't hate yourself, little A-chan. Be full of love.*

He didn't hate himself. Maybe thanks to Grandma. But loving himself? That might be a stretch.

He looked at Masami, her hard eyes scanning every detail of the room, absorbed in the task at hand.

Is there any love in her heart? he wondered. *Because it sure doesn't look like it.*

He moved carefully past the bedroom doorway. *Footprints be damned.*

Masami was looking at a photo on the nightstand of a couple standing with trees behind them, smiles on their faces. The young woman's head rested against the young man's shoulder. They were happy. These were the same faces from the paper, from a photo that Masami had probably gotten from the press club for her article. This was a different photo, but the faces were the same. They had been so impersonal then. But now Akio was standing in their bedroom. A room where they had lived, slept, made love, argued, planned for the future, and ultimately where one of them had been murdered.

He saw Masami give a little shiver and her eyes twitched slightly. She breathed sharply out of her nose and stepped back toward the bedroom door.

This is affecting her. Maybe she is human.

"The initial police report said the front door had been locked and there was no sign of forced entry," she said, not looking at Akio. "Since the murderer dropped the head of the woman's boyfriend, he or she was obviously the boyfriend's murderer as well. Therefore it wouldn't be a stretch to assume that the murderer would now possess the key." She looked over toward the window. "Then again," she continued, "maybe she had just left the window open."

"Yeah," Akio chimed in as he walked over to look at the view himself. "But we're on the fourth floor. Even if the window was open already, how would the murderer get up here? It's a sheer drop."

She gave him a queer look that he couldn't decipher. It felt like she didn't see him.

She went on. "And why would the murderer trade out the boyfriend's head for the woman's?"

He started to answer, but she continued before he could make a sound, leaving him with his mouth half open.

"He's never done that before. The heads of the previous victims haven't been found. So it makes more sense that he didn't mean to drop it. Something made him leave it behind. But why would he be carrying it in the first place?"

"Maybe he liked to torture his victims with it," Akio said, startling Masami. She seemed to have come out of some kind of trance. Perhaps she hadn't realized she had been thinking out loud.

"Yeah," she said, regaining her composure. "Maybe. Maybe he's becoming more attached to his victims. Maybe he thought she would want to see her boyfriend before she died."

Akio grimaced at her.

"Morbid, I know," she added, "but we're obviously not dealing with a humanitarian here. According to the police report," she continued, apparently more eager to discuss the possibilities with him, "the boyfriend's head appeared more preserved than it should have been for being dead that long."

"Maybe he kept it in the freezer," Akio suggested.

"The reporting officer said it looked like it had been dead for maybe a few days. Except for the eyes. They looked as fresh as the victim's. They were still moist."

"Weird." Akio got a shiver down his spine. "And more than a little creepy."

He heard a sound from the front of the apartment. *Oh no, the police. We're screwed now. I hope she has a plan to get us out of this.*

"How's it going in there?" It was the manager.

Akio and Masami both slipped out of the bedroom. She headed toward the front door and Akio followed. There were no police to be seen. "I guess we're done for now," she said to the manager. "We'll have to come back later. Got another story waiting."

"Okay." Th e manager seemed relieved. Th e two journalists squeezed past him in the entryway breaching an invisible cloud of smoked cigarette stench.

"Hey," Masami said to him as they passed, "don't tell the detective we were here. I don't want him to feel bad that he was late. We'll give him a call later."

"I understand," the manager said. "You got it."

As they walked back to Masami's car, Akio asked, "Why didn't you tell me about that police report before? I thought we were working on this together."

"You're just the photographer, remember?" She loved putting him down. But there was something else about that statement that . . .

"Dammit!" Akio hadn't taken a single photograph in the apartment. In his daze at Masami's brazenness, he had completely forgotten his job. *Why hadn't she said anything?* He turned to go back. "I'll just get him to let us back in for a minute," he said, red-faced.

"I'm sure Powell wouldn't have forgotten," she said calmly.

Akio stopped and glared at her. That was his weak spot, and she knew it. She knew he didn't think he was as good as the American, and he wasn't. She knew it and twisted that knife in deep.

"Don't even start with that damn red-haired misfit!" he railed. "He'd be lucky if he remembered to take off his lens cap." Akio knew that was an absurdity. Powell was a master with a camera, and Akio was immensely jealous. His only cherished victory had been getting the American to recommend him for this assignment. Through a bit of trickery, yes, but it had been genius. Now he couldn't screw it up and not have any good photos to show for it. His anger was really at himself, but he didn't want Masami to realize that. The childish insults probably weren't helping his cause.

He started back toward the building.

"I wouldn't," Masami said.

He turned back at her, ready to spout, "Oh really, Miss Bribery? What wouldn't you do, really?" But before he could say anything, he saw the police vehicles approaching down the road.

"Fine," he said, and with a huff, he turned his camera on the apartment building behind them.

"You already got that shot on the way in."

"I know!" Akio fired back. "I'm getting another one, okay!"

"It's all right, Akio." The corner of her mouth turned upward ever so slightly. Something in his puerile suffering had ignited the beginnings of a grin in her impenetrable facade. A small chip in the ice. "We wouldn't be able to print any shots of inside the apartment anyway. Not only were we not supposed to be in there, it would be in poor taste."

Akio paused, gave a sigh and lowered his camera. "Yeah. I know that." Then he spun around and snapped a photo of Masami, trying to grab that fleeting, little smile.

"Dammit, Akio!" Masami stormed off toward her car. Akio jogged up behind her, having fully regained his good spirits.

They sat in the diner near the hotel again. Jonathan's was brightly lit with extremely clean floors. Th e highly polished hardwood walkways reflected the ceiling fans like a mirror. It was a very brown place. Brown walls, brown tables, brown chairs and brown booths, the latter two both covered in brown and beige striped cushions. Masami was looking through local publications they had picked up at the newsstand, while Akio flipped through a handful of tourist brochures he had grabbed for free from the hotel.

A fly buzzed over Akio's teacup and he brushed it away. He picked up his chopsticks and waited for the insect to come back. Soon it did, and Akio tried desperately to snatch it from the air with only the wooden utensils.

"I am Musashi Myamoto," he mumbled to the zigzagging insect. "You will die in the grip of my chopsticks."

After several failed attempts, he dropped the sticks and swatted at the fly with his open hand. He made contact, but only succeeded in knocking the bug right into his tea. He was watching it flail around in the hot liquid when Masami spoke up.

"There was something else I noticed in the bedroom."

"Did you find some soiled panties?" Akio joked and instantly regretted it from the evil eye Masami gave him. Her eyes could cut diamonds.

Ignoring his crass comment, she went on. "There were gouge marks on the wall leading up to the open window."

Off Akio's blank stare, she continued, "Small ones, like the kind that hand claws and foot spikes would make."

His eyes lit up. "Like a ninja?" he said excitedly.

"Yes, Akio," Masami frowned. "Like a ninja."

"So our murderer is a ninja?" Akio was grinning. "How awesome is that?"

Masami looked at him disapprovingly. "Number one," she said. "People are dying, so it's definitely not awesome. Number two, no, we are not looking for a ninja but maybe for someone who has read too many comic books and is trying to be one."

Akio giggled a bit, thinking of his own comic collection and the times he had pretended he was a ninja or a superhero. He lifted his tea to take a sip. As the liquid touched his upper lip, he noticed the fly still flailing about on the surface. He set the cup back down.

"Um, now what?" he leaned back in his chair, having abandoned his drink to the spinning insect.

"Now we talk to the cops," she said, a passionless victory behind her steel eyes.

"Because of the ninja?"

Masami ignored the question.

4
Kuramoto

The Kofu police station was not the most aesthetically pleasing place. The dull gray, three-story building stood like a giant, concrete block against the cloudless sky. Inside, the walls were yellowed from the cigarette smoke that hung in the air. Masami's brain was firing rapidly through possible scenarios of how this meeting would go, but she sat stone still next to Akio, both in plastic chairs with thin, worn-out cushions that provided no extra comfort. They used to be green cushions, but now were gray.

Masami felt tense, but projected calm as she silently judged every cop in the room. Some seemed intent on whatever case they were working, a couple were interviewing civilians, while others laughed like boys at crass jokes. One looked her way and whispered comments to a fellow officer who snickered. There were no women officers in the room. The only woman she had seen was the uniformed receptionist, a plain but hardened woman, makeup as thick as her skin. Masami didn't want to know what she put up with daily. It was bad enough at the newspaper.

They were waiting for a detective named Kuramoto. Masami had spoken with him on the phone after visiting the crime scene. He had expressed interest when she mentioned the notches in the exterior wall of Sayaka Inawa's apartment building.

"So your boss thinks a ninja crawled up the wall, huh?" he had said, his mouth clearly too close to the receiver; she could hear his every breath as if they were scraping against her eardrum.

"No," Masami had countered. "There are notches in the wall, and *I* think that might mean someone used ninja-type equipment to gain access to the apartment."

"Hmm," he had said. "Maybe a ninja did this, huh? Crazier things have happened. I'll meet your boss."

"Me, sir," Masami had said, trying to hide her irritation.

"Yeah, yeah." He had been dismissive. "Come by this afternoon."

When they arrived, they were directed inside the station to a long table. Kuramoto wasn't there, but they were assured he would return soon. So they waited. Twenty minutes passed. Akio seemed to have a hard time sitting still, which was nothing new. He kept trying to get a closer look at the bulletin board across the room.

"It looks like it has pictures of dead bodies on it," he said. "Maybe they're our dead bodies." He pulled his camera out and started to lift the telephoto toward the board. Masami immediately slapped it down.

"They *will* be our dead bodies if you start shooting photos in here!" she shouted in a whisper. "Do not screw up this meeting for us!"

Akio stopped, a dim light apparently going off in his head as he realized that taking photos of unreleased information inside the station wasn't a good idea if they wanted a working relationship with the police. He put his camera away and zipped the bag shut. "Us," he said, leaning back on the squeaky chair. "I really like the sound of that."

Masami ignored him.

A thickset man with a broad, drawn face and a round, black mole on his cheek stepped up to them. He had the look of someone who was about to either jump on top of a desk and start singing or fall asleep standing up. It was a strange dichotomy and a little unnerving.

He wore a cheap blue suit and a clashing purple tie that hung slightly crooked. He was clearly single. No—divorced. His ex-wife would never have let him go to work like that. His face was pale and pasty; clearly he'd never had a full night's sleep in his life. And he smoked. Probably two packs a day. It oozed from him like a chemical spill.

They both stood to greet him.

He spoke to Akio.

"You are the journalist?"

Akio looked like someone had asked him if his eyes were made of cream cheese.

"I am the journalist," Masami spoke up quickly, introducing herself politely with a slight bow. "I am Masami Sato, journalist from the *Dainichi Daily*." She indicated Akio. "This is Akio Tsukino, photographer, also from the *Dainichi*."

Kuramoto looked her up and down, glanced over at Akio and then back to Masami. "Journalist, huh? What is the *Dainichi* coming to?" he asked rhetorically, looking at a pack of Seven Stars cigarettes he had pulled out of his suit pocket—a white box patterned with tiny gray stars. He gave it a once over and then put it back in his pocket without taking one out of the pack. Then he sat at the table.

Masami and Akio sat as well.

She knew she should have brought a gift—a bottle of *sake* or tickets to the Seibu Lions, or whatever baseball team the detective followed. That was how the information game was played. But she hated the game. She could only play it as much as she absolutely had to. She hoped the marks on the building wall would be enough.

The detective turned to Akio. "So you think a ninja is the perp, huh?"

Again, Akio had that cream cheese look in his eye for a moment but then spoke up. "Uh, yeah, yeah," he stumbled. "Sure looks that way."

So this is how it's going to be.

Masami jumped in. "Sir, we hate to waste your time, but there were clearly some fresh gouges in the outside wall that appear to be leading up to the open window in the apartment.

Kuramoto glanced sideways at Masami but was still facing Akio. "So you crossed a police line and investigated the bedroom, huh?" he asked dryly.

"Well, it wasn't my . . . I mean," Akio stuttered suddenly. "We didn't think that . . ."

"We saw them with Tsukino's telephoto lens from the outside of the building," Masami spat out quickly.

"Hmm, telephoto, huh?" The detective was still talking to Akio.

"Um yeah, of course," Akio struggled to recover his composure. "From the outside."

"Let me see the photos."

Akio froze again. It looked like his tongue was moving around in his mouth, but no words were being formed.

"That's just the thing, sir," Masami said, the word "sir" tasting like acid in her mouth. "Tsukino's camera malfunctioned at that moment. We could see them in the lens, but we were unable to get a photograph of it."

Kuramoto gave a little smirk. "Do you always let her talk for you?" he asked Akio.

Masami was boiling inside, but she showed only a calm, unaffected exterior. She would sit there and pleasantly take this abuse from another misogynistic idiot. If she didn't, they would lose their chance at getting any intel. She wasn't sure she could contain her anger much longer. There had been too many times.

"Um, well," Akio sputtered. "You know how it is." He attempted a knowing glance and a wink between men, but what displayed on his face was much closer to a sneer with a slight eye twitch. Masami cringed.

She spoke up again in the most convincing, polite tone she could manage. "Yes, sir. We apologize for our clumsiness with this, but I assure you that if you investigate the building you will discover these marks."

"Hmm," the detective grunted. "Okay, boss," he said to Akio. "We'll check it out. If this pans out, we may have some little tidbits of information for you. Give us a call tomorrow."

He fondled his pack of cigarettes again, but still didn't take one out. He nodded to them both slightly and left them in their uncomfortable chairs.

"Whoa," Akio laughed when they got outside. "I've never seen you kiss so much ass in my life."

"Drop it, Akio," Masami said.

Akio laughed harder. "No way. After all the times you've ignored me and treated me like I was a bug. Finally, there's a little karmic revenge for you."

Too far.

Masami blew up.

"If I hadn't kissed ass," she turned on him with the fury meant for Kuramoto. "If I hadn't saved us from your stupidity, we wouldn't have this connection right now. You are a photographer who forgets his camera. You try to take photos inside the police station. What is wrong with you? Have you no common sense at all? If I hadn't been polite to that asshole of a cop who treated me like I was your secretary, we both might as well be on our way home to Tokyo. You are completely useless."

She looked him over as if figuring out the best way to skin him alive.

"Give me some scissors, Akio, and I'll show you how it feels to be a woman in this business." She indicated his crotch.

Akio immediately shrunk away from her like a scared rat.

"Yikes," he said. "No thank you. Why would I want to be a woman?"

Masami glared at him. *Did he really just say that?*

"I mean, uh, I'd be okay being you, of course," he added pathetically. "I mean you're not really a woman. I mean, I mean, you're a woman, you're just so like a man, like in a good way, you know, like except not that I think you look like a man, but . . . I . . . mean . . ." Akio had worn himself out backpedaling.

"There aren't words, Akio," Masami sighed. "There really just aren't words."

Early the next morning, the phone in Masami's hotel room rang. It was Kuramoto.

"Ah, Miss Sato. Can I speak with your boss, please?"

It was too early for this. Masami fought back the urge to rip into him with words unfitting a proper Japanese woman. But he was her only inside connection right now. She had to be civil.

"My apologies, sir, but my boss is in Tokyo." *And is going to get a real mouthful when I get back there for sending Akio with me.*

"Tokyo? He left already? Ah well, his loss. We checked out your lead. It seems there may be something to this ninja idea after all."

"Thank you, sir." *What is with men and their fascination with ninjas?*

"I have some information your boss might be interested in. If he still wants it, that is."

"Yes, yes, absolutely, sir. He has assured me he does." She nearly gagged on the words, imagining Akio as her boss. But she knew that was exactly what Kuramoto wanted. *Prick. You know that Akio isn't actually in charge.* Her unfortunate companion had made it clear he was an idiot. The detective was just trying to get under her skin. Or his humanity had truly been crippled by outdated, patriarchal thinking. Either way, the game must continue if she was to get to the finish line.

"Come by the station then. I have something for him."

Masami got ready quickly and left, not bothering to wake Akio. She hurried out of the hotel, hoping to avoid accidental contact with him. She was afraid he might have snuck down to grab a donut or something from the complimentary breakfast spread. Fortunately, she made it out unscathed, only passing a couple of arrogant-looking businessmen and bumping into a young couple who appeared to have been out all night.

At the police station, Kuramoto made her wait in the drab lobby for almost thirty minutes. When he finally showed up, he appeared disappointed to have to talk to her at all. Reluctantly, he handed her an inch-thick manila envelope.

"A lot of this is public information," he said. "Hope it helps though. Let us know if you find any more ninja tracks."

5

The Spy Shop

"So our ploy worked!" enthused Akio at breakfast. "I just knew it would."

Masami groaned. Her ability to not show irritation seemed to be weakening.

"I still don't understand why you didn't wake me to go along," he continued. "He clearly wanted to speak to the boss." Akio grinned and leaned back in his chair, patting his skinny stomach.

"Exactly why I didn't," she snapped. "The day you are the boss is the day the world weeps."

"Happy, happy tears," he smirked.

He felt bad about what he had said to her the day before when he had joked about her kissing the detective's ass. Part of him felt she deserved it. She could be so cold-hearted. Finally someone had made her feel like he always felt. But he still didn't like it. He didn't like the idea of anyone having to feel how he felt. Because it sucked. He didn't buy that "misery loves company" bullshit. He really just wanted people to get along and be happy. But people were jerks. The detective was a complete ass. He knew Akio wasn't the boss. He was just a misogynistic a-hole.

Still, it was fun to tease Masami a little bit, to see some emotion on her robot face. Until the teeth came out and she made comments about scissors. If Akio had ever imagined Masami thinking about his crotch before, that was certainly not what he had in mind. The image made him cringe and close his legs.

"Back to work, Akio," Masami said, clearly not in the mood to play his games this morning. *Was she ever?* She slid the envelope across the table to him. "This is what we have. There's not much that I didn't already get from the press club and the local news, but if we play our cards right, we may get more."

"Cool," he said, flipping through the file folders inside. Each folder contained information on one of the previous victims: crime scene photos, evidence lists, witness accounts, and so on. "Ooh, gross!" His demeanor quickly changed as he came across a photo of a headless man on a train platform, his white collar stained with blood. "Eichi Himura – third known victim" was written below the image. The salaryman's blue-suited body was sitting against the wall, a dark pool under the legs, and a large advertisement for perfume above it. The windswept hair of the pop star in the ad curled downward, pointing as if to indicate where the head should have been. "I hope I'm not gonna be taking any photos like that on this trip," he said, disgusted.

"Not if you don't remember to take them," Masami answered.

"Ha, ha, ha," he said sarcastically. But it stung. "It's not going to happen again."

"Let's hope not. We have a lot of work to do. And I'm not going to let you ruin this story for me."

"Ruin?" Akio was flabbergasted. "What makes you think . . . I'm not going to . . . maybe you're going to ruin it for me, huh? What about that?" And even though he said it impetuously, maybe she *was* going to ruin it in a way. But it wasn't the story of the headless victims or their murderer that he was all that interested in, as creepy as it was. It was the story of Masami. He had hoped that maybe they could make some kind of connection on this trip, be friends of some sort. That was the story that concerned him. If he honestly thought about it, it ran tandem with his desire to be more respected as a photographer. It might even surpass it. He'd rather be as far away from any head-chopping maniac, ninja or not, as he could be. But he hoped to break through some of Masami's defenses, to get a little closer to the robot queen, to find a bit of that humanity that must be buried inside her somewhere. But she was thwarting any and all attempts at connecting. He had been fooling himself to think otherwise.

Masami ignored his little rant, took the envelope back from him and perused one of the folders again. She was on her third cup of coffee already and more impatient than usual.

Akio sat sulking with his tea, thankful that there were no flies at present.

Then he remembered something. It pulled him out of his wallowing.

"Oh!" he nearly shouted. "I have some information too, Miss Smarty Pants."

Masami could only raise an eyebrow.

"After you conked out to get your beauty sleep," he began. "Not that you need any," he deftly inserted. "I was a little restless. I figured 'the boss' needs a drink, so I went out."

Masami sighed but ignored the comment. The look in her hard eyes made it very apparent she was more than a little skeptical.

He continued. "I met a guy who knows a guy who owns a . . . stealth . . . uh . . . spy shop in town. Of course, I was very discreet about the whole thing, not letting on for a minute that I was here as a reporter. I made it sound like I was interested in getting a hold of some ninja gear for hobbyist purposes."

"Hobbyist purposes?" Masami interjected. "You just enjoy climbing buildings on weekends?"

Akio giggled. *Did she just crack a joke?* He continued. "Turns out this guy at the bar, Okada, mostly buys surveillance equipment there, spy stuff—hidden cameras, wiretaps, that sort of thing. Do you know that you can buy a *Daruma* doll with a camera mounted in it?"

"Seems like bad luck to me," Masami opined. "I don't want to know what he was doing with these cameras."

"Oh, he said just keeping an eye on his wife, you know. He was worried she was cheating on him. Nothing serious."

Masami stared at him like he was an alien.

"Anyway, the place isn't far from here. I think we should check it out. Maybe our ninja wannabe shops there."

He watched as she considered, his knees bouncing from nervousness. He moved the handle of his spoon back and forth in a tick-tocking motion on the table. He knew that visiting the spy shop wasn't exactly on track with simply telling the story of what happened, a sideline, impartial view of events. But he also knew that Masami liked to go deeper than most journalists. She hated the press clubs and wanted her own scoop. Akio had heard her rant about it to Tanaka, who was clearly on her side and allowed her plenty of leeway. She had helped solve cases in the past, not that the Tokyo Metro Police had ever given her much credit. But still, there was a good chance she might want to investigate this.

"Hmm," Masami hesitated, but then, as if she might regret it, added, "Maybe you won't be completely useless after all."

Akio beamed. "Not completely useless," he mused. "Well, it's a start."

"Okay," Masami seemed keen to get back on track. "We have the spy shop. We can hit that today. We also have this." She pulled out a paper with a stapled photo from one of the file folders.

"Oh," Akio's eyes lit up. "Now that's more like it!"

The photo was of an extremely cute and brightly made-up young woman in a red and white maid costume. Her adorable, innocent smile and rosy cheeks bounced off the print. She was seated next to Himura, the third victim, her head cocked toward him, at what appeared to be a diner booth.

"Keep it in your pants," Masami huffed. "This is one of the few tidbits in the envelope I didn't know about already. Her name is Emiko Kanemashi. She works at a maid café and was apparently the only person this salaryman, Himura, was in regular contact with outside of work."

"So we get to go talk to her?" Akio was suddenly much more excited about the investigation.

"No, Akio, we don't get to, we have to. The police have already questioned her and ruled her out as having any valuable information, but she's one of the few connections to the victim we have. Maybe she'll be more willing to talk to us. Who knows, but we have to try."

"Oh, what a bummer," he answered with heavy sarcasm. "I don't know if I want to hang out with a hot maid girl on the company's dime. I'd feel so guilty!" he laughed.

"Well, that's good," Masami said. "Because I don't think Tanaka is going to shell out for this. Which means you're buying."

"Wha . . . ?" Akio looked at her stone face, trying to decipher if she was serious or not. He decided she was. "How is that possible? We are working for the company. The company should pay our expenses."

"Doesn't work that way and you know it. We'll submit our receipts when we get home. If we get a good scoop and break something big before anyone else can, then maybe Tanaka will pitch in. In the mean time, this one's on you."

Akio's spirits sagged. He barely made enough to get by. If he had money for maid cafés, he'd surely be spending more time at them. He glanced at the photo again, and his spirits lifted a bit. She was really cute. He looked up at Masami, who was scowling out the window thinking whatever dire thoughts constantly ran through her head, and then back at the photo.

Hmmm, he thought and joked to himself. *Who is more appealing? Super cute and bubbly, or angry, robotic and completely unattainable? I just can't decide.*

Emiko didn't work until evening, so that left them the spy shop for the daytime.

It was located in a less trafficked, industrial part of town. In Tokyo, Akio had seen a similar shop right in the midst of the hustle and bustle of Shinjuku, but the stuff they sold there was mostly trinkets and souvenirs. He wasn't convinced any of it was actually functional.

This place was different. A-chan's A-Team, it was called. A small rectangular sign above the metal-framed glass door confirmed the name. It was not something that would catch your eye from the street. And that's probably how the owner liked it.

Inside it was fairly small. There was one main room with two aisles separated by a rack of simple shelves that you'd see in any convenience store. Only they didn't have candy bars, chips and blind boxes with collectible toys in them. There were far more sinister-looking things placed there: tiny microphones, pen recorders, GPS trackers, lock pick sets, a spray that allowed you to read letters without opening them, and lots and lots of innocent looking items with cameras hidden inside of them, including that ever present symbol of fortune and perseverance, the *Daruma* doll.

Behind the checkout counter there were even scarier things displayed on the wall: *kama, sai, nunchaku,* and whips. And in the counter case: throwing knives, knives disguised as cell phones and pens, *shuriken,* and . . . yes, *ninja shuko* hand claws and foot spikes.

The man behind the counter was a middle-aged man with a bowl cut and randomly sprinkled facial hair. He was looking at a newspaper spread out before him. When Masami and Akio approached, he looked up at them without raising his head. It made him look sinister and sleepy at the same time.

"I love the name of your shop!" Akio enthused to the man, who still didn't lift his head. "A-chan is what my mother used to call me!"

He saw Masami roll her eyes. It was a common thing to call someone with "A" as the first syllable in their name, A-chan. Although it was an affectation generally reserved for children and pets. Still, Akio remembered it fondly.

A little tickle of a smile started in the shopkeeper's face that quickly spread into a big grin. "Me too!" he said like a joyful boy. "That's so cool! My name is Akira. What about you?"

"Akio!" He smiled broadly.

"Both A-chans! Crazy world, huh?" The shopkeeper seemed genuinely pleased.

Masami, however, looked horrified at the thought of Akio having found a kindred soul.

"Why is your shop the A-Team?" Akio asked excitedly.

"A-team means the best. But also, I like the American TV show."

"No way!" Akio couldn't contain himself. "You know that show? Who is your favorite character?"

"B.A. Baracus, of course! Mr. T!" Akira answered happily.

"Me too!" Akio almost shouted. "I pity the fool!" he boomed, making his best Mr. T grimace.

Both men laughed heartily like old schoolmates on the playground.

Masami was not amused.

"I hate to break up this little love connection, boys," she interrupted, "but I have a few questions I'd like to ask about some possible purchases that may have been made here."

Akira suddenly became serious, eyeing Masami suspiciously. Akio also straightened up and tried to be cool, leaning casually on the counter, but only succeeding in knocking over a miniature stand holding a toy katana.

"Purchases?' Akira asked. "What kind of purchases?"

"Particularly these ninja shuko spikes."

"These spikes? I haven't sold these spikes yet. They are still here."

"Yes, of course," Masami said impatiently. "But perhaps you've sold some like them?"

"Hmm . . ." The storeowner pulled at one tuft of facial hair, eyeing Masami carefully. "Why do you want to know? Are you the police?"

"Well . . ." Akio started, but Masami cut him off before he could say anything stupid.

"No, sir," she said quickly. "We are reporters for the *Dainichi Daily* in Tokyo and we are just following up on a lead."

At the word "reporters," Akira winced a little. "I don't want any bad press about my store. Everything I sell is totally legal."

Akio felt bad for him. He could tell Akira suddenly felt like he was under the spotlight and wanted to hide.

"We don't want that either," Akio said. "This store is cool."

"He's right," Masami added and forced a smile. "We have no intention of smearing your good name. We're just trying to identify a person that may be connected with a story of ours." She set her hand lightly on Akira's hand, which was resting on the counter. It was a soft touch, surely just meant to assuage the man's fears, but Akio quickly saw the effect it had on the shopkeeper, who turned a light shade of crimson, sweat instantly beginning to form at his temple.

Brilliant! Akio thought. *But so devious too! The charms of a woman hardly make the playing field fair!* And then immediately he felt jealous. *She's never touched me like that! And she's smiling!*

"Can you remember anyone who may have purchased something like that," Masami said, sounding extremely seductive all of sudden. "Maybe anytime during the last six months or so?"

Akira stumbled over his response, obviously rattled by Masami's attention. "Uh . . . uh, yeah. I think so," he sputtered. "There was a guy. Um. Let me look at my records." He motioned toward the back room with his free hand. His other was still under Masami's and he was clearly reluctant to move it. Masami did him the favor of removing hers instead.

Akira smiled uncomfortably, but in an attempt at being suave, he stammered. "You c-could . . . uh . . . come back with me to look, if you like."

Akio found himself immediately offended. *The nerve of this guy! Really?* And then suddenly worried. *Would she do that? To get information?*

Masami smiled demurely. "I'll wait right here for you."

Thank goodness, thought Akio. He had been ready to intervene on her part. He shot her a look that said, *good for you*. It was a little nod and a half smile. It was meant to be a moment of bonding, an acknowledgment of their team effort. She glared at him in response as Akira went into the back room. There was no remnant of her recent smile or any connection between them at all.

A moment later Akira returned with a black binder.

"Yeah, yeah," he was saying as he returned to the counter. "Here it is. It was a few weeks ago. He was a short, muscular guy, bald I think. Credit card says Tatsuo Miyahara."

"Thank you," Masami said, all hint of seduction evaporated. "Did he purchase anything else at any time? A katana, maybe?"

"No, no," Akira responded nervously. "I don't sell katanas, no. These weapons you see here are for display only. They are not sharp." Akio had a strong feeling that Akira probably had a stack of unlicensed and perfectly sharp katanas in the back room.

"But . . ." The shopkeeper seemed to be rethinking his tactics. Masami had turned off her seductress act. Maybe she'd bring it back if he spilled more info. "I know where you could get one with no registration needed."

"Really?" Masami asked, stone-faced. "Where?"

Akira hesitated. He appeared to take inventory of his entire shop in the moment before he laughed nervously. "No, no. I'm just joking." Apparently Masami's sway had worn off. And it didn't look like she was going to switch on seductress mode again to try to get it back. Akira wasn't going to be spilling all of his secrets.

"Are there any other stores in the area that might sell spikes like these?" she asked.

"No, I'm the only one nearby. Other places only sell trinkets and toys. There's one guy out toward Chuo called Life Check that may have some decent stuff, but still not great quality like mine."

"Thank you," Masami repeated, and headed for the door.

Akio turned to the shopkeeper with an awkward smile. "A-Team high five!" he said, holding his hand up high.

Akira just laughed nervously again, leaving Akio hanging with his hand in the air, and went back to looking at his newspaper.

Akio deflated. He felt like he had lost a potential friend, another odd soul like himself bumbling through the universe, all thanks to Masami's trickery. He followed her out the door.

"So, that's our man then," Akio said as they walked to the car. "This bald guy, Miyahara."

"Hard to say," Masami said, pulling out her keys.

"How is it hard to say? He bought the ninja shuko. He climbed the building. He killed the girl. Case closed."

"We'll see," Masami answered.

They still had a few hours before Emiko would be arriving for work at the maid café, so they returned to their hotel. They sat in Akio's room; Masami at the desk, Akio slouched on the bed.

He was replaying the seduction incident over and over in his head. Masami was so much more devious than he had realized. *How could she just turn that on so effectively when she is normally an ice queen?* Akira had been duped. But at least they had gotten the information they needed. It made Akio nervous though. *What else is Masami capable of? If she can just flip a switch and be Seductive Susie, what else could she become? Or is this a trait that all women have? Can they all turn emotions on and off like a faucet?*

Akio had little experience dating. He had had a girlfriend for a little while about three years back. He was just twenty. She was nineteen. The whole relationship only lasted about four months.

Her name was Chie. She was this absent-minded, faraway girl. She always seemed only half present. The other half was dreaming and dancing in some distant corner of the universe. She was smart though. And she was fun. They had played video games together for hours. She was obsessed with *Dark Souls* and could slice up undead like nobody's business. They had laughed a lot, and at the dumbest things. He would poke her round cheeks and she would make farting noises as he did. It was stupid, but they would laugh themselves silly. She was the dead opposite of Masami.

But Chie had gone to America. She decided Tokyo wasn't enough and that she had to see the world. She joined some exchange program and went to school for a bit in California, then ended up being an au pair for a rich family in Silicon Valley. She had written him for a few months on Mixi, but then stopped. She still posted for a while, but then those stopped too. She had moved on. And he let her go.

He thought of her a lot. He missed her. He had been crushingly sad when she left. But he had never imagined she would stay. She was too flighty to begin with, too impermanent. She had spun his world around and left him dizzy and alone. But he had been alone before, and he expected to be alone. Women just weren't that into him. So it was just an enjoyable fluke, a temporary escape from the norm.

Maybe he was so enthralled with Masami because she was Chie's polar opposite. He was attracted to her because she wouldn't run off somewhere on a whim. She was solid and predictable. She was a veritable Rock of Gibraltar, as unshakeable as a mountain. That was why the seduction act had been so unsettling. The mountain had shook, even if it had been on its own terms. Akio felt on unsure footing. But it was not as if he had a thumbtack's chance in concrete with her anyway. He would never shake that mountain. It would shake when it wanted to shake.

So there was that.

"Look at this," Masami said, breaking into his reverie. She turned her laptop toward Akio. He got up from the bed to get a closer view.

On the screen was the image of a park and an old *sukiya*-style building, like a traditional teahouse. In a second photo to the right were the ruins of a small castle. The heading at the top of the page read, "Learn kendo in a classic nature setting next to Maizuru Castle!" Underneath the banner image was a photo of a short, stout, mostly bald man in his fifties. In the caption below was the name, "Sensei Miyahara."

"Miyahara," Akio read out loud. "Hey! That's the name of the guy who bought the ninja shuko!"

"You're quick," Masami said sarcastically. "And he's a kendo instructor."

"Okay." Akio didn't make the connection. Kendo had been part of his physical education in grade school, and his strongest memory of it was getting whacked across the back with a *shinai* by Ryu Nobunaga when he had lost his balance. It had stung like crazy, and he had been sore for days. "Is that relevant, Dr. Watson?"

Masami glared at him with blank astonishment. "The murders were all committed with a blade of some kind, probably a sword. A very sharp katana would be my guess. Who would be more proficient at sword fighting than someone involved in a kendo group? Possibly even the instructor."

"Yeah, of course." Akio feigned knowing all along, and rolled his eyes at her. "I was just testing you."

"Uh huh." Masami sighed. "You make a poor Sherlock."

"Whatever." He twisted his face with childish disdain. "I knew it was that guy. This just confirms it."

"We'll see," Masami answered blankly. "We'll pay him a visit tomorrow."

6

The Hot Maid Girl

he café was brightly lit. So much so that it was a little blinding, but to Akio it was like a palace made of candy. He could hardly contain his excitement. Masami appeared to be trying to contain it for him with the sheer force of her will.

It wasn't working.

The place was called Red Riding Hood, and all the servers were dressed like a version of the fairy tale girl if she had been made to clean bedrooms and serve food. They wore white-laced red petticoats with white aprons over the top and, instead of pinafores, simple red blouses with white collars, and short, puffed, white sleeves. In place of a traditional maid's bonnet, they each had pinned into their hair a loose, soft red hood sporting a red bow off to one side. Their feet glowed with thick-heeled, polished red pumps with ankle straps and long, frilled white socks leading up slender legs, capped with a tiny red bow just at the knee.

Prints of idyllic forest scenes adorned the walls, replete with fairy mushrooms, colorful flowers and butterflies. All of the prints appeared to have a pair of eyes peering from a dark place between trees, and a few even exposed the eyes as belonging to a large wolf. The curtains that were tied off at the windows repeated the mushrooms and butterflies theme.

At each table, a small picnic basket held the usual array of condiments and seasonings found at any diner: ketchup, mustard, salt, pepper, and hot sauce, as well as the dessert menu and rules of the café.

As Akio took all of it in with a schoolboy's relish, one of the servers skipped up to them with a smile as bright as her demeanor. She looked all of sixteen.

"Welcome home, Master and Mistress!" she beamed. "I've prepared your favorite table for you!"

Akio was dumbfounded and couldn't respond. This was what Heaven must be like.

Then, addressing him directly, she added, "Will anyone else be joining you today, Master?"

He was pretty certain that his heart had stopped, and he knew without a doubt that he had forgotten how to use his mouth to form words.

Masami came to the rescue.

"I'm sorry, but we are looking for a particular maid, uh, server." It seemed even Masami was uncertain how to act in such a place. "Her name is Emiko."

"Of course, my mistress," the girl bowed, and her face took on a tint of the red of her hood. "I will send for her immediately." She retreated into the restaurant and skipped through the swinging door that led to the kitchen.

Akio watched her go, unable to take his eyes off her.

"Snap out of it," Masami demanded. "I can't have you drooling through the entire interview."

Although the girl was already out of sight, Akio found it hard to turn his head back to Masami. When he did, he was startled by her scowl, even though he had expected it.

"Is that what you want?" she asked to his blinking eyes. "A young, pretty girl that will do your bidding whenever you please?"

Akio was pretty sure that, yes, that was exactly what he wanted. But something about the way Masami had posed the question made him certain that was not how he was supposed to answer.

"Uh . . . no," he stammered. "Of course not. I want a . . . a . . . strong woman . . . who can be her own boss."

Masami grimaced. It still didn't seem like the right answer. Or maybe she just didn't believe him. What was he supposed to say? The maid girls were really damn cute.

Very soon, another server in the same outfit, but looking a few years older, came skipping out from behind the swinging door. She was the girl from the photo, and Akio reacted with a dumb smile as if he had not expected her to be real.

She bounded up to the two of them trilling in a high squeaky voice, "Welcome home, Master and Mistress! It's so good to see you again!"

"Drop it," snapped Masami. "We're not here for the show."

"Uh . . ." Akio tried to interrupt. *We're here; we might as well enjoy the show too, right?* he wanted to say, but Masami shut him down with a glare and a hiss. She actually hissed at him.

"I'm very sorry, Mistress," said the young woman in the red hood. "Can I take you to your favorite table?"

"We've never eaten here before," said Masami.

Akio had to butt in again. "You're ruining the game. It's all part of —"

Masami ignored him and cut him off. Addressing the maid, she said, "Are you Emiko Kamenashi?"

"Yes, Mistress. I am here to serve you."

"Take a break, Emiko," Masami ordered. "We need to talk to you about Eichi Himura."

At that name, all of the color fell from Emiko's face. Her bright makeup fought to hide the ghost-white shade her skin had become.

Akio thought he might have to catch her if she fainted, and instantly two conflicting thoughts fought each other in his head. *I could be her hero if I save her from hurting herself in the fall, but I know I'm not supposed to touch the maid girls, and I might be arrested!* He froze again, unable to make a decision.

Thankfully, she remained upright.

"We're from the *Dainichi Daily* in Tokyo," Masami said. "We won't take too much of your time."

"Yes," she hesitated. "Please excuse me. I'll check with my manager."

Emiko walked quickly through the kitchen door, abandoning her buoyant skip. A few minutes later, she returned with her red hood in her hands.

"I have ten minutes," she said far less bubbly than she had been. "It's not quite dinner rush yet."

"Can we talk here?" Masami asked, dropping into a more concerned tone of voice.

"No," Emiko answered quickly, "I'm sorry, not while I'm in uniform. There's a Doutor next door."

The three found an open table at the bustling coffee shop. It was just far enough away from the smoke billowing out of the semi-enclosed smoking section, where suited men and women sat next to hip twenty-somethings all sucking in mouthfuls of tar and nicotine euphoria as they sipped coffee drinks and tapped away at their smart phones.

Akio was a little miffed that he wasn't going to get the full maid café experience, but at least he was sitting with a hot maid girl, and in public. He tried to imagine what it would be like if she was his girlfriend. It was pleasant at first, imagining her on his arm, all the envious men looking as they walked past. But then, he imagined her being sugary sweet to all those men who came into the maid café and her treating them as if they were her masters. He started to get jealous and even a little angry. Involuntarily, his face made a little sneer at her, right when she looked his way, and she turned away quickly. *Dammit!* he thought. *Now I've made her think I'm a jerk! My stupid face can't control itself!* He harrumphed and hung his head, staring at the scratched black surface of the coffee shop table.

"I didn't know him very well," Emiko answered Masami's first question, her squeaky voice less affected than it was before. "But he was a nice man. He visited me three nights a week. I don't think he had a wife."

"He didn't," said Masami.

Akio stared a little vacantly at Emiko before coming to his senses. He had to be a man. He couldn't let Masami down. So what if this maid girl was ridiculously cute. He was a news photographer and hoped to be the best. He pulled out his camera. He started to lift it to aim it at Emiko, but Masami put her hand on it and held it down. She looked at him as if to say, "Not appropriate. Not now."

Dammit. Akio had failed again. He slumped into his chair. *Why wasn't this a good moment?* Cute maid girl talking about a victim. It seemed all right to him. But he knew the drill. In delicate situations, when dealing with loss and whatnot, the right thing to do was get permission. But didn't all the renegade photographers with the best, most thrilling shots just snap away when they felt like it? They had no need to respect the situation; they just got the shot. They captured life as it happens. But Akio wasn't like that. Some part of him felt you had to be a dick to be successful. And he didn't want to be a dick. He was just a nice, awkward guy. With poor timing. Maybe that was why he only got assigned low priority stories. He was useless. He couldn't handle the pressure of a headliner like this. He shouldn't even be here. He shouldn't have finagled his way in by making a deal with Powell.

No. He had to do this.

He had to be good at this.

He would get the picture later with Emiko's permission. Barring that, he would just snap a shot of the exterior of the maid café. That would be good enough, he figured. It would work for a basic, boring news photo.

He was too flustered to think straight, because he wanted so badly to be amazing, to be respected. And because this maid girl was so cute. And because for some reason he felt guilty thinking about the maid girl with Masami sitting next to him. He wanted so badly to impress Masami. *There.* He admitted it to himself. But his irritation at the situation made him nervous. And when he was nervous, he had a tendency to talk. In a burst of what sounded like strange jealousy that surprised even himself, he asked Emiko, "Do you think he loved you? Do you think he thought you were his girlfriend?"

After he said it, he thought he had been too forceful. He thought he had really attacked her with the question, so he drew back into his chair.

But Emiko just looked at him thoughtfully. She didn't seem to have been affected by his aggressiveness. "Maybe," she finally answered. "A lot of men who come to the café seem lonely. Others are just having fun, but some really seem lonely." She said it as if she were genuinely concerned about these sad, lonesome men. It made Akio like her more.

"Is there anything he ever mentioned that was odd?" Masami asked. "Did he have any enemies? Was there any reason someone would want him dead?"

"No, he was kind," the young woman sighed. "He would talk about the people at his work and about living with his family when he was young. His older brother picked on him. His mother didn't seem to care about him, and his father was disappointed. There were co-workers he mentioned that he thought didn't like him, but I think it was mostly in his head. They didn't threaten him or anything. They just didn't invite him out for drinks. They laughed a lot, and he was sure they were laughing at him. But I doubt it."

Then as Masami was forming a follow up, the maid girl blurted out, "I've seen him since."

Akio and Masami both looked at her inquisitively, but while Masami remained stony, Akio involuntarily screwed up his face and narrowed his eyes in suspicion.

"Since when?" Masami asked tentatively.

Emiko seemed reluctant to answer. She fidgeted with her coffee mug, swinging the handle back and forth almost causing it to spill.

"Since he died," she finally said.

Even Akio had no response to that.

Emiko tried to explain. "I didn't know he was dead until the police came to question me. I thought he had just gotten bored of me and moved on." She nervously sipped her coffee, trying to gather her thoughts.

"But about a week later, I saw him." She couldn't look either of them in the face. "He wouldn't come into the café, but it was him. I'm sure of it. He came by for a few weeks, and then I never saw him again."

Akio watched the young woman peering sadly into her coffee. She looked like she was about to cry.

Masami broke the silence.

"If he didn't come into the café, where exactly did you see him?" she asked suspiciously.

"I know it's hard to believe," Emiko answered, "but I'm sure it was him." She sighed before continuing. "He would just stay outside in the shadows. He would watch me through the front window."

Akio was mesmerized now. Emiko really appeared to be telling the truth, which was crazy. She truly believed what she was saying. Even he could tell that. If she was lying, she was a world-class actress.

"When I would go outside to talk to him," she continued, "he would disappear."

"Disappear?" Akio questioned. "Like literally vanish?"

"Yes. I mean . . . I could see him through the glass, but when I opened the door, he was gone."

"Do you think it was his ghost?" he asked, trying not to sound like he was mocking her.

She gave a sad little smile at Akio, who blushed.

"Yes," she said. "It was." She smiled a little bigger, apparently thinking about the salaryman's visits from beyond. "He must have been a very old soul," she added, "and very powerful in his past life."

"Why do you say that?" Masami asked.

"His face was clearly Eichi's," Emiko answered, "but his body was large and muscular, and he was in full samurai armor."

7
The Kendo Instructor

"So we're dealing with a samurai now?" Akio asked as he sat across from Masami at the diner. "A samurai who's also a ninja?"

"Apparently." Masami wore her usual scowl as she picked at her food. Tonight she was having spaghetti and meatballs in a red sauce. She pushed her garlic bread through the sauce and it crunched as she bit into it.

"I think we're dealing with a lunatic," Akio said, his mouth full of hamburger and pickles. "If we're talking about that waitress, that is." He grabbed a couple french fries and shoved those in as well.

Masami stiffly wiped some sauce from the corner of her mouth and took a sip of water before speaking again. "I thought she was a hot maid girl."

Akio sighed. "She was! Until she started talking."

He was being mean. He still liked Emiko. He even believed her on some level. At least, he really wanted to believe her. She seemed so fragile and honest. And she was still very hot. But a samurai back from the dead had shown up outside of her café? Really? It was too much. His fear of hot women intensified when they were also crazy. But it wasn't that. Not really. It was Masami. He assumed Masami must think Emiko was crazy, and he wanted Masami to know he was on her side.

He didn't want to look like the weak-kneed boy that he felt like, someone who could be swayed into believing something absurd because a pretty face said it. So he lied, sort of, to save his dignity in front of Masami.

The diner was fairly empty. It was that odd hour between lunch and dinner. There were only three other patrons: a Chinese couple sitting in the corner looking unimpressed and a large Caucasian man in a baseball cap digging into a Chef's salad.

"I don't know." Akio was starting to question if he had read Masami correctly. "Do you think I'm being too hard on her?" He asked this as if he and Emiko were a couple going through a rough patch in their relationship.

"Maybe," Masami said. "She seemed sincere at least. Even if it is hard to believe. Let's let her go for now. We can't very well go chasing after ghosts, especially if they aren't showing up anymore."

So diplomatic. I'll never read her correctly. "We could become ghost hunters. Maybe that'd be a new career for us after we get fired for botching this story," Akio joked.

Masami's mouth twitched as if she wanted to laugh at his comment. But she didn't. She got serious. "We're not going to botch the story. We have more leads."

"Like what?" Akio asked, shoving a handful of french fries into his mouth.

Masami pulled out the envelope she had been given by Detective Kuramoto. "The second victim was a homeless man found in Maizuru Castle Park."

"I remember you mentioned a homeless guy in your article," Akio said.

"Yes, there's a little more info in here, though not much that's useful." She pulled out a document with an attached photo and passed it across the table. "Please don't get grease on that," she added as an afterthought.

Akio wiped his hands thoroughly on a napkin. "Wait, Maizuru Castle Park? Isn't that where the kendo class is?"

Masami only nodded.

"That's kind of scary." Akio looked at her, trying to see if she was freaked out by that information too. Miyahara, the guy who bought the ninja shuko, held his kendo class at the same place where this homeless guy was killed.

Masami's blank look gave him nothing.

"The body was found by a couple of picnickers a few days after his beheading." Masami saved him the trouble of reading the report himself. "He was off to the side of the park in some brush and trees," she went on. "Apparently, their dog ran in and they followed. From the report, it looks like the police didn't get very far in their investigation because the victim was homeless. He had no connections to anyone. It was only after they found another beheaded body that he was considered a potential victim of the same killer. It also says that the scarring of the neck bones clearly showed a blade of some kind had severed the head."

Akio gulped down some Coke. "Wow. Well, we should talk to these picnickers then, right? Maybe they'll know something."

"I don't think so. There's no reason to think they would. They only found the body. They're a schoolteacher and an artist who live nearby and take their dog for walks in the park. They don't know anything about it."

"Well, what then?"

"We need to go talk to this kendo instructor," she said.

"Uh huh," Akio reluctantly answered. "That's our man, right? The guy who's slicing off heads?"

"Possibly," Masami looked at him disapprovingly. It was the look that his mother used to always give him when he would talk too loudly in public. "But we don't know anything yet. We're going to talk to him is all."

"Is it safe?" Akio asked, genuinely concerned.

Masami looked at him deadpan. "I have you with me, Akio. We should be fine."

Akio gagged on a french fry. He tried to decipher if she was being serious or not, but couldn't.

It was Saturday morning and the burger and fries were not sitting well in Akio's stomach. It was earlier than he wanted to get up, but there wasn't much choice. He relegated himself to spending some time on the toilet, collecting monsters playing *Puzzle & Dragons* on his phone.

Breakfast was at Jonathan's diner again.

"Not much for variety, are you?" Akio asked sarcastically as they sat at the same brown Formica table. It was noisier today. A large family sat nearby and their kids were shouting at each other. The parents seemed oblivious.

"We're not here on vacation." Masami, as usual, was in no mood for his sarcasm. "This is simply quick sustenance so we can get back to work."

Akio found he couldn't eat much. He was nervous about the day. *What if this kendo instructor really is the killer? What if he just attacks us on sight?* He had to get himself together. He had to find some courage. After all, maybe Masami had meant what she said about him being with her. Maybe she really saw him as someone who could protect her, someone who could handle himself in a fight. Against a master sword-fighting murderer.

Right.

Masami got up from the table when Akio had a mouthful of salted mackerel and half of it still on his plate. He hadn't even started on his *natto*.

"Time to go?" he mumbled through his food. But Masami was already out the door.

"I thought she wanted me to protect her," he muttered to himself as he stood from the table, slurping down a few mouthfuls of natto. He looked at the server, a girl in her twenties and probably a student, who just waved goodbye at him with a bored smile. Apparently, Masami had already paid. He hoped so.

She was nowhere in sight when he exited the diner. *Great.* He knew she was headed for the park though, and he knew that was east. He headed that way.

A block and a half later, he turned left on Heiwa Boulevard. It was the same route that took him past their hotel and back toward the train station. He saw Masami coming out of a side street a block ahead of him. *She must have taken a short cut. Dammit.*

She was moving fast. Traffic lulled at the crosswalk in perfect time for her to keep her brisk pace and cross the street without pause. Akio had to stop and wait for a hundred cars to pass.

He finally caught up to her half a block away from the park.

"Don't worry," he said, half out of breath. "I'm fine. I needed my morning jog anyway. It's all good."

Masami ignored him.

Akio followed her up the pathway into the park from the north side. He tried to stay with her step for step, but she didn't slow until she rounded a stone wall and reached the flat of the walkway. The castle ruins loomed above on their right, its huge slanting stone walls standing defiant as they had for 400 years. The spire of a monument spiked at the sky. A short, white castle tower was further along the path in front of them, a reconstruction of days gone by.

On their left was a sukiya-style building that looked like a samurai home from ages past. Its slender dark wood crisscrossed in perfect squares, eight panes to a window with smaller rectangular windows above, designed to let in vast amounts of sunlight. They reflected the beauty of the park around them. White walls separated the windows. The double doors were also dark wood and had more windows above. One door stood open by a sign that read, "Kendo class today." Noises and cheery voices came from within.

I'd better get a few shots now. Akio turned on his camera. *Just in case we don't make it out alive.* He snapped a few of the building and one of the doors and sign.

Peering into the brightly sunlit dojo, they saw several young people putting on the final elements of their blue *bogu* armor. A few were inspecting their shinai, their bamboo swords, for splinters. Many heads turned when the two journalists appeared at the door. Akio snapped a shot of the kendo group from the hip before he slipped his camera in his bag.

Masami removed her shoes and bowed before entering. Akio followed suit, aware of the proper etiquette for entering a dojo, even if he did think it was an empty gesture since they were entering the dojo of a murderer.

A short, thick, balding man approached them with a pleasant, but impatient look on his face. It was Miyahara, from the website photo.

"Can I help you? Are you interested in observing a class?"

Masami bowed and introduced herself and Akio as representatives of the *Dainichi Daily* in Tokyo. The man returned the pleasantries and offered his name as well, adding that he was the instructor.

"Sensei Miyahara," Masami said respectfully, "we'd just like to ask you a few questions about some recent events."

"Ah, yes," the older man answered. "The recent murders. Do you think me a suspect?"

"You cut right to the chase, don't you, sir?" Masami said, her expression softening into almost a smile. "But we are not the police, just journalists looking for a story."

"Perhaps you think it's one of my students then." He indicated the group with a wave of his hand. Bright young faces with ruddy cheeks and pimply foreheads looked back at them.

"I apologize, sir," offered Masami. "I don't mean to offend you. We aren't here to implicate anyone, especially these youngsters. We were just wondering if you had any thoughts on the matter."

"I mean," Akio chimed in, "if we were police, you know, your kendo skills might be a little suspect."

Masami gave Akio a glare full of daggers. These were worse than the usual daggers. Th ese were twice as long and razor sharp. "I apologize for my associate," she said quickly. "We do not mean to suggest such a thing. Please disregard his comments."

Miyahara did. He didn't address Akio at all. Looking at Masami, he said, "All that I know, I've read in the local paper." He emphasized the word "local." "I'm not sure why we need someone from Tokyo to rehash what we've already learned."

"With all due respect, sir, people in Tokyo deserve to know what's going on too."

"Yes, they do," he acknowledged. "And my students deserve to get their money's worth today. If you'll excuse me." The instructor turned his back on them and walked barefoot across the room to where his class was gathered. "You are welcome to stay and watch," he added, before barking at his students to line up for the start of class.

Akio wanted badly to call to the man, "Why did you buy ninja shuko? Been climbing up apartment walls lately?" But he didn't dare. The daggers from Masami's eyes were still hovering. He could be impaled at any moment.

They watched as the students bowed to Miyahara and he bowed back. A boy with a wide face and wider eyes looked straight at Akio. For an instant, he seemed to be pleading, asking for help. But he followed along with the other boys as they lined up for drills and didn't look their way again. As Akio was trying to dissect the boy's gaze and wondering if they were actually going to stay and watch, Masami bowed from the doorway and abruptly turned and walked out.

Akio jumped to follow. He must have just imagined the boy's look. It was just some weird kid. Anyway, if he mentioned it to Masami she would just think he was stupid.

Well . . . more stupid.

"That didn't go quite as planned," Akio said as they were walking from the park. "Did it?" he asked sincerely.

"It wasn't planned, Akio. I didn't have any preconceived notions."

"He's definitely the killer." Akio did a little skip and clenched his right hand in a fist as if in victory, punching the air. "He's so guilty."

"There's no proof," Masami corrected him. "But he does seem like he's hiding something, doesn't he?"

"Yes, totally!" Akio almost shouted. "It's gotta be him." He clapped his hands once as he said so. "The homeless guy was found there, he knows how to use a sword, and he's clearly hiding something! I'm convinced."

"Yeah," said Masami. "That's kind of what makes me question it."

Akio sighed loudly in frustration. "Great," he said. "Just great." He resisted saying anything sarcastic back to her. "What now then, oh wise one?" he asked.

"The base of Mount Fuji," she said.

"Why? Do you wanna go on a nature hike?"

"If you'd looked through the envelope the police gave us or had paid closer attention to my article, you'd know," she said, in her disappointed yet unaffected *and oh-so-endearing* way. "The first body was found there. Aimi Matsuoka. She was the co-owner of a *ryokan* in Fujikawaguchiko with her husband, Minoru. We should go talk to him."

Upon returning to the hotel, they retreated to their respective rooms first. Masami said she needed to take some notes. Akio scanned through the photos he had taken, marking the ones he liked and taking some brief notes of his own. He couldn't stop thinking that the kendo instructor was guilty as hell. He imagined Masami, when it was all over, telling Tanaka that she had her doubts but Akio knew all along.

An hour later, they were in the car. Masami pulled away from the hotel and toward the highway.

"So I'm still wondering," Akio said to break the silence of their drive. "Do we think the kendo instructor is a suspect or not?"

"We're not the police, Akio." Masami kept her eyes on the road, as steady and blank as an automaton. "We are not here to accuse anyone. We're journalists. We are just trying to get some information." Akio had the feeling that she was also trying to convince herself.

"But he was pretty damn suspicious, don't you think?" he said.

"I don't know. Maybe he's just a grumpy old man."

"Who's good with a blade."

"Look, when we get back from Mount Fuji, we'll investigate him a little closer."

"Good idea. But we're not the police?" Akio grinned.

"No."

"Okay."

8

Fujimaki

The thrum of the road was the only sound for miles. Akio wasn't talking. *I should be grateful for the silence,* Masami thought. But it made her nervous when things weren't as she expected them to be.

They were going to meet with the husband of the first victim. *How will this go?* Detective Kuramoto had said the innkeeper was crazy, that the death of his wife had made him nuts. Masami had called the station from the hotel after they met with Emiko, the maid girl, who was probably crazy too. It seemed everyone was. She had dreaded the call but asked to speak to the detective. Unfortunately, he came to the phone.

"Miss Sato," Kuramoto answered. "The boss still in Tokyo?"

"Yes, sir," Masami said, gritting her teeth. "He usually is."

"Hmph. What do you need?"

"Just a small favor, if it's no trouble."

"I'm sure it is trouble," Kuramoto droned. "It always is."

"I apologize, sir." Masami hated hearing herself be submissive to this jerk, but she had to play along. She always had to play along. "It's a simple request that would help our story, and we would be sure to pass along any pertinent information to you about the case."

There was a long pause.

Kuramoto wasn't getting anywhere with the case. She knew that. He had run out of leads. In that way, he needed her. And she could tell that he hated it. *Good.*

Finally he said, "The ninja tracks did pan out," rehashing what he had told her last time. "In fact, it turns out there are two sets."

"Two?"

"Yeah, two going up, only one going down."

Masami didn't know what to think. She hadn't considered that there might be two killers.

"Anyway," Kuramoto continued, "we're hot on the trail now. Probably have it all wrapped up by tomorrow," he said hollowly.

"That's great, sir." Masami said. "I'm glad we could help."

Another pause, and then, "Fine," he said. "What?"

"Thank you, sir," she said begrudgingly. *You dick.* "The address we have for Minoru Matsuoka is out of date. All we have is the address of the inn that he owned."

"Yeah, he used to live there," Kuramoto groaned. "Closed now."

"I'm aware of that, sir. That's why I'm calling. I could probably track it down at the town hall in Fujikawaguchiko, but I thought going to you would be more efficient. I imagine your information is far better than what they would have on record." *A little flattery can go a long way with these jackasses.*

There was another pause.

"This Matsuoka is a complete nutbag," Kuramoto said. "He lost it when his wife died, or when he killed her, probably. His marbles are rolling around ten ways to Sunday. But what can you say? Evil cause, evil effect. He didn't make a lick of sense when we talked to him. You're wasting your time." He went on like this, ad nauseam, about how foolish he thought it was to interview Matsuoka.

When he relented, Masami asked again, "So . . . the address?"

"Hmph." A pause. "Yeah, we got that."

"Thank you, sir. It would be a big help."

"Come by the station tonight and I'll give it to you. I'm working late."

"Sorry, sir, would it be possible to just give it—"

Click.
—*over the phone?*
He had hung up.
Dammit.

The station hadn't been any prettier in the evening. The dingy walls somehow seemed very clean. There didn't appear to be any cobwebs or dust. The room was just a faded yellow that made Masami feel like she was breathing in ancient toxins of some kind. *There must be lead in the paint*, she thought. *Asbestos in the ceiling.*

The reception officer was different than before. A very stone-faced, skinny man greeted her. He could have been a gargoyle in a uniform. Drooping eyes and a long nose, too much space between his eyes. He was someone who never opened the blinds in his apartment. He had no artwork on the walls, just a reminder list. Pick up mother on Tuesday for her root canal. Garbage day is Wednesday. Things like that. He was jaded from working the night shift. Masami wondered what kind of off-kilter characters showed up in the evening. Probably no one selling cookies.

Masami always dissected people when she met them, sometimes creating their entire life story. She couldn't help herself. She took in every detail and made a judgment call on their character before they even said a word.

After she announced that she was expected and who was expecting her, she sat. The same worn plastic covered with thin, useless cushions greeted her butt. But she didn't wait long this time.

After only five minutes, a young cop entered the lobby. He was probably in his late 20s, 30 at the most. His black hair was short but not buzzed. It had a little flip to it, but not enough to peg him as an overgrown kid. It was a serious cut with a hint of free spirit.

His clothes were sharp but a little creased and lived-in from the day's work. His dark blue suit jacket fit him well. It showed the cut of his chest, and his muscled arms filled the sleeves. His tie was tight and subtly colored. There was a thin sheen of sweat across his forehead. Professionalism was important to him and he put in the hours, both in the office and the gym. He was no slacker.

The cop had a gleam in his eye—that dangerous gleam that confident, handsome men have. But this gleam was friendly and empathetic, not arrogant like most of those type of men. *Even more dangerous.*

Normally Masami would have pegged him for a patrol officer, but he wasn't in uniform. *Was he off-duty and just on his way out or was he actually a . . .*

"Detective Tadao Fujimaki," he said, bowing respectfully. "You must be Sato from the *Dainichi Daily*. It's a pleasure to meet you."

"Yes," she answered, returning the bow. "It's a pleasure to meet you as well." She hated these formalities. And where the hell was Kuramoto? Not that she wanted to see him, but he had the address she needed.

"I apologize," Fujimaki said. "My partner had to leave, so I hope you don't mind me meeting you instead."

"Your partner?" she asked. *Was this guy really that prick's partner?*

"Yes, Detective Kuramoto."

Didn't see that coming. Fujimaki smiled disarmingly. Masami felt the pull of her lips trying to curl into a smile of her own. She wouldn't let them.

Kuramoto had told her he'd be working late. That he suddenly had to leave seemed suspicious. More than likely, he was just trying to screw with Masami, doing his utmost to show her no respect at all. *Typical.*

"Oh," she answered. "That's completely fine." And it was—assuming she could still get what she came for—except for the lack of respect. But she didn't need Kuramoto's respect. That would be akin to getting respect from a cockroach. The less time around that prick, the better. She was regretting even calling the station again. She could have gotten the address through other means, but she was trying to build a relationship; she was trying to play the game, as much as she loathed it.

"I have the address you requested," the young detective said, presenting a piece of paper.

"Thank you," she said, retrieving it. She glanced at it before putting it in her pocket. "I don't want to keep you. Thank you for your time," she said and turned toward the door.

"Wait a second," Fujimaki said. "If you don't mind, can we talk?"

Masami stopped and turned back.

"If you have the time, that is" he added, that respectful sparkle glinting in his eyes.

Ugh, she thought. *What's this about?* "Okay." She eyed him carefully but didn't get the hint of any ill intentions. She began to move toward the interior door of the station, to where she and Akio had spoken to Kuramoto.

"No," Fujimaki said, "Pardon me. Can we go for a walk? It's too stuffy in there." And by "stuffy," he meant crowded with testosterone and misogyny—from the look in his eyes, she was pretty sure.

"All right," she said, showing not one iota of the trepidation she felt. "Lead the way."

The detective opened the door for her, and they walked down Heiwa Boulevard as evening overtook the daylight. Subtle oranges faded from the buildings and shifted into grays.

"This is a strange case, isn't it?" Fujimaki asked.

Masami only nodded, wondering what the detective wanted from her.

"There seems to be no connection at all between the victims," he continued.

"Apart from missing their heads," Masami answered flatly.

The detective laughed quietly. "Yes, that's true." After a few steps, he added, "Pardon my laughing. It's not really funny, is it?"

Masami said nothing. But no, it wasn't.

"I'd like to hear your opinion on something," the detective continued. "It may sound crazy, but I can't stop thinking about it."

Masami remained silent, but a glance and a small nod let him know she was open to hearing him out.

"This killer went back to the apartment of one of his victims," Fujimaki said. "Now, I know on the surface that doesn't seem odd. He could have gotten the address from the vic's wallet. He might have thought it would be an easy place to rob since the guy was obviously dead. But the wallet on the corpse didn't appear disturbed. There were no fingerprints anywhere actually. Sure, maybe he's a pro and was able to remove it and then put it back. But it doesn't seem right. Our forensics guys found that the body hit the ground and stayed there. It wasn't jostled."

Masami walked and listened. He was making some good points. These are things she had thought about too. But she had nothing to add just yet.

"So this opens some other possibilities to me," he continued. "Maybe the killer knew the vic and already knew where he lived. Maybe this was personal. In the apartment, he didn't seem to be looking for valuables. The only thing that was disturbed were boxes of playing cards. It's possible the perp thought whatever he was looking for was hidden in those boxes. Maybe he found it and then was interrupted by the girlfriend, so he killed her."

"Sounds feasible," Masami finally offered.

"Right?" he answered quickly. He was on a roll. "In a self-contained little world, it seems like the obvious answer. We just need to figure out what the relationship was with the vic, what he was after, and we should have a good idea of who. But this scenario leaves out a ton of other obvious evidence."

They had walked about a block and had come to a small park. There was a cement pathway between a lawn and a few maple trees. Fujimaki gestured to a bench as he continued talking, and they sat.

"For one, why did he take the girlfriend's head? Why did he take the vic's head in the first place? Why did he take anyone's head? And that opens it up to the other victims. They have no connection with each other that we can establish. Nothing. The only two that are connected are this latest couple. But that seems like an accident, like he wasn't intending to kill her. She just got in the way. And then, he leaves the boyfriend's head behind. He'd never done that. Why?"

Masami was about to reply, but Fujimaki kept going.

"There's something else going on. There's some other reason he went to the apartment. I just can't see it yet."

Masami was starting to like this guy, even though he talked too much. She liked that he was passionate about his work, that he didn't just accept a pat answer and close a case. He was intuitive. He was smart. That's good. But why was he opening up to her? They had just met.

The detective smiled at her. "You're wondering what the hell I want from you," he said.

Damn. He can read that? Masami prided herself on her flat, unreadable expressions. She only screwed up the corner of her mouth in response, and raised an eyebrow.

"I know you," he continued. "Well, I know your writing."

Masami hoped her complete surprise was not also visible on her face.

"I lived in Tokyo through my twenties. I paid my dues at Tokyo Metro before winding up here. I read the *Dainichi Daily*. Your articles were something else, always fascinating. And there were a couple guys on the force that swore you were key to solving their cases. They would never admit it, not publicly, but I've heard your name whispered with some serious respect."

Masami was floored. She had no idea. The cops at Tokyo Metro were not generally much better than Kuramoto, though there were a few exceptions.

"Your exposé on the owner of Nakama Robotics was fantastic. There's no way they would've caught that bastard without the info you uncovered. Intentionally covering up dangerous defects in their OfficeBoy helper-bot and infidelities with three staff members! What a slimeball that guy was."

So he really had read the article.

Masami didn't know what to say. She wasn't good with receiving compliments. So she just nodded and said, "Yes, he got what he deserved."

Fujimaki smiled at her with obvious admiration. She avoided eye contact, wanting to get back to the topic at hand, not wanting this conversation to be about her in any way.

He seemed to be a good guy, but he wanted something from her. That was clear. He wanted to work with her so she wrote well about him probably, so he would get some kind of promotion or recognition. Or maybe—did she dare think it?—he just wanted her insight. Maybe he was simply a good cop that wanted to do what was right and didn't need to be cagey and overly protective of information. Maybe he recognized that Masami wasn't just out for a good story at anyone's expense. She wanted the real answers. She wanted the evil, ugly, and hateful to be put away. Did he want the same? She hoped so.

"There's something else you should know," Masami finally said, deciding to take a chance on trusting him. She told him about the visitations that Emiko the maid girl claimed to have. "If it's true, on any level, it could be that the killer is masquerading as the victims. But what reason would he have to come back and torment the people that were close to them?"

"And would he have been wearing the third vic's face?" Fujimaki asked. "The fourth vic's head was still in one piece."

"Gruesome thought," Masami said.

"I know, I know. But I saw it on TV once." He smiled.

Stop that. You're not going to make me swoon. I don't swoon. Masami pressed her lips tighter. It was something that helped her stay in control. It helped her keep her edge.

Then the detective got thoughtful. His eyes started to go distant, and he looked away. Something else had struck him. But she wouldn't ask. He'll tell her eventually, whatever it was.

"I think you're right," Masami said. "There's something else at play here. But I don't know what it is either. I'm sorry."

Fujimaki came back to the present, shaking away whatever it was he had been thinking about. "You know," he said. "There was something weird about the head too."

"What's that?" This was not what he had been thinking about. This was something else.

"Fibers," he said. "There were strange fibers in his hair and on his face. Some sort of cloth or rope, very damaged and old, maybe even ancient. Don't know what to make of it."

"Maybe it was wrapped in something," Masami said. "Some old family heirloom."

"Yeah, maybe," he answered, but didn't seem convinced. "There's something else too, something the first vic said, this Matsuoka you're going to see." He had that distant look again.

Masami raised her eyebrows, waiting.

"Nah," Fujimaki said, and looked at his watch. "It's pretty crazy. Maybe another time. I've got a few things to wrap up at the station."

Masami didn't press. She refused to look desperate, or even curious for that matter. But then she remembered something that had been bothering her. "Just one thing before you go, please." she said. "I know you're busy, but—"

"No, go ahead."

"Two of the murders were at the train station. A public place. Isn't there security camera footage?"

"Oh, that." The detective seemed to be struggling with whether he should tell her or not. "Can we leave this out of the paper until we have more solid information?"

Masami was intrigued. "Sure."

"There wasn't any footage, not really. The cameras were recording, but the image was distorted. We could see the victims, but around them it was like . . . like someone had smeared the image. It's not useable. After the murders, the footage goes back to normal. We're still trying to figure that one out."

Masami didn't respond. That was not what she expected. She had assumed that the police just weren't releasing any images to the press yet. She wasn't sure why Fujimaki trusted her enough to tell her this, but she was glad he did.

The detective broke the silence. "I don't want to take your time any longer. Let's meet again when you get back."

"Okay," she said, hoping he wasn't viewing this future meeting as some kind of date. His smile came back. It was meant to be disarming, whether Fujimaki knew it consciously or not, but Masami would not be disarmed. "I'll check in."

Masami thought of Detective Fujimaki as she sped along the highway toward Mount Fuji. She didn't want to admit it to herself, but she wished he were there with her, if only to talk to and help her make sense of this crazy story. He was smart and honest, at least he seemed to be. Her instincts were usually good about these things. He was dedicated to something more than himself. And he wasn't hard on the eyes.

Instead she had Akio, a scrawny, fidgety, motormouth of a pest, who was sitting very still and very quiet at that moment. He wasn't being annoying at all. And that was somehow more annoying than anything.

9

The Crazy Innkeeper

The route to Fujikawaguchiko by car was much faster and more direct than the train. With the way Masami drove, it was faster yet. What would have been an hour with normal morning traffic, took them about fifty minutes. If they hadn't gotten stuck behind that truck in the Shin-Misaka Tunnel, it would have been forty-five.

Akio gazed out the window at the trees along the road. His view was repeatedly interrupted by the zigzag patterns of gray brick retaining walls, where the mountain had been cut away to make room for the road. But he tuned those out like blips of static on the radio. The broad leaves of the trees were lush, green, and inviting. He wondered what kind of trees they were. Part of him longed to run through them like a little kid. But at the same time, the thought of it frightened him. He had grown up in the city. Who knew what strange, evil things lurked in the forest?

And they weren't that far from Aokigahara, the forest where around a hundred people committed suicide every year. What if he ran into a decaying body hanging from a tree branch? *Ugh. I'm happy right here in the car, behind steel and glass.* He slunk down into his seat and pulled out his mobile phone. *Puzzle & Dragons sounds like a great idea right now.*

They pulled up in front of the ryokan just after 9:00 a.m. The name of the inn, Sōkai, was written on an arcing wooden sign hanging above the glass front door, which was covered by a wooden lattice. A coating of dirt clung to the lattices where wind and rain had kicked it up over time, collecting it there. The glass was equally grimy, dotted with dirty water spots that hadn't been cleaned off after an aggressive rain, or several. The paving stones in front of the building were in an even sorrier state. Dead leaves and dried mud caked the area, looking like a landscape where tiny rivers once ran.

A banner spiraled down from the balcony above like a twisted and flattened animal that was strung up to bleed out. It was evidently once yellow, but now the mud caked it too, making it a grayish brown. It was impossible to tell what it might have said.

Akio shot photos as they took in the sorry state of it all.

"They're closed," said a strident voice behind them, startling Akio.

They turned to see a thin man, probably in his late sixties. He wore an equivalently thin mustache that was completely gray. A newspaper was clutched in one hand.

No one spoke for a moment, so the man spoke again. His creaking voice made it sound like it was a trial for him to form words.

"You can't stay here. But there are plenty of other nice places in town."

Masami took the opportunity for information gathering. "Do you know why it's closed?"

The man paused, frozen for a moment, evidently considering how he should answer that question.

"It's haunted," he croaked finally.

That's no surprise! Akio almost blurted out but stopped himself as Masami grabbed his arm tight enough to hurt. Despite the pain, he kind of enjoyed the contact.

"Really?" she said, sounding surprised. Although Akio thought she laid it on a little thick.

"Yes, I don't want to scare you though." The man gave a friendly smile, but with a hint of mischief, as if he might actually enjoy scaring them.

"No, you wouldn't," Masami answered. "You've certainly piqued my curiosity. We'd love to know the story, right, Akio?"

"Yes, yes, of course!" Akio spluttered.

The man's momentary restraint melted away, and he launched into the story as if he'd been waiting for just such an audience.

"Not that long ago, a woman was beheaded in there," he began. "She was one of the owners, with her husband, Matsuoka. My wife and I live right next door, so we heard everything. I saw Minoru—Mr. Matsuoka—out on the porch smoking when I was taking out the trash. I waved to him and he waved back. It was something we had done a hundred times. He seemed fine. Just enjoying a smoke and the evening air. But soon after, there were screams and things crashing. We heard the crashing first but didn't think much of it. Then we heard his wife screaming at him to get out of the house. Maybe he had been drinking too much. I don't know. They never argued much and were always friendly. So it was a surprise for sure."

The man paused for a moment, reflecting.

"After that, there was a blood-curdling scream. It had to be Matsuoka. I'm sure he woke up everyone within fifty kilometers. The police found him weeping over his wife's headless body. They never found the head. That's why they haven't convicted him yet.

"My wife thinks he did it," he continued, "but I'm not so sure. I don't think he had it in him." The man sighed, reflecting. "He was a good man. Even though, now he's as crazy as they come."

"Where'd he go?" Akio asked suddenly, caught up in the story and wanting more. Masami's fingernails dug deeper, but then released as if what he had said was okay after all. *Ow.*

"Toward Mount Fuji. He bought a shack out past the Lakeside Country Club. He hides there now. The weasel's last fart."

Masami wrinkled her nose at the rude expression to describe a desperate act, but Akio chuckled.

Ow!

"If he didn't do it, Mr . . . um?" Masami began quickly.

"Yamauchi," the man replied. "Harmless Yamauchi," he added with a tired grin. Then he finished her sentence. "Who did? Who can say?" The man formed an almost cartoonish frown. "Only Matsuoka knows for sure. And his brains are mush."

"How are we going to find his place?" Akio asked as they started driving again.

"With the address," Masami answered curtly, handing him her phone with the coordinates already inputted.

"Where did you get this, mystery woman?"

Masami didn't respond, eyes on the road.

"And if you had this already, why did we go to the inn?" Akio was flabbergasted.

"I wanted to see it," she answered. "I wanted context. And I thought you might appreciate the photo op, since you are the photographer on this assignment, if you haven't forgotten again."

"Of course. It was on my list," Akio lied; he hadn't made a list. "It just woulda been nice to know ahead of time what the plan was." Akio glared at her from the passenger seat, but she remained stone-faced, cold.

"Just tell me where I turn next."

The dirt driveway was almost hidden by bushy alders that leaned in toward each other from either side. The Logo's tires crunched into the dirt as branches scraped against its roof and windows.

Akio was already getting goose bumps.

"Do we really have to talk to this guy?" he asked, nervously. "What if he attacks us?"

"I guess your judo training will come in handy," she answered coldly.

Akio gulped.

The house appeared, also flanked by alders, the branches reaching out as if to protect or hide it. It was a small, two-story, *gassho*-style home, its triangle A-frame shape covered with a dense thatched roof. It was not a shack exactly, as the neighbor, Yamauchi, had called it, but Akio could see why he had. It was in decent shape but certainly old.

There was something foreboding about it. Or maybe it was just Akio's nerves.

The Logo pulled to a stop next to a faded blue, scratched and dented, old Toyota Hilux. The pickup looked like it shouldn't run, but it was clean and there was fresh dirt in the tire treads.

They stepped out of the car and surveyed the property. Trees pressed up against the roof, with a tangled mix of live and dead branches. Overgrown bushes and weeds covered much of the area, but what looked like a fenced and cared-for garden peeked out from the far side of the house. A weed-ridden stone path meandered toward the porch. The sun shone through the trees behind the house, playing in Akio's eyes.

The front door burst open, sliding violently against its frame.

A short, scrawny man in his later years rushed forward from the porch toward the two intruders. His face was twisted into an angry, puffy wart of an expression. He looked murderous. In his right hand he held a long, unsheathed katana. Its blade sparkled in the sun, except for where it was slick with fresh blood. In his other hand, he carried a human head, gripped by its white splay of hair, a tortured, lumpy face below.

Akio nearly fainted. His breath caught in his throat; he couldn't utter a sound.

The wart face let out a shout that was unintelligible to Akio, but he heard Masami respond.

"We just want to talk. We don't mean any harm!" she said to the rampaging man, as if she wasn't all that concerned that he had just murdered someone and was about to do the same to them.

Just want to talk? Akio couldn't believe it. *No, no, we don't! We just want to get the hell out of here!* He gripped Masami's shoulder trying to convey that message physically since he still could not form words. She shrugged his hand off and actually stepped forward.

"Get off of my property!"

Akio heard the man clearly this time, and he involuntarily stumbled back toward the car.

"He's . . . He's . . ." *the killer!* Akio was trying to warn Masami but couldn't quite get the words out.

The old man raised the sword higher as if he would bring it down on Masami's head, but he was still six meters away. He might have thrown it at her at that distance, but it seemed unlikely.

"We are sorry about your wife!" Masami said. "We know you didn't kill her!"

Oh really? Akio's thoughts were dizzy. *Have you lost your . . .*

But then he saw the man lower the weapon slowly. And although it certainly could be used with deadly force, it was not a katana. It wasn't a sword at all—it was a baseball bat. It was just an old scarred baseball bat that probably belonged to Matsuoka's son, if he had one. Maybe it was Matsuoka's himself from when he was younger. There was no blood, just a long patch where the wood was darker, or maybe worn and dirty; it was hard to tell.

Akio looked to the man's left hand and saw he was holding a transparent plastic bag that appeared to have lumps of greens and vegetable bits in it. He saw a carrot stem pressed against the front center. It made a protrusion that he must have mistaken for a nose.

I'm losing it, he thought. *I'm seeing things now. Great.*

"I don't want to hurt you," the man said, his whole being appearing to deflate. "I just want to be left alone." He seemed pathetic now, a sad empty man. He let the baseball bat drop to the ground.

He was not the killer after all. He hadn't been carrying a sword or a severed head. Akio shook off his fear and tried hard to focus. He had to make sure that what he was seeing was reality.

Yes, that's a baseball bat on the ground, not a bloody katana. Yes, that's only a plastic sack full of garbage, not a human head.

He hadn't been sleeping well. *That must be it,* he thought. *I just need to sleep. I need to relax.*

He took a step forward to stand by Masami. She was looking at the man with kind eyes, with concern.

"Do you mind if we just talk for a little bit? I want to hear your story," she said, her voice like a caress, like a dear friend.

"You are reporters?" he asked. "Students?"

"Reporters," she confirmed. "We're from Tokyo, the *Dainichi Daily*. We have no biases from local politics or this community at all. We've heard what some people around here think, and we don't believe the rumors. We want to hear *your* story." She emphasized the "your" with a caring that held the weight of a loving hug.

How is it that she can be so compassionate to strangers when she's such a cold, emotionless stone toward me? Is it all an act? Akio thought. *If it is, it's a really good one.*

The old man gave her a far away, defeated look. "Let me go dump this in the compost heap," he said, indicating the plastic sack. "I'll be right back."

He shambled off around the side of the house.

"Are you okay?" Masami looked at Akio with none of the concern she had just shown the man. "You look a little pale."

"I . . . I'm fine." Akio was trying to discern if she really cared about him when he got his answer.

"I just want to make sure you're not going to pass out on me," she said. "Maybe you should wait in the car."

"No!" Akio said a little too loudly. "I'm going with you. I'm not a child." *Thanks for your mock concern.*

He quickly grabbed his camera and snapped a photo of the house just before Matsuoka reappeared from around the side with the plastic sack, now crumpled and empty.

The old man stopped by his porch and looked them over for a moment, apparently reassessing whether he could trust them or not. His expression betrayed no decision, and maybe there wasn't one, but he silently waved them toward the house, a feeble pawing at the air with his hand.

Inside, they sat on the floor at a low table, which was centered over a tatami mat. He offered them both sitting cushions. Akio accepted one, but Masami politely refused. He brought out tea and small sweet breads filled with bean paste and set them on the table. It seemed his skill—and perhaps his need—for pleasing guests at his ryokan was still in him. Masami waited patiently and watched as the man went through his motions. Akio followed her lead and remained silent.

The man's puffy wart face seemed to have deflated along with his anger. He sat gazing at the two journalists with a look of loss and some skepticism.

He poured the tea. "It should be ready now," he said feebly.

The two offered their thanks in unison.

"It hurts to lose the person you love more than life." The old man said it out loud, but there was no indication he was actually saying it to them.

"That . . ." *sucks*, Akio started to say, but stopped, realizing that even though it was all he could think of as an expression of sympathy, it probably wasn't appropriate.

"I'm sorry," Masami said softly. "I can't imagine what you've been going through."

Yeah, that was more appropriate.

Matsuoka looked at Masami and then at Akio. "You two are together?" he asked.

"No," Masami said, a bit too quickly and sharply for Akio's liking.

"Oh," the man said and dropped his head to stare blankly at his tea. "Just as well," he added, after a moment.

The steam curled up from Akio's tea, and he braved the silence to take a sip. It was warm and earthy. He thought of what it would have been like to taste it as a guest at Sōkai when Matsuoka was happy and his wife was alive.

The innkeeper's eyes remained downcast for a long while. Then he took a deep breath that rattled in his chest and let it out slowly. "You will not believe what I have to say," he said, completely detached.

"Try us," Masami said, her voice barely a whisper.

The old man shifted on his cushion, his posture straightening slightly. He closed his eyes momentarily and opened them again. "I will tell you what happened," he said with a sigh that threatened to break him. "It is my suffering."

He looked at both Masami and Akio in turn, seeming to map their faces one by one, to take in their essence. Then he began.

"I was on my balcony, having my nightly cigarette. It was the only one I would smoke. Just one per day. I used to smoke a pack and a half a day. But I got down to only one. I told everyone I was a non-smoker. One a day doesn't count as being a smoker. Now I don't smoke at all." He coughed suddenly, as if the long years of that bad habit were trying to expose him.

"It was around 10 p.m. There were not many stars because of the clouds. It was a little chilly and I had forgotten my sweater, but I was too committed to my cigarette to go back in for it.

"Aimi, my wife . . ." He paused and closed his eyes briefly, clearly conjuring an image of her behind his eyelids. "She was watching television, I think. Or cleaning up our dinner mess. We had *okonomiyaki* that night, one of my favorites. She cooked so well. Without her, there would never have been a ryokan.

"I kissed her and said, 'I'm going to meditate.' She knew that was my slang for having a smoke. She smiled and rolled her eyes. I will never forget."

Matsuoka took another deep, rasping breath. The wrinkles at the edges of his eyes deepened as he fought back tears.

"I was sitting in my chair, my rickety old worn out thing, looking down the empty street. It's slow that time of the year . . . It was slow then. A car would drive by occasionally, but mostly it was dark. Just a couple street lamps glowing."

He paused again, seeming to try to find some reserves of courage. He looked up at Akio and Masami for just a moment, as if checking to see if they were still there, to see if what he was saying still mattered.

"I don't know where it came from," he said. "It was just suddenly there. This big, wide monster of a thing, dressed like an ancient samurai. It was on my balcony. Just dropped in from nowhere.

"I was too shocked to even speak, to ask what he . . . it was doing there. It took only one long stride and grabbed me by the shoulder. Its dark red mask was right in my face. It was an ornate piece with flames and clouds etched across it. But there was no face behind it. There was only blackness. It had no head under its kabuto."

No head? Akio wanted to laugh, but he held it in. *Oh boy, we've got another crazy one.*

"The thing grabbed its katana and unsheathed it," Matsuoka continued. "I knew what it meant to do. It was going to cut off my head. I could tell in a moment. It didn't have a head, and it wanted mine.

"I had no hope. It was so much bigger than me. I wanted to run, but it thrust its mask closer to me. It was almost involuntary, but I reached up and grabbed the mask with my left hand. When I did, my fingers locked into the eyeholes and mouth. The teeth on the mouth cut into my thumb. I could feel the blackness behind it. It felt cold, like hate. But I pulled at it. As hard as I could.

"The samurai crouched over me, almost like it was waiting for me to take the mask. It came free suddenly, like pulling something from a vacuum cleaner that's too big to be sucked in. As soon as I had it free, I took my lit cigarette and shoved it into the blackness where its head should have been. I don't think it was expecting that.

"It screamed somehow, some dark, guttural curse from within, and staggered back. I don't know if it was from the cigarette or from losing its mask or both. But it let go of me. And I ran inside. I stumbled through the door, shouting as I went. Aimi met me in the living room. She had heard the shouting.

"'Run!' I told her. 'Get out of here!' But she didn't. She stared helplessly, just as I had, at the horror that followed me. I turned to face the thing again, to do anything at all to protect my wife. But I tripped. As I turned, I tripped . . . on nothing. When I looked later, there was nothing. My heel just caught the floor and I fell backward."

Akio had become engrossed in the story. He was rethinking his opinion of the old man. He didn't seem crazy, even if his story was.

"I saw the monster stop and look at my wife, my beautiful Aimi. It looked back at me on the floor, trying to scramble to my feet, and then again at my frozen wife. It made a decision then. I could see it even though it had no face. Just like I knew it wanted my head before, now I knew it decided that her head would do."

The old man's breath caught, and he gasped out a few tortured sounds like a whimpering animal.

"It took her head instead." He began weeping in short bursts between words. "He cut it off and carried it away. I couldn't stop him. I couldn't save her. He walked back out to the balcony with her head gripped by her hair. I screamed at him. But I couldn't stand.

"If only I had let him take my head on the balcony. If only I hadn't fought him. She would be alive. He would have taken my head and left. She would still be alive," he repeated, sobbing freely now.

Tears pushed out of Akio's eyes, and he cried too. He didn't know what to say. The man was in such pain. Akio had never even been in love—he was pretty sure—but he could feel this man's anguish so intensely that he couldn't help it. The love of his life murdered—beheaded—right in front of him! It was horrifying. As crazy as the story was, as implausible as this giant, headless samurai seemed, he could tell the man was painfully sincere.

Masami was stone-faced. *Of course.*

But she did apparently have some compassion—that compassion reserved for strangers.

"You saved her," she said softly.

The ruined man looked up at her, confusion showing through his wet, red eyes. He looked like he was going to be angry.

"If you had died, she might not have been able to go on," Masami explained. "She was not as strong as you. She could not have handled your death. But you are strong. You can go on, despite the pain. You can be strong for her."

The man's head dropped, and any inclination toward anger fell away with it. More tears fell to the tatami mat below.

Akio looked in awe at Masami and then at the old man. His tears stopped as he thought about what Masami had said. It was brutal in a way, but was it true? *Would things have been worse if Matsuoka had been beheaded? Would his wife have killed herself or really gone mad?*

Matsuoka's neighbor had said he was crazy, but he didn't seem crazy. Not at all. Even though his story was hard to swallow. The killer was probably just a man with a black balaclava on—probably Miyahara, the kendo instructor in Kofu. He couldn't have had no head. People see things. Akio's own vision had played tricks on him at the front of the house. No, Matsuoka wasn't really crazy. He was just a man bereft of the love of his life. *Wouldn't that make anyone seem crazy?*

Matsuoka's breathing slowly calmed. He found some hidden strength in himself to control his emotions. Perhaps it was simply the strength that Masami had suggested he had. Maybe she had given it to him.

"Oh, she was strong," he finally muttered reflectively. "So very strong. But thank you." Even though Matsuoka may not have agreed with Masami's suggestion, something about what she said had diffused his self-loathing.

There was a long silence in which Masami poured more tea for the old man, who was regaining his composure, one breath at a time. The only noise was from the myriad birds that sang outside in the late morning sun. The bunting's chirping whistle mixed with the shrill chattering of a thrush and what was clearly the knocking of a woodpecker on a nearby tree.

Akio was barely aware of the birds. He was mesmerized by the old man's emotions. He wondered if he would end up like this man. Or worse, he might end up never knowing love at all.

Matsuoka shifted his pillow beneath him and tried to sit up straighter. He managed an embarrassed smile and said eerily, "But that was not the last time I saw her."

Matsuoka had that empty, far away look again, like he was outside himself. Keeping that distance from his own feelings might have been the only thing that kept him upright.

"It was ten days later," he muttered, "after I had been held by the police and grilled for three of those days. But they could not get me to admit I killed her. I would not sign any statement for them, so they let me go. But they still watch me, I know. When I returned, Aimi's family grilled me too." That part clearly hurt him. "They all wanted to believe that I was guilty."

He looked right at Akio and asked, "Why would I kill her?" He was earnest and full of pain. Akio could only return the look with his own confusion of concern and horror.

Yeah, why would you? There's no way.

"I would sit in the room where she was murdered by that thing. I tried to disbelieve what I saw. It must have been a person, not a monster. But I couldn't. It was too real. No matter how I tried, I couldn't make it something I could understand. It was a monster.

"So I accepted it." A mild cough cut into his narrative, and he sipped tea to quell it.

"I prayed to see her again. I wanted so badly for her to come back. I knew that if she could come back, it would be to the room where she had died. So I waited there.

"We only had two rooms occupied the night it happened, and of course they had checked out quickly that evening." He paused, reconsidering. "No, I don't think they checked out at all. They just left. I can't blame them.

"I closed the ryokan. And I waited."

Matsuoka shifted again and closed his eyes, as if he was back in the living quarters of the inn, waiting for his wife to return to him.

"I sat every night in the same position on the floor where her body had collapsed. Praying. Crying. Sometimes screaming. Sometimes calling for her to come back, or for the monster to return and take me too. It's why my neighbor's think I'm crazy, I guess."

He opened his eyes again and looked at Akio and Masami in turn. "But I'm not crazy." It sounded almost like a question.

"No," Akio grunted softly in reply, even though he could still not come to terms with the monster story. But it was the second time they had heard a description of a big samurai ghost person. *Could Matsuoka and Emiko, the hot maid girl, both be nutjobs? And be having the same hallucination?*

"Both of my wishes came true, in a way," the old man continued with a momentary, joyless smile.

"It was nearly midnight when she first came back to me." He gulped down the anguish that the memory was causing him. "First, I only saw the monster. Its hulking shape blocked the moon through the balcony window. I jerked alert and stood up, awaiting my fate. I wanted so badly to join my wife, wherever she was. 'Take my head too,' I thought. 'Take my head too!'

"But then it opened the balcony door, slowly. It was so unlike how it had crashed into my home the time before. It was calm. It was even graceful. It walked . . ." He paused, not wanting to admit it. "Like my wife."

Okay, now things are getting weird, Akio thought. *Maybe he is nuts.*

Akio was sure the man could see the doubt creeping across his face, but Matsuoka continued. "It walked up to me, its katana was still sheathed. It wore all its armor, and its kabuto like before, but no mask." He gave a small smile. "Because I still had that. But it had a head this time. It had a face." Tears began to well again in his eyes. "It was my Aimi's face." He buried his head in his hands. "It had put on her head."

What? Akio was dumbfounded. *Put on her head?* He wondered if it had just been a different samurai. The salaryman's ghost that Emiko saw had been wearing armor too. Maybe this was just what happened to certain people when they die, he thought, to people who were beheaded. *They become ghost samurai.*

"Was it . . ." Akio stumbled. "Was it a ghost?"

"No," Matsuoka replied with certainty. "It was no ghost. Ghosts do not leave dirty footprints. Ghosts do not slice off people's heads."

Anger was starting to bubble up in the man's demeanor again. He pulled at his bony fingers, cracking each knuckle, one at a time.

Masami's soft, soothing voice—*Where does that come from?*—reached out to him again. "Please, continue," she intoned. "What happened next?"

The man took another deep breath and looked straight at Masami. "You look nothing like her," he said, and then added, "but you sound like her."

He finished his story with short fits of tears and one moment of uncomfortable, anguished laughter, but mostly with that distant look of loss.

"She reached out to me," he said. "She put her hand on my cheek and a tear fell from her eye. It was the monster's gauntlet that my skin felt, but it was her soul in there. It was her touch." Akio's skin prickled at the thought.

"Then it shoved her away from me. It took over and pushed itself back. I could see it take control of her face for a moment. It reached for its katana and began to withdraw it, but then it stopped." This was the moment of laughter. He giggled softly between tears. "She stopped him. Her face was back in her control and I could see her determined look. It was that look she had when she put her foot down, when there was no way I was staying out late, drinking and smoking my head off with my fair-weather friends in my thirties. She stopped him. I had stopped fighting that look decades ago. And this monster, this terrifying beast, couldn't fight it either.

"'Let him do it,' I begged her. 'Let him take my head. Let me be with you.'

"But she wouldn't. She shook her head. She looked at me with such love. She wouldn't let that happen," he whimpered. "Even though I let it happen to her."

"No," Masami whispered, but he ignored her this time.

He steeled himself again to finish the story. "Then the monster— my wife—turned and ran out the door, leaping off the balcony into the night.

"It came back every night for two weeks, but it wouldn't come inside. It stayed at a distance. She kept it there, because she was afraid it would kill me, I think. But she made it come back, so she could look at me. So she could show me she loved me.

"But then it stopped. For a week there was nothing. I knew she had moved on and that I had to move on too. It was torture letting go of her. Not seeing her anymore, even in that monster's body. But I knew she wasn't coming back. So I closed for good. I bought this house, and I have not returned to the inn."

He stood simply to stretch his legs, groaning as he rose. "My bones are old. I can't sit so long without getting stuck."

He seemed embarrassed for a moment as he looked at his guests, possibly considering whether or not he should regret telling these strangers his story. "Can I get you anything else?" he asked. "Some cookies, maybe?"

"You mentioned that you had taken its mask," Masami said, ignoring the offer.

Cookies had sounded like a great idea to Akio, especially after a good cry, but the mask was intriguing too. He had forgotten about it.

"Yes," Matsuoka answered. "It was laying on the floor after the creature left. I must have dropped it at some point. Would you like to see it?"

He brought out a square cardboard box with a removable lid, like a hatbox. He set it on the low table and lifted the lid. A bundle of thin towels were inside. Akio could see "Sōkai" printed on one. Matsuoka unfolded the towels, unwrapping the mask hidden within.

It was a *somen*, a full-face mask with round eyeholes and a jagged-toothed mouth. It was a deep, blackish red, like blood that was nearly dry. The nose pointed sharply down with large round nostrils flaring out. The whole of it was etched with clouds and flames.

Akio wanted to hold the mask. He really wanted to hold it, maybe even put it on.

But Matsuoka offered it to Masami. "Be careful of the teeth," he said. "They are sharp."

Masami flinched as she reached for it, retracting her fingers momentarily, but then she took it and leaned over it intently.

Akio squeezed closer to her and looked over her shoulder. She didn't move away like he had assumed she would. But at this moment, he was far more interested in the mask than in her. It was sinister looking, as most samurai masks were, but there was something more about this one. It felt like it was looking at him, speaking to him.

Its detail was stunning. Swirls of clouds were etched into the forehead. Flames whipped under the eyes and into the cheeks where they met with intricate wisps and puffs of clouds. These continued under the nose to form what looked like a flaming, cloudy mustache. More flames that seemed to almost jump off the mask licked around the jaw, beginning at the chin, where three short metal tubes protruded downward. This was for sweat drainage, Akio remembered reading in a comic book. There was no neck guard attached to the mask.

Masami handed it to Akio suddenly, nodding to him. She had a strange look on her face, and he wasn't sure what the nod meant. Was she giving him the okay to wear it? He really wanted to wear it. It *was* speaking to him. He was sure of that now. Low voices came from it, as if from far away. Soft, raspy voices like jagged metal dragging across skin.

It was heavy, surprisingly heavier than he had anticipated. It pulled like a weight to the floor. But that made sense somehow to Akio, though he wasn't sure exactly why. He couldn't tell what it was made of, but it seemed like some kind of stone. It didn't feel like the usual iron or leather. And he really thought he should put it on.

He started to bring it to his face.

"Akio!" Masami interrupted. "What are you doing? A photo, please."

Right! A photo! That's what the nod had been for.

He looked at the mask, and the low voice prodded him to wear it. The words he heard were not Japanese. They were not words he had ever heard before. But he understood them.

Masami glared at him.

With an intense effort, he set the mask on the table. As he let go, he regained some control. He still heard the voice, but only faintly, further off, and then it was gone. He must have imagined it. He really needed sleep.

He retrieved his camera.

"Do you mind if I take a photo of this, sir?" Akio asked.

"No, no," Matsuoka replied. "I don't care. It will make a better picture than me."

Akio snapped a few shots, adjusting his camera for the nearly noon light angling in through the window from the garden. The mask lit up in his lens, reflecting the light like a finely cut gem. It was beautiful. So much better than his own face.

"Did the police examine this?" Masami asked, indicating the mask, as Akio zoomed in on some of the detailed flames. Each lick of fire looked almost real, like it was flickering in a breeze. It was intoxicating.

Matsuoka looked away for a moment, as if ashamed. "No," he said. "I hid it. I'm not sure why. I think it wanted me to hide it. So I did."

"The mask wanted you to hide it?" she asked.

"Yes."

Masami nodded as if it made perfect sense. And somehow it did.

"Do you think the monster just wanted his mask back?" Akio interjected, grateful that whatever or whoever Matsuoka thought was a monster had not gotten it back.

Masami looked at him with a queer little twist of her mouth that said, "Okay, that's actually an acceptable question. I'll let it slide."

Akio didn't wait for an answer. He switched to a macro lens to get the mask's detail even better.

"I thought maybe so, at first. But I could see it in her eyes. She brought that monster back so she could see me. And if it wanted that mask, she wouldn't let the thing have it. I'm sure of it. She wouldn't let it get close enough."

"And it's never shown up here?" Masami asked.

"Never. It's moved on."

To Kofu, Akio thought. *It's slicing heads off there now.*

"Do you watch the news?" Masami asked. "Or read the paper?"

Her question pulled Akio's attention from the mask for a moment. He knew what she was getting at.

Matsuoka laughed. "No. I want to be alone now. I stay here. I read. I grow what food I can and shop only if I have to. I don't care about the outside world. Let them think I'm crazy. I don't care."

He has no idea what's happened since. And maybe that's best.

"I'm sorry I won't be reading your article," he continued. "I'm sure it will be great. But I don't care."

"It's okay," Masami answered. She smiled ever so slightly, as if it somehow made her happy that someone was so detached from the world, so free of concern about others. It was a world that had abandoned him. Why should he care?

"That's enough, Akio." Masami said, indicating the photos.

Akio slowly lowered his camera as if coming out of a trance. *How many did I take?*

A look passed between the two journalists, and it was silently agreed that it was time to go. Under normal circumstances, Akio would have been secretly thrilled at that connection, but he didn't want to leave the mask.

"We don't want to take any more of your time," Masami said, rising.

Akio packed up his camera, not taking his eyes off the mask lying on the table. He was sure it was looking back at him.

"Take that thing," Matsuoka said, startling Akio. "I don't want it anymore. It reminds me of what happened."

Yes! Akio was thrilled. He wanted to take it. The mask wanted to go with him. It should go with him.

"Sir, are you sure?" Masami asked. "We have no need of it."

Yes, we do! Akio wanted to shout.

"Please. You would be doing me a big favor. I swear that thing talks to me sometimes. And it's getting louder. Maybe I am crazy. Please, get it out of my sight."

Akio barely registered the last part of what Matsuoka said. He was giddy that they got to keep the mask. It was the single coolest thing he had ever seen.

"We will then," Masami said, and packed it back into the box.

Akio wanted to carry it, but she held on to it. He was jumping out of his skin at the fact that they were taking it with them. He felt giddy. He wanted to dance.

"We are very grateful for your story," Masami said as they stood by the door.

"But do you believe it?" Matsuoka asked.

Masami smiled this time, a genuine smile, however stiff. "We don't have to believe," she said. "We only have to tell it fairly."

This seemed like a good enough answer to the man. He waved them off, sliding the door shut behind them.

IO

The Wide-Faced Boy

Akio's thoughts were spinning as fast as the tires on Masami's Honda Logo as they whizzed down the highway back toward Kofu. Their encounter with Matsuoka kept replaying in his head. The mask hovered in front of everything, its flames and clouds glinting in the sun, swirling like tiny eddies about the sinister face. It had spoken to him.

Or was this just another hallucination like the bloody katana that was really only a beat-up baseball bat?

Probably.

He had wanted to carry the mask with him in the front seat, but Masami put it in the cargo hold. She had just looked at him like he was stupid and shut the hatchback door. It made him angry at the time, though he hadn't said anything. Now that he had some time to think, he wasn't sure why. It was just a mask. It was beautiful. It would have been nice to put it on. Maybe he'd get a chance later.

Slowly, the mask faded into the background. The vibrations of the road lulled Akio's thoughts to Matsuoka's story.

"It hurts to lose the person you love more than life."

He wasn't even sure he could wrap his head around it. To love someone more than life. That was huge.

He looked over at Masami, her sharp, dire face intent on the road. She held a focus like daggers. Her mind was somewhere far away though. He wondered if it was at a similar location to his own.

She's so mean.

Could he ever love . . . her?

She treats me worse than a filthy, stray, mongrel dog.

That much?

If she would just . . .

More than life?

He shook the thought away as shivers ran up his back.

He pulled his mobile phone out of his pocket and started to enter the passcode. Then he locked it and shoved it back in his pocket. He wanted a distraction, something to take him away from his thoughts. But a game wasn't going to work. Maybe if he had the mask. That would keep him occupied.

"It didn't have a head and it wanted mine."

The image of the headless samurai attacking the old man was too vivid. It couldn't be real. The crazy old guy must have made it up. He must have imagined it. The neighbor had said his brains were mush. That was the only answer that made sense.

A headless samurai? Seriously?

But he seemed so truthful. He was so sad. Nobody's that good of an actor.

Except maybe a crazy person.

Was Matsuoka so crazy that he killed his wife and then made up a wacko story to cover it up? A story that no one would ever believe?

Akio slipped his hand back in his pocket, touched his phone again, but then withdrew it. He looked out the window at the blur of trees interspersed with flashes of zigzag, gray brick.

"It took her head instead."

Akio couldn't imagine the emotional pain. *The person you love more than life. Beheaded in front of you. The killer walks away from you holding her head.*

He glanced at Masami again. He couldn't help it.

What would that be like? Her, headless. That thin-lipped, pale, severe face hanging from the gauntleted fingers of some ghostly samurai.

But he didn't love her. Certainly not more than life.

Probably not at all.

He couldn't fathom it. It was a train of thought for which he had no ticket.

The sun was high in the passenger window pricking at Akio's left eye as the road leveled out. They would be back in Kofu soon, and it was still early afternoon.

Masami swung the car to an abrupt stop into a parking space in a lot near the hotel, not bothering with the hotel's own stacked car park. She got out quickly and slammed the door. When Akio exited the car, she glared at him.

"Are you okay?" she asked him flatly. "You haven't said a word the whole trip."

Akio was completely taken aback. *Did she just express concern for me? And for real this time? Or is she just annoyed with me for something I don't understand?* He looked back at her blankly, unable to process the situation.

And did I really not say anything for almost an hour?

He wasn't sure which was stranger.

No . . . no, he knew. Her expressing concern would definitely be stranger. So she was probably just annoyed at him.

She didn't wait for an answer. As he stood there dazed, looking at her like she had just sprouted dragon wings, she stormed off into the hotel.

Akio sat on his hotel room bed wondering what they were supposed to do next. Masami hadn't said anything. He assumed she was in her room, but he didn't dare knock to find out. She seemed in a royal foul mood.

But she had asked about his well-being. Th at was certainly progress.

The wallpaper had tiny pink lines in it. He hadn't noticed that before. It had tiny green lines in it too. He had thought it was brown, but it was a mix of pink and green lines. It wasn't brown at all.

Then he remembered the mask.

It was still in the back of the car. When they had gotten back, Masami had stormed off without taking it, and he had forgotten all about it. It must still be there.

He instantly knew what he had to do. He had to go get the mask.

He headed to the elevator and punched the button for the lobby. After an agonizingly slow ride down, he hurried out the hotel doors, dodging a woman carrying a small dog at the last second.

"Sorry," he said, as he shot out of the hotel.

"It's okay. It's okay," said the woman, giving him a look of concern that he didn't register.

Masami's car was a block away in the public lot. He moved quickly toward it, almost running down the sidewalk, then abruptly stopped.

Someone was standing by the car, looking at the license plate.

Akio's heart jumped. Was it the kendo instructor? Had he come to kill them for questioning him at his dojo, to take them out of the picture before they could cause him more trouble?

Against his better judgment, Akio moved forward. The figure was too tall to be the kendo instructor, and too slim. Whoever it was lifted the driver's side wiper blade and was about to put something under it.

As Akio got closer, he saw that it looked like a teenage boy. It was just some punk distributing fliers. He called out, "Hey! Whatever it is, we aren't interested." And then added, "And you know that's illegal anyway."

He was feeling bitter and it made him bold. It was a weird feeling for him and not something he was entirely comfortable with.

The boy looked up and Akio recognized him. It was the boy with the wide face and eyes from the kendo class. He looked at Akio, startled, his wide eyes even wider.

"I'm sorry," he said. "I just wanted to talk to you."

Akio walked up to the boy, bolder now that he knew who it was. He assessed him like he was some kind of detective, like he had the inside scoop and already knew why the boy was there.

But he didn't have a clue.

"So . . ." Akio began, putting on his best movie detective drawl. "You followed us here, huh?" He leaned on Masami's car with one hand and fished in his pocket with the other, as if for some cigarettes. He didn't find any though—he didn't smoke, he remembered. So he awkwardly put that hand in his back pocket.

"Well, kind of," the boy said. "When I was walking home from the dojo, I saw you two drive by. And well . . . I have a thing for license plates," he said, a little embarrassed. "I remember sequences, like numbers and letters. It's like a stupid game I play by myself."

"So you're some kind of numbers genius? Like a savant?"

The teenager didn't answer the question, but gave Akio a queer look, somewhere between confusion and pity. "I figured you'd be staying near the train station, so I just wandered around the closest hotels, hoping I'd see your car. I'm glad it wasn't sandwiched in that stacked car park."

"Is that so?" Akio asked. "You're a regular spy guy, huh?"

"Uh . . . no," the boy stammered. "You two were talking about the beheadings and I just thought I should talk to you."

"Oh!" Akio said accusingly. "So you know about the beheadings, huh?"

"Uh, yeah. Everyone does."

"Hmm . . ." Akio's upper hand was suddenly diminished. "I guess that's true." But then he had the boy with his next question. "Why did you think we were staying near the train station when we drove here in a car?" He was good. That would surely trip the boy up.

"Well, two of the murders happened there, and the other one not far off. I assumed you'd want to be close to the crime scenes, for efficiency's sake if nothing else."

"Hmm." This boy was clever. "Yeah, yeah, of course we would," Akio said as if it had only been a test.

"I just have some information for you," the teenager said. "Since you were asking about it."

"I know exactly why you're here," Akio said, trying to convince himself more than anyone. He had to regain the upper hand. "You're here to defend your sensei. You think he's a great guy and there's no way he could be involved. And you want us to back off. Well—"

"No, actually," the boy interrupted. "That's not it." He fidgeted with the note he still held in his hand. "Can we go somewhere else to talk, please? I don't want Sensei Miyahara to see me talking to you."

"Uh . . . sure," Akio answered, trying to remain cool despite being completely wrong, despite losing the upper hand yet again. He looked around nervously to see if the kendo instructor might be hiding behind another car or a building. His neck felt hot suddenly, like he was being watched. But there was no one.

"There's a 24-hour manga café a few blocks away called Sheep Box," the teenager said. "Sensei wouldn't be caught dead there."

"Good plan," Akio said, and meant it.

"I'll meet you there in ten minutes," the boy called and hurried off without waiting for confirmation.

Akio didn't know what to do. He tried to be casual, as he watched the boy go, but then felt uncomfortable standing on the street without a purpose. He shoved his hands in his pockets and started walking slowly in the same direction. Half a block later, he pulled out his phone and looked up Sheep Box on his maps app.

He had forgotten all about the mask.

Sheep Box reminded Akio of a pancake restaurant, or maybe a church, from the outside. It had a tall sloping roof that went up three stories on one side but then flattened out to one level on the other. There were signs everywhere advertising their weekly specials for games, manga and curry.

Inside, it was brightly lit. It wasn't that busy in the early afternoon. The place would probably get more crowded after work hours, if it were at all like the ones Akio had visited in Tokyo.

The wide-faced boy met Akio at the front counter.

"I already have a spot rented," he said, "but you still have to pay for your time. Get a booth next to mine."

Akio knew the drill. He requested thirty minutes, which was the minimum time allowed. If their conversation took longer than that, he'd have to pay another 100 yen for every 15 minutes. In Tokyo, when he knew he was going to camp out all day at a manga café and binge an entire series, he'd pay the discounted rate for up to eight hours. That was the rate people paid when they were using the café as a cheap place to sleep through the night.

Akio selected a booth next to where the teenager pointed on the seating map and took his receipt. He'd pay on the way out depending on how long they stayed.

"Follow me." The boy led him into the café.

They passed a long table surrounded by shelves and shelves of manga. Two young men sat at the table reading intently. Beyond it were two rows of cubicles with curtains for privacy. Akio followed the boy to the end of the second row.

The boy ducked into the cubicle that Akio had selected and pulled the office chair out of it, carrying it into the next one over. He squeezed it in next to the chair that was already there leaving no room available to actually get into either chair without climbing over them —which is exactly what the boy did, plopping himself down in front of the computer screen.

Akio followed suit, feeling a little ridiculous in the cramped space that was most definitely not meant for two people.

From a few cubicles away they could hear the grunts and mumblings of someone playing an online game and talking quietly into the headset. Other than that, there was very little noise. Pages turning, occasional stifled laughs or involuntary mutterings of surprise.

Manga cafés were like libraries. You had to be quiet so people could read. In that way, it really wasn't the best place to have a conversation. But the kendo instructor wouldn't be there, that was certain, and Akio hoped the young men and boys who were there would be too engrossed in their reading and video games to pay attention.

"I'm Yoshio Hirakawa," the teenager whispered, looking into the computer screen at Akio's reflection.

"Akio—" Akio started to whisper back.

"Tsukino," interrupted the boy. "I know."

Akio snapped his head toward the boy, astonished. Yoshio continued looking at the screen's reflection. "I'm good with names too," he said, still whispering. "You introduced yourself at the dojo. You and Miss Masami Sato."

Akio's hackles were raised when he heard Masami's name. Some protective instinct deep inside him was awakened. "You're good," he said softly, turning his head to gaze at Yoshio through the screen. "I can't remember my own phone number half the time." He looked at Yoshio, daring him to speak the digits of his own phone number. If the boy knew that, he would know that he had some demented stalker on his hands. He needed to be careful.

But the boy didn't say Akio's phone number. He just looked at Akio's reflection as if he felt slightly sorry for him. *'The poor man can't even remember his own phone number,' he must be thinking. 'And I can remember your credit card number forever after one glance.'*

Akio felt a little inadequate in front of this apparent memory wizard, but he also felt calmer. Something about the perceived threat to Masami actually settled his nerves. It made him focused and confident.

"Tell me why you brought me here," he whispered to the boy's reflection, hoping he sounded like some hard-boiled detective with a mean streak, or a yakuza crime lord bent on vengeance.

The computer screen had a scratch across the middle that made Yoshio look like he had a scar on his cheek. A smudge a little higher up made one eye look blurry and somehow devious. "It's about Sensei Miyahara. I think he's up to something." He dropped his voice further and leaned forward in the chair, closer to the screen. It was as if he was talking to someone online instead of the person who was actually sitting right next to him. "I think he's involved in the beheadings."

Akio didn't respond. He had thought the boy was going to be a staunch defender of his sensei's honor, but instead he was implicating him.

"I think he might be the murderer," Yoshio said in the lowest whisper.

Akio leaned back in his chair, completely forgetting his previous suspicions of the boy's intent. "I knew it," he said, a little too loudly. "I knew it the moment I saw him."

"He's come into class with his shoes covered in dirt, his shirt sleeves torn, sometimes green and brown smudges on his clothes, like he's been out in the wilderness. He's been late many times over the past couple months, and he was never late before. He was always sitting still, meditating at the dojo. No one ever got there before he did." The boy seemed to feel bad for what he was saying, but there was more. "And he stinks sometimes too. He's sweaty and musty smelling. Once, he had blood on him. I'm not sure it was his own."

Akio was entranced, nodding his head. "He's the killer. He's got to be. It's the only thing that makes sense." He found himself looking into the computer screen too, talking as if he was in a video call. "What else?" he asked.

"He brings a real katana to class now too," Yoshio whispered nervously. "I don't think that's even legal. But he always has it close. He used to only bring the shinai."

Akio was convinced. He knew it all along, but this was proof, surely. What else would that old, angry man be doing with a real sword? He was out chopping off heads and burying the bodies in the woods somewhere, or maybe right there in the park. And he had almost started to believe Matsuoka's crazy story about a samurai monster. Of course, that was probably a trauma-induced, delusional load of crap. The real killer was just some psycho kendo instructor. *Samurai monster, my eye.*

Akio's mobile phone rang. It was a flowery sort of tune that made him think of cherry blossoms and graceful ballet. Ironically, this was his ring tone for Masami. He answered quickly, embarrassed for the noise. The rules of the café said to silence your phones.

"I want to go to the train station," she said, without a hello. "Where are you?"

"I'm meeting an important connection. Secret location. Lots of good intel. Stuff you'll want to know." Akio felt like a secret agent in that moment, whispering to his spy comrade.

"Can it, Akio," Masami cut through his fantasy. "Meet me at the diner in fifteen. I'm hungry."

She hung up before he could answer.

On the walk back, Akio remembered the mask.
Dammit!
He hurried his pace. He had to get it out of the hatchback and still meet Masami in time. He started to jog.

Then it hit him. How had it not occurred to him before? He didn't have the car keys.

Dammit, dammit, dammit!
He had been going down to the car earlier as if he could magically open it somehow. Then he got distracted by Yoshio and forgot all about it. Of course, he would have realized it had Yoshio not been there, but then what? How was he supposed to get the keys from Masami?

But then he had an idea. He started jogging again but a little slower. He had to time it right.

The car wasn't parked far from Jonathan's. He would pass the diner before he got to the car. He didn't want to get there too soon and run into Masami while she was passing the car park from the other direction. He had to get there just when she was getting to the diner.

He rounded the corner and saw Jonathan's a block away. And there was Masami. He knew that perfectly metered, staccato walk anywhere. It was her black jacket and her cropped black hair. He slowed to a walk and watched her turn into the diner.

Perfect. He accelerated to a brisk walk and entered the diner a couple minutes later. He'd get the keys from her, let her know what he wanted to eat so she could order, then he'd get the mask and take it up to his room. When he got back, his food would be ready, no time wasted.

She was just being seated in a booth not far from the door. He approached, wearing his most innocent face.

"Hey," Akio said, as casually as he could muster. "I've got some good info, but can I get your keys first? I left my phone in your car."

Masami didn't move. She didn't reach for her bag to retrieve her keys. She just stared at Akio with a curious look in her eyes. As well as Akio knew her, it was about as close as she ever came to smiling at him, even though the corners of her mouth didn't move up; they only kind of stretched back in an expression that was somewhere between mirth and disappointment.

"Akio," she said. "I called you on your phone 15 minutes ago and you answered. What are you up to?"

Dammit!

How that had not occurred to him, he really wasn't sure. His perfect plan had just crumbled to dust.

"Did I say my *phone*?" he said, after a moment that was far too long to be natural. "That's funny. I meant, uh . . . I meant my lens cap. Ha. Yeah, that's what I meant, my lens cap. I guess I'm just really tired."

Masami wasn't buying it. This was obvious. "We'll get it later. The car is on the way back to the hotel. Let's eat. Sit down."

He hovered there for a moment beside the booth, his brain working to find some way out, some way to get back to the car and get the mask without Masami around. He had nothing. So he sat.

After sulking for a while over another hamburger and fries, Akio started to get annoyed that Masami hadn't asked about his intel. "So . . ." he said, leaving the rest of his thought in the air.

"I figured you'd tell me when you were ready," she answered.

Great, so she's a mind reader too.

Akio filled her in on what Yoshio had told him, that the kendo instructor had been behaving very suspiciously. At the end, she was nodding her head slightly, as if agreeing with everything he had said. Her eyes were far away, contemplating. Then, possibly to herself, she said, "But Matsuoka's story . . ." She didn't finish.

"He's lost it," Akio said. "He's cuckoo. What's more feasible here? A samurai ghost monster or a nutjob kendo instructor?"

She nodded again. "Yeah," she said. "Yeah." But that was it.

They stopped at the car on the walk back. Akio didn't know how to approach the mask issue. And why did he want it so badly anyway? He wasn't sure, but he did.

Masami unlocked the car, and Akio went to the hatchback door.

"Why would your lens cap be in the back?" she asked.

"Right, right," He veered around to the passenger door and opened it. He feigned looking on the floor and the seat. "Damn. Not here. Not sure where it got to."

"Uh huh," Masami said, going to the rear of the car. She opened it and lifted the cargo lid. "Looks like we left the mask in here. I guess we should keep that closer."

Akio perked up. "I'll take it if you like. I can keep an eye on it."

"Uh huh," she said again, with the absolute connotation of "no way in hell." She hung onto the box, eyeing Akio suspiciously. She was going to keep it for the sole reason that it was obvious he wanted it. If he had been somehow able to play it cool, to make it look like it was the last thing he wanted, she probably would have given it to him. He was so bad at those types of ploys. People always saw through his intentions.

On the ride up the elevator, Akio had visions of wrestling Masami for the mask box. He could probably take her. He really did take judo. But who was he kidding? For all he knew, Masami was part of some secret ninja organization, and her reporter job was just a front. He slunk against the elevator wall, staring at his reflection in the polished metal.

They walked down the hallway and into their separate rooms, and the mask was gone.

II

The Snake Woman

In the hotel room, Masami was fidgeting. She couldn't sit still. None of this made any sense. And it gave her chills.

She had felt the mask's pull. She understood why Akio wanted it. It was one of the reasons she had left it in the cargo hold. But she decided having it close might be better than letting him figure out a way to get to it. Now that it was in the box and out of sight, she didn't feel the pull so strongly.

At Matsuoka's house it had been different. The pull on her had made her almost sick. She had felt it reaching out to her and she resisted. Nothing good would come of putting that thing on. She hadn't even wanted to hold it when Matsuoka handed it to her. But oh, she *had* wanted to, despite the nausea. And badly. She would have to find a way to lock it up somewhere safe and inaccessible.

She thought about turning it in to the police. After all, it was evidence. And it would give her more leverage, more bargaining power for information. *No,* she thought—or was it the mask? *I can't. I have to keep it. The police wouldn't understand. It has to go on the right face.* The police were the wrong face. She didn't know why, but they were.

What was happening? She didn't know if her thoughts were her own. It was just a mask. It couldn't have any power over her. It couldn't put thoughts in her head. *It's just a mask,* she kept telling herself. But she wanted it out of sight. It was difficult to not think about it. Inevitably, she came back to the idea that it needed to be stowed away —somewhere deep beneath the earth, preferably.

Her thoughts moved to Matsuoka. There's no way that what he said could be true. But it felt true. And her instincts were rarely wrong. He certainly believed it. He believed it with every fiber of his being, the poor man.

There was something else about his story that bothered her, something else that made her consider its veracity. It had brought back a memory, something she had suppressed a long time ago, something she had no desire to think about.

She was only eleven. It was summer and she had gone with her father on a camping trip to Yamanaka Lake. Her mother had been sick and told them to go without her.

It was a somber time. Her mother had cancer, a tumor next to her brain that was inoperable. Her older sister stayed with her while they went off to the lake.

"You need to get outside," her mother had said. "Take your father fishing. He loves that. I'm not going to die before you get back."

And she didn't. That didn't happen for another six months.

So they went camping.

Her father barely spoke on that trip. He set up the camp mostly by himself, giving Masami softly spoken orders to fetch the spikes, hold that rope, etc. But then he went off to fish. He sat there for hours, not catching anything. Masami wasn't sure he had even put a worm on his hook. He ignored her, left her to her own devices.

She wandered the shoreline, tossing stones, skipping a few, and looking for interesting ones that she thought about keeping but never did. The rocks gave way to tall grass and dirt, and she found herself on a small stretch of marshy coast where no else was around. The giant swan boat that the tourists rode was on the far side of the lake. Mount Fuji loomed in the distance with only a few wispy clouds near its snow-topped peak.

Out at the end of an arm of grassy land that jutted into the lake, she saw a woman in the water, holding a baby and washing its hair.

The woman looked up from the child and her deep black eyes saw Masami. Th e eyes had flecks of green in them. Th ey looked like gemstones.

The woman smiled and beckoned for Masami to come closer. She lifted up her baby, a beautiful naked child. A boy. He had a horribly cute smile on his face and seemed giddy to be in the water. The woman didn't say a word, but it was clear that she wanted Masami to come hold her baby.

The woman seemed friendly enough, and the baby was adorable. Masami took a few steps toward her. Her foot sunk a few inches into the marshy land, and she stopped. She looked for firmer ground.

As she did this, something in the woman's demeanor changed just for a moment. A flash of annoyance crossed her face before she resumed her inviting smile.

Masami did not move forward. She stood still in the muck, watching the woman beckoning to her. She didn't want to hold the baby anymore. He looked too squirmy, like he would wriggle right out of her grasp. And between his legs . . . it looked like a snake's head, not a penis. His hair looked like worms. She started to back away.

The woman's smile faded quickly. She hissed at Masami as the baby fell from her arms, separating into chunks that were fish, serpents, worms, and mud, splashing into the water and falling or squirming away.

With one last snarl and a guttural sound that seemed to lurch up from the depths of the lake, the woman dove into the water. The body of a giant snake followed her head and arms, undulating once above the surface before disappearing into the wet dark.

Masami picked up the phone. She had to call Detective Fujimaki and let him know what Matsuoka had said. She had to do anything to put the memory of the snake woman out of her head.

"How'd it go?" he asked, when he came to the phone, his voice soothing and confident at the same time. Masami was ecstatic that it was him and not Kuramoto, but no outside observer would have detected it.

"Interesting," she said. "Not sure he's all there, but he's passionate about his story."

"Yeah," Fujimaki agreed. "He's a heartbreaker."

I should tell him about the mask.

NO.

There was an uncomfortable pause before they both started talking at once. The detective let Masami speak first. They politely agreed that Matsuoka clearly believed what he said, but that there had to be a rational explanation. Masami was afraid to tell the detective what her instincts told her.

It's real. His story is real.

She couldn't say that. She couldn't sound like some disturbed teenager who's afraid of monsters in the dark. Somebody must be masquerading as a samurai.

And a snake woman that lives in the lake.

"The thing you were going to tell me yesterday, but didn't," Masami said. "Was that about his samurai story?"

"Yeah," he answered, and then paused for a long moment. Through the silence on the phone, Masami could feel his struggle to say what he wanted to say. Finally, he did. "It's completely insane, isn't it? But I believed him. It creeped me out. It makes no sense and couldn't possibly be true, but I believed him."

Masami didn't answer. She knew the feeling exactly.

"I know that sounds crazy," Fujimaki added.

"No." It was all she could say.

12

Kofu Station

It was nearly evening when they arrived at Kofu Station. The setting sun's rays caressed the clouds into dwindling wisps. They approached from the south, following the patterned sidewalk to a small cement landing with a few trees and a prominent statue. The whole of it was surrounded by tall buildings, a parking lot, and streets busy with people. The statue was a large patinaed bronze figure of the samurai warlord, Takeda Shingen.

They paused there, and Akio gazed upward at the figure hovering over them on its high, gray brick pedestal. The seated warrior was in full armor with a horned kabuto helmet; a squat face rested between the horns with a crest of four diamonds on a circle above it. In his left hand was a double string of large prayer beads, and in his right, a *gunpai*, the wooden fan that shogun used to direct their warriors. The warlord's mustached face looked off to his left as if uninterested in any who would view him, too preoccupied with thoughts of war and conquest. Under his eyes, sagging cheeks hinted at sadness from a bitter life of betrayal and death. Th ere was obvious pride in his countenance, but also hidden regrets.

"The Tiger of Kai." Masami spoke with an odd, reverent tone.

"This guy?" Akio indicated the statue, pointing.

"A mostly fair ruler, but ruthless as well." Masami talked toward the statue and not necessarily to Akio. "He taxed people evenly, fined criminals for minor offenses instead of torturing them, but then he would occasionally boil people alive."

"Sounds like a real gentleman."

"He also betrayed his father to take over rule."

"A hero too," Akio snickered.

"But that was after his father had betrayed him by planning to choose his younger son as heir. Can't really blame him, given the patriarchal rules as they . . . still are."

"Killed his father, though. That's not very nice."

"He didn't kill him." Masami remained gazing at the statue, not addressing Akio directly. "Just sent him away to Suruga."

"Suruga? Where the hell is that?"

"It's Shizuoka now. Don't you know your history?" She finally looked at him, disapprovingly.

"Uh, I know Princess Kako just came of age."

"That's pop culture, not history," Masami said flatly.

"She visited a shrine all on her own!"

"The royal family is only fodder for the tabloids. You realize that, right?"

"Whatever. I think it's history."

"You should work for *Flash*, not the *Daily*. You'd be right at home there." Irritation was creeping into Masami's tone.

"She's amazingly cute too."

"Some 'cute' girl visiting a shrine when she turns 20 is not history. It shouldn't even be news!" Masami was getting visibly riled. This was not like her. "Who cares if she has royal blood, whatever that is."

"Well, at least she won't have to sit on the throne since her little brother was born."

Masami mashed her teeth together and turned on Akio, seething. "And what is wrong with a woman on the throne? I knew you were an idiot, but I didn't think you were also a sexist!"

Akio couldn't help but grin. "What does it matter? It's not like the royals have any power anyway." There was something he loved about getting under her skin, even though she had called him an idiot. At least he was affecting her in some way. "What are you so upset about? Thought you weren't interested in pop culture."

Masami stormed off toward the huge Celeo department store, which was the south entrance of the train station.

Score one for Akio. He was thrilled to have turned the tables on Miss Smarty Pants before she saw it coming.

The sugary smell of cream puffs came from a Beard Papa on the station side of the department store. It was underscored with the gray cough of diesel fumes and a note of pungent human sweat, all of which was mellowed by the light chill in the air. Normally, Akio would have queued up to get a chocolate-covered cream puff, but not today. His stomach felt uneasy.

The station itself was ground level and open to the outside. Walkways accessed by escalators passed over the tracks to get to the further platforms.

The whine of a train braking sounded over the bustle of the station's patrons. Automated machines dispensed tickets next to ones that dispensed good luck charms. A photo booth gave temporary sanctuary to a group of giggling girls delaying the moment they had to head home to face tiresome chores, a strict father, and an overly protective mother.

It was just starting to get busy as the workday ended. People were mostly rushing about, intent on being somewhere else fast. But some didn't seem to be in much of a hurry at all; their destination was evidently no more appealing than where they had departed. One man with a flat expression shambled his way down the wide walkway, his black shoulder bag nearly dragging on the platform. He moved like a satiated zombie—he had eaten all the brains he could handle—not intent on getting anywhere or doing anything anytime soon.

Masami scanned the main terminal with a slow sweep of her robot eyes—Akio was pretty sure she had lasers in them. She was so methodical.

"It's early," she said. "Let's look around. Two of the murders happened here late at night: Eichi Himura and Katsu Fukui, both salarymen. All of the murders were about a month apart, and he's just killed again recently. So he won't be killing anyone tonight, but we can still get a feel for the place, try to figure out why he's killed here twice."

They set about getting the layout of the place, slowly walking the length and breadth of the station, perusing each platform. Akio discreetly eyed each person they passed. Was one of them the next headless victim, or perhaps even the killer himself? *Doubtful, since we know who that is already.* They separated to peer into restrooms and even gave the ticket agents a good once-over.

Nothing seemed unusual. People were going about their business, despite the killings. The last murder in the station had been a month previous, and no one was running down the platform slicing off heads at the moment. People had to get on with their lives, after all.

They killed about an hour observing, but found nothing interesting. Akio suggested they question one of the ticket agents. He was making a decision, taking charge. *Good.* And Masami agreed. Her recent irritation with him seemed to have disappeared completely. But then, she was a master of hiding her emotions.

"Just let me do the talking, okay?" she insisted.

After easing into the topic with a few harmless questions and a hint of the same charm she had used on Akira, the spy shop owner, she asked if the ticket agent knew where within the station the killings had taken place.

"Easy," he replied. "They were both down on platform 6."

Masami thanked him, and they headed back down the corridor and down the steps to platform 6, which was on the northeast end of the station. Nothing was unusual there either. The tracks sped off into the night in both directions. East or west appeared roughly the same, except that to the west the tracks were covered for a length by a large canopy, while to the east they crossed below a bridge and exited under the darkening sky.

Half a dozen people sat on benches and leaned against the wall, waiting for a train that wouldn't be there for another twenty minutes. They passed by a row of vending machines, selling ice cream, hot or cold tea and coffee, soft drinks, and lastly, beer.

"I could use a drink," Masami said.

Akio's brain did a double take. He wasn't sure how to respond. *A drink? As in alcohol?* "Uh, okay" he finally spit out. "I saw a bar not too far from here."

"No." Masami was authoritative but not demeaning this time. "We can't leave here. Do you have any small bills?"

Akio looked at the shiny, white-framed vending machine with surprise. Its window displayed a variety of cans containing mostly beer, but also *sake* and mixed *shochu* drinks. "Wait, they still have these? I thought they got rid of beer vending machines!"

"Most places did. It was a voluntary ban, not strictly enforced. I'm surprised to see this here too. Mostly it's the small towns that still have them. But I'm not complaining." She looked at Akio and raised her eyebrows. "So do you have any small bills?"

Akio fumbled for his wallet. "Yeah, I've got a couple 500 yen notes."

"Great." Masami took the bills from Akio and purchased two large Asahi beers. She handed one to him and then walked over to a bench near the exit and sat down.

Akio followed.

"This isn't exactly the kind of date I had in mind, but it'll do," Akio said, sidling up to her on the bench.

"Very funny, Akio. That's a good one." She scooted a few inches away from him.

"Is it that unlikely that we might actually have a date?" Akio knew all too well the answer to that question and tried in vain to play it off like he was joking.

"You really don't want me to answer that."

They sat sipping at their cans, watching the last few trains of the day come and go, the people bustling and swirling like a river with ever-changing rapids, getting dangerously close to flood levels then sputtering out to a drizzling drought.

The beer slowly made Akio relax, and he became contemplative and dreamy. It was strange being in a train station without having a destination, not going anywhere himself, but watching throngs of others with their minds on their objectives, simply in a transitional state. It was oddly meditative. He thought of all the times he had been in a hurry, not paying attention to the things around him, only focused on getting somewhere. Gotta get to work, get home, to the grocery store, to the bar, the cleaner's, his parents' house, his latest assignment. He couldn't recall once having just stopped and observed, having taken in his surroundings without any end result in mind. It was a completely foreign feeling for him. It was uncomfortable at first, but he started to feel centered and calm. The compulsive need to interrupt the scenario with a smart comment faded.

If he hadn't been sitting next to Masami, he likely wouldn't have been able to accomplish this. She was there with her hard, thin lips and black eyes that could sever any man's genitalia with a look, but something was different. She was contemplative too. Her steel exterior had softened somewhat. She was drinking beer with him! That was something he never thought possible. Granted, they weren't saying much to each other, but it was okay. He could smell her presence, feel her heat radiating next to him like the low breath of a warm lover sleeping.

This wasn't a common sensation for him.

How he craved to be inside of her head. *What is she thinking?* Was she just analyzing the facts, sifting through evidence? Or was it something deeper? Some secret she would never share with him, most likely. Certainly she wasn't thinking about him. This was probably as close to her as he would ever get.

The image of a deep red face swirling with clouds and flames slipped into his head. The mask floated there for a moment, questioning him, rebuking him. It asked him wordlessly, why hadn't he managed to retrieve it? Why hadn't he taken it from Masami and put it on?

But Akio pushed it away. It was too weird. Why had he wanted it so badly anyway? It was odd that Masami seemed so intent on keeping it from him, but he didn't care in that moment. *Whatever.* Sitting there next to her was far better than having any creepy mask, however amazing it looked. It's funny that he thought it had been talking to him. His imagination really had been getting the better of him.

Soon the tide of people slowed to a dry trickle. Then only Masami and Akio sat there, both staring off in different directions. He remembered a gloomy painting he saw once, a man sitting alone on a bench—or was he leaning against a wall? He couldn't remember. But there was a glass of absinthe next to him and an empty bottle at his feet. The man was in a ridiculous top hat, staring off at something unknown, something disturbing, Akio thought. He was pretty sure the man was afraid. He felt as if Masami and he were in that painting, or a similar one, a knock-off from some unknown, depressing artist. They were in shadow, and their beer cans sat on opposite sides of the bench, empty; Akio's was slightly crushed and crooked.

Akio looked around at the empty station, feeling uncomfortable again. It was getting late and he wasn't sure why they were still sitting there. What were they waiting for? Masami had said the killer wouldn't show up tonight, and they'd certainly gotten a "feel for the place." But Masami wasn't moving. He was conflicted between suggesting they leave and just staying there on the bench. After all, he may never have the chance to sit that close to her again.

The air around them began to vibrate, and a low rumble crept up through the floor and the bench. Then the not-so-distant hum of a locomotive was heard from the eastern darkness. Only seconds later, lights illuminated the tracks from around a bend in the night, spilling past the far wall as the train curved up to the platform.

"This is the last train," Masami said. Something about the way she said it seemed so final, like there would never be another train again in the history of mankind.

Akio shifted nervously on the bench. *Why are you such a pansy?* he asked himself. *It's just a train.*

It stopped with a coarse whine and halted in front of them. The doors hissed open.

A few passengers exited from each set of doors—one here, three there—and quickly disappeared from the platform and out of the station.

At the other end of the platform, where the train curved into the night, and furthest from where the two of them sat, a lone man in a business suit stepped off the train. Everyone else had cleared out. He was the last, and it appeared the train was now empty.

The salaryman was clearly not in a hurry. He paused on the platform while the doors closed and the train chugged on. He dug in his jacket pocket for an object that materialized as a pack of cigarettes. He pulled a single one out and admired it for a moment before inserting it between his lips. Then he found a lighter and brought it up to his mouth. He clicked twice on the lighter to create a flame, the click echoing in the silent dark. It felt like the world stopped breathing for him to inhale. A rapture of nicotine and the slight burn of tar hit his lungs like a secret lover.

Then a sudden shape loomed up behind him. It was large and dark, a humanoid shadow cast from some giant of the night. But the shadow itself was the giant. It was not cast from anything. Its darkness, crowned with a hideously shaped head, rose high up above the man, who remained oblivious to its presence.

Masami stood, but didn't speak. Akio remained frozen on the bench.

Nothing was supposed to happen tonight. That was what Masami had said. Masami was always right.

The shadow was not a man. It was too dark a presence. It couldn't be. Even from the distance, Akio felt that it was some kind of malevolent soul, a manifestation of hate and death. *How can he not feel it? It's breathing over his shoulder!*

But it had to be a man. What else? Akio's imagination was getting the better of him again. He tried to shout. *Look out! Behind you!* But his mouth wouldn't form the words.

A sliver of light flashed—only for a severed second—under the arc of the night sky, and the man's head fell to the concrete, the cigarette still hanging from his lips. Masami and Akio remained still as statues as the huge figure removed an ornate helmet, revealing what appeared to be a normal human head beneath. *It is just a man after all.* But as the dim light played over its face, the head appeared female and far too small for the massive body it sat upon.

Then—as if watching a person being decapitated wasn't scarring enough—something happened that made Akio nearly collapse with horror. The huge shadowy figure reached up with one hand, and, gripping its chin with fat fingers, it tore off its undersized head and stuffed it under one arm. Then, headless, it reached down and picked up the salaryman's newly severed head, placing it between its own shoulders to replace the one it had just removed, briefly twisting it back and forth to set it properly. In doing this, the beast had moved closer to the light and revealed its presence more completely.

It appeared to be a large man who was dressed in full samurai armor. The yoroi carapace was worn and had evidently seen battle in its time. The cloth between the interlocking pieces of armor was frayed and ragged, and the armor itself was scarred with scrapes, slashes and dents. The helmet that lay next to the prostrate body of the man had a face and horns mounted on it like the one on the statue of Takeda Shingen, but the similarities ended there. This one had twisting, spiral horns, like an antelope's, jutting upward above a toothy dragon face with ears like leathery wings flaring out to each side.

The salaryman's head slowly began to twitch and blink as it came back to life on its new body. The face stretched and the neck turned from side to side, adjusting and setting itself like an anime hero getting primed to tackle his final boss fight. For a moment, the cigarette still dangled from its lips, but having fully gained control of its new appendage, the beast grimaced and spat the cigarette onto the train tracks.

Then its fresh eyes fell on Masami and Akio.

The warrior cocked its new head like a dog, as if trying to make out what it was actually seeing. Then it put an enormous gauntleted hand on the handle of its sheathed katana.

Akio let out an involuntary whimper. The thing lurched forward a foot in their direction causing him to exhale louder and nearly faint. Masami stood immobile as a rock, but Akio didn't know if it was from fear or courage.

The samurai stopped where it was and stared at them. Then it bent down and retrieved its kabuto helmet and placed it on its new head as if preparing for battle.

"A photo," Masami whispered. "Get a photo."

Right. A photo before we die. At least they'll know what killed us. Akio's left leg began to twitch. He tried to steady it, but it persisted. Then he realized the camera was already in his hands, his finger on the shutter release. He only had to bring it up, focus and shoot. The samurai was lit by beams of light from grouped rows of fluorescent bulbs overhead. The light glinted off the horned, dragon-faced kabuto, intensifying the darkness of the night around it, the contrast making the dragon's toothy grin more sinister, the horns sharper, deadlier. Akio lifted the camera only to his hip, aimed, and shot. He held the button down and let the shutter fire.

The samurai had paused again. It looked at its old head still wedged beneath its armpit, then at the headless body that lay on the concrete. It looked back at Akio and Masami at the far end of the platform. It seemed to come to a decision and abruptly turned and leapt onto the eastbound tracks.

Akio couldn't move for what seemed to be full minutes. Masami was still as well, a slim figure breathing in and out next to him, but finally she broke the trance.

"We have to follow him."

"What?" Akio exhaled as if he had been holding his breath for the last five minutes, and he might have been.

"He's getting away."

"And a good thing too!" Akio wanted that thing as far away from him as possible. Mars would be fine.

"This is our story, Akio!" Masami started moving toward the other end of the platform.

"This is our lives! Where are you going?" Akio reluctantly began to follow, but only in the hope of preventing her from the madness she seemed to be attempting.

"I thought you wanted this assignment. You said you were going to protect me or some such nonsense."

Akio could only make an unintelligible whine in response.

"Did you get a photo?"

He lifted up his camera and gazed at it as if it were something he had never seen before.

"Never mind. Stay here." Masami increased her pace.

Yes, he tried to say but the word didn't come out. Akio paused for a moment, considering actually staying there like she said. Then he summoned courage from a deep reserve he didn't know he had and hurried to catch up, though his whole being shivered with the desire to run for his life in the opposite direction.

Masami was just lowering herself down onto the tracks, when Akio stopped her with one last plea. "What about the body? We have to report it."

"Nothing we can do about it. Someone else will find it. It's not like we can save him." She disappeared into the darkness.

Akio looked down at the headless body. An immense amount of blood had spilled out over the concrete, but the man's suit had somehow remained clean. He had fallen relatively straight, and the body looked like a poorly faked display of a murder, legs at even angles, one hand still clutching the lighter. The cut where the neck ended was perfectly straight and smooth. If it hadn't been for the blood, it would have looked like it was meant to be that way, like it had never owned a head at all.

Akio turned away just as his stomach lurched. He emptied his dinner and the beer, splattering it over the platform edge onto the train tracks. Wiping his mouth with the back of his hand, he snapped a couple photos of the corpse, jumped down to the tracks, and forced himself forward into the darkness.

The stars glinted warnings above him as he caught up to Masami just past the curve in the tracks. In the distance, beyond the bridge arcing over the railway, he could see a large figure loping with long strides down the tracks. Its previous head was swinging from its left hand, gripped by the hair.

The armor-clad creature seemed to want to barrel straight along like a train following the rails, when it suddenly veered from its course and leapt over a high fence to its right nearly in one bound. It caught itself on the top and flung its girth over to the other side with one arm, as if it were as light as an autumn leaf. It shot across a road and ran up a sharp hill on the other side.

Masami and Akio reached the fence, huffing, and looked up at the tall boundary blocking their way. Masami only paused for a few seconds, then laced her fingers into the fence links and began climbing. Akio reluctantly followed and they both dropped down to the other side.

They had lost sight of the samurai. The steep hill across the road was not a hill at all. It was a castle wall. In the darkness, they hadn't realized where they were. They were back on the north side of the park.

The samurai had scrambled up that wall like a spider. It hadn't even slowed down. They were not going to be able to do the same. But the entrance was just off to their right. Masami realized this a split second before Akio and bolted in that direction.

Rounding the corner of the pathway, they saw a sukiya-style building on the wide flat area to their left. It was the dojo, where they had visited the kendo class.

"Well, isn't this interesting?" Akio gasped out between breaths. "Maybe our kendo instructor has something to do with this after all."

"Maybe," was Masami's only reply.

13
Maizuru Castle Park

asami slowed her pace and gestured for Akio to do the same. She wanted a story, not to become another victim. They had to make sure they kept their distance. Now that they had lost sight of the killer, they needed to be extremely cautious. The way the samurai had run straight up the wall made her very nervous. How would they ever escape him if he chose to chase them instead?

She hadn't expected to see the killer tonight. She had been certain they wouldn't. The timing was off. He had just killed less than a week ago; why was he killing again? It broke the pattern. But if she really hadn't expected to see him, why had she stayed at the station for so long? Was it just to see what it was like late at night when it was quiet and the last train had come and gone? After all, that was when both station murders had happened. It would give her a sense of environment for her next article. It would give her firsthand descriptors of the eerie quiet night, and the rumble and squeak of the last train disappearing into the darkness.

Is that all it was? She wasn't sure. There was a whisper within her that she knew all along.

She went slowly into the park, looking for signs. There were dirty scuffs across the path, like something a pair of oversize boots might have made. A small dark spot lay by one boot print. It could have been anything in the darkness, but Masami had a gut feeling. She bent down and touched it with the tip of her finger. It was wet and cold, blacker than it should have been, but she was sure it was blood.

It seems he's going to make this easy for us, she thought as she followed the scuffs and drops down the path. Akio followed close behind.

The trail led them away from the dojo. It seemed as if the creature had gone right past it.

"I knew it," breathed Akio. "He's definitely involved in this. So what if it didn't go into the dojo? He's here in the park. Right here where that evil kendo dude is. I'll bet it's just him, wearing an extra large samurai suit."

It seems damn suspicious, Masami thought, but didn't say it out loud. She didn't want to make any assumptions yet, and didn't want to give Akio any more fodder for his rant.

The tracks seemed to head straight up the side of the castle ruins, ignoring the long switchback path that made it easy for tourists. A fence picket was freshly broken, its tip in splinters on the path.

Masami picked out signs of the thing's rough passage easily. *The thing, the man, what the hell is it?* She was good at tracking. She was a natural. Her father had said so. She had always been quick to spot animal tracks when they went camping. And human ones too.

She followed these tracks to just below the monument spire, aimed at the night sky like a pale spearhead, and to the side of a newer white, wooden building. A snapped branch on a tree pointed directly to another broken fence picket. A stone stairway went down next to the building on the other side of the fence.

Masami went cautiously down. Akio followed, strangely silent, probably scared out of his wits. She wasn't exactly calm herself. She clenched her jaw, her heart raced but she moved slowly, taking long, deep breaths.

At the bottom of the stairs was a doorway sunk into the stone beneath the base of the monument. A battered, heavy wooden door stood partially open, still swaying slightly from some recent disturbance. A sign above the door read, "Service entrance. Do not enter." And below that was another sign: "Unsafe. Closed for repairs."

The two of them stood, grim faces in the dark, gazing over the doorway, each weighing out their options privately.

Akio finally broke the silence. "I'm not going in there. Let's come back when it's light out. This is crazy."

Masami didn't answer for a moment, torn between getting the story and perhaps not getting out alive. But she had to get in that building now. By tomorrow, the killer may have destroyed or hidden all the evidence. But it was more than that. She had to see it. She had to find out if it was real. She had to know if the monster was truly a monster, or if the head swapping had just been some elaborate trick. If she turned back, she might never know. She couldn't let it dissolve into the water and disappear like the snake woman. It had to be now. She was about to voice this to Akio, when they heard a noise from within. Heavy footsteps were ascending stairs toward them.

"Up the stairs!" Masami whispered urgently. "Into the bushes!" They both charged up the steps as if the devil were behind them. And maybe he was. They dived behind some photinias that flanked the trees by the monument. She heard Akio whimper and gave him a glare. He was holding his arm and biting his lip. He had apparently scraped against a thorn.

The door creaked open, followed by a waft of a pungent, sulfurous smell and low, husky breathing. Masami tried to remain still despite the rush of adrenaline, and saw Akio was desperately trying to do the same. She positioned herself to get a view between the branches.

She could see pieces of the thing emerging from the stairway. First came the spiral horns jutting into the night, then the grinning dragon face of its kabuto helmet, covering the samurai's stolen head. Broad shoulders followed, bulky arms and a thick waist. A sheathed katana protruded from its side. Then its tree-trunk legs moved away from the stairs, and it lumbered off into the park.

A long moment passed, their breathing drowned out by the noise of cicadas.

Akio was trembling. His left foot was vibrating involuntarily, and he was sure it was going to give them away. He tried to will it to stop but to no avail. They were doomed. His breathing was getting louder too. He was going to get them both killed.

But then there was nothing. The heavy footsteps moved on, and they were left with only the disproportionately loud buzzing of the cicadas. Akio had always been a little disturbed by the noise the insects made. From the sound of them, he imagined six-foot long monsters hiding in the trees and laughing at him.

When he was a boy, his father had tried to get him to hunt the bugs with a net and a little insect cage like the neighborhood boys would, but he had refused. He wanted nothing to do with them and had dreaded them in the summer nights, unable to sleep for thoughts of them eating through the walls. But just now, he found himself extremely grateful for their deafening racket.

"Now's our chance," Masami finally urged and started to move quietly around the photinias.

Akio grabbed her arm, wishing he were still sitting on the bench with her, sipping beers together, imagining they were on a date and that at any moment she might turn and look at him with a yearning gleam in her eye, moist lips awaiting a kiss. A kiss he would eagerly plant on her. But no, they were hiding behind a thorny bush in a darkened park, about to expose themselves to a giant, head-swapping samurai who would surely kill them without blinking . . . someone else's eyes.

"I don't want my head to be next!" he screamed in a whisper. He knew it sounded pathetic, but he couldn't help it. With his eyes, he pleaded with her to find some sliver of reason. He begged her to come to her senses. They could both go sprinting headlong from the park and collapse in their beds, laughing that they had escaped with their lives. He didn't even care about the impossible thought of a kiss anymore. He just wanted to survive the night.

Masami looked at him with caring—this time there was no mistaking it—it was a concern he had never before seen in her face. It was a concern for him. He could feel it emanating from her, see it in her black eyes. Maybe she actually did care about him. "It'll be all right," she said. It was a comforting voice, despite the madness of what she intended to do. "We'll make it out before he comes back. I just have to see what's in there."

He? Akio thought. Maybe it was only a *he* and not an *it*. He couldn't see how, but maybe. It made it a little less frightening if it was just a man. A man could be stopped. Either way, Masami cared about him. That was enough for now. Somehow that was enough.

"Okay," Akio acquiesced.

The door opened onto a descending stairway. Akio balked at the pitch dark within, but Masami lit it with her key chain light, a blue beam cutting through the sinister blackness, casting long shadows as it flicked about. Akio wished for a proper flashlight, but it would have to do.

Better yet, we could just go back to the hotel and not die.

The smell from inside was a dank, moldy odor with a hint of the same sulfur they had smelled twice before, once when the creature had opened the door and that brief hint of it at the murder scene. It was intermingled with the musty smell of a mausoleum, the smell of death and loss.

The stairs were ancient stone, uneven, chipped and worn in the center from ages of use. Their footsteps reverberated off the walls louder than they liked, causing Akio to flinch with each step and continually check behind him.

Reaching the bottom of the brief stairs, perhaps twenty steps in all, they moved carefully but quickly down the dark corridor. They passed a small, disused room, no bigger than a large closet, and then a slightly larger room that appeared to have once been used as an office of some kind; a battered desk stood against the wall in front of a chair with only one leg, lying on its back. Shining her light on the floor, Masami pointed out an obvious trail that had been worn through the thick dust. Footsteps had gone back and forth along this corridor many times but never into that room. So they continued forward.

Several steps later, Masami paused at a corridor that headed off to the right, away from the main.

"The trail goes that way," she whispered.

Akio trusted her instincts, so much so that he dearly didn't want to go that way. But on they went.

The corridor ended at a door, twenty paces further. The door was open.

Peering in, they saw another stone stairway descending.

Akio looked back down the dark hallway. He couldn't decide what was worse: continuing on, deeper into this scary dungeon or heading back in the direction where they knew the monster/man/murderer was. Either way, he was not certain he'd be able to contain his bowels if that thing, or any other thing, showed up. *Maybe there'll be another way out,* he thought. But going downstairs further didn't seem likely to increase the odds.

He waited for Masami to make the decision, partly because he had no idea what to do and partly because he was immobile with fear. *Why did I follow her in here? What am I trying to prove? That I'm a complete coward? Done.*

Masami touched his shoulder, firmly. He couldn't see her face—the only thing illuminated by her tiny torch was the crooked, stone stairway down—but he felt caring in the touch. He felt courage.

Masami started downward.

The temperature dropped as they descended, and the stink of decay and sulfur became gradually stronger. It bit into his nostrils, and Akio unconsciously began to grind his teeth.

The stairs ended in a short, straight corridor with a dirt floor. One door stood at its far end. It was a wooden door, not stout, but reinforced with makeshift crossbeams, which appeared to have been added as an afterthought and not by the original builder. It hung at a slight angle from its hinges but was effectively closed. The source of the smell was without a doubt behind this door.

Overwhelming fear gripped Akio. He couldn't go in there. Something dead was in there. He had seen only one dead person before this day, before the decapitated man at the train station. It was a man that had jumped from a thirty-floor building. It wasn't a story he had been covering; it had been sheer happenstance. He had grabbed his camera from his bag while the man still stood on the roof, but before he had the lens cap off, he looked up horrified to see the man bouncing from the pavement. He had not known that a person would bounce. The cartoons and movies never portrayed it that way. His camera only hung limp from his hand after that. He had been unable to bring it up to his eye to shoot.

But this situation was vastly different. They had sought out the abattoir of some twisted serial killer. Akio was still grappling with what he had seen the killer do at the train station. He had swapped heads! No, not *he*. Masami was wrong. Akio kept trying to tell himself that it was just a man, and there was some trick of the light, but it was not a person at all. It couldn't be. It was some horrid creature, some otherworldly thing. And they were about to enter its lair.

Masami seemed paler than ever. Her normal blanched skin appeared alabaster in the dim blue light, bleached as a whale bone on a desert island. She wasn't rushing into the room any faster than Akio.

But it was her who finally reached for the latch.

The door was not locked and opened without creaking. Akio had expected it to creak, and its silence somehow made it worse, more frightening than a creak ever could have been. No sound at all would greet his death, no warning, no prayer.

They were surprised to be welcomed by a dull glow. The room was oblong in shape with earthen shelves built into the walls on either side. Small candles were lit at even intervals along both surfaces. Masami let her thumb off the button on her key chain, and the blue light died.

In between some of the candles were shapes, ovoid shapes with hair and drooping faces. Human heads, severed cleanly at the neck. Eyes stared out blankly from some of them, glinting dully in the candlelight, empty glass pools, void of any soul.

The smell of rot was severe, but the sulfur stench almost overpowered it.

Akio turned around in the room, looking at each severed head. He saw his own face in each one. He began to count them.

One, two, three, four . . . seven?

There were seven heads. That means there were at least two, no three, killings they didn't know about. They only knew about six, which were the ryokan owner's wife, Aimi Matsuoka; the homeless man in the park; the maid cafe patron, Eichi Himura; the salaryman, Katsu Fukui; his girlfriend, Sayaka Inawa; and the man killed tonight at the train station, but his head wasn't in here, because the samurai creature was wearing it.

Katsu Fukui's head had been recovered by the police, so that didn't count. Did that mean it was four more that they didn't know about? That would depend on whether the creature still possessed the head he had been carrying—the one he had removed from his shoulders. The smaller, female one. *Sayaka.* Was that one here?

Akio scanned the shelves. The heads were in various stages of decay. A couple were nearly skulls with hair, but others still had sagging flesh. One looked nearly hale with life and had long black hair, high cheekbones and a small sharp nose. It was her. It was the one that had been too small for the samurai's body. It was Sayaka, the girlfriend who had been murdered in her apartment. She looked at him, pleading, her eyes still moist.

So that's three we don't know about.

The horror of the monster removing her head from its shoulders so it could replace it with a fresh one replayed in Akio's mind. *It might be back at any second to do the same thing with my head. Or Masami's.*

Akio was quivering now. It took every ounce of inner strength he had to not run from the room. He began to mumble something, unaware that he was even doing it. At first it was unintelligible, but slowly it began to make sense, and he became louder. He repeated it quickly, faster with each repetition, and slowly it dawned on him what he was doing. It was a Buddhist mantra, something he used to chant when his mother took him to the temple, and especially when someone had died. It was a prayer for the souls of the deceased, an homage to the infinite light.

"*Namu amida butsu, namu amida butsu, namu—*"

"Pictures." Masami only spoke the one word.

Her interruption jarred Akio from his involuntary chanting. In a lurch, he yanked his camera from his bag and began snapping shots like a man possessed. Putting the camera lens in front of him helped to distance himself from the gruesome scene. They were only photographs; it wasn't real.

After capturing the heads and candles, he turned toward the back of the room. Masami was crouching by a large metal chest that sat on the floor in a small alcove. He moved to get a closer look.

The chest was engraved with sharp, angular symbols, some cryptic language he had never seen before. A large and ancient-looking keyhole was prominent at the front, the shape of which appeared to be a symbol as well. It was rounded at the top with a smaller half circle above, crossed like a "T" and then it zagged downward, ending in what looked like two curled tentacles.

He shot a picture of Masami next to it, her notepad and pen in hand.

"Get a close up of this keyhole," she said.

He crouched down to do so, and then his attention was drawn upward to a mounted wooden weapon rack positioned behind and above the chest. It was painted with a black sheen that made it nearly invisible in the dim light, though its contents were at eye level. It was a two-tiered stand, and it held a katana and a *wakizashi*—a smaller sword traditionally used for ritual suicide—respectively. They were a matching set with black handles that looked like bones—tibias— wrapped in black hair. They each had a gleaming red guard, the whole of which appeared to be cut from some kind of gem.

Akio paused in his frantic shooting to admire them. Swords were illegal to own in Japan, unless the owner was granted a rare permit. He had looked up the law once and found it amusing that a sword license could be granted for hunting or for the "eradication of noxious birds and animals." He suspected there were probably more efficient methods of extermination these days than hacking about with a katana. They were also granted for "artistic" purposes, plays, or for display only. Despite these restrictions, he knew that many people still kept family heirlooms that were unregistered or even secretly collected swords. The weapons were available but expensive. The two displayed before him must have certainly been priceless, and Akio would have been surprised if they were licensed to anyone.

He reached up toward the katana, the longer of the two swords.

"Don't touch that," Masami snapped. "Evidence."

"Right." He withdrew his hand, and took a few photos.

Masami moved on to examine the heads closer, and Akio squatted down to the chest. It was a roughly 30-centimeter cube of what looked like solid steel, reinforced at the corners with more pounded steel. On the surface of every side was an oval design with barbed edges like tiny flames coming off it. Inside the oval was an intricate yet angular symbol carved in thick strokes and painted black. *No, burned in, not painted.* Outside the oval were more angular symbols, though smaller, written in vertical rows.

Akio leaned in to get a closer look. Unthinkingly, he brushed his fingers over the symbol on the top. Instantly, a jarring vibration buzzed through his hand and up his arm. An icy pain zipped along his nerves. He jerked his hand back and cried out.

"What is it?" Masami rushed over to him. She had been as mesmerized by the severed heads as he had been by the chest. "Did you touch something? I just told you . . ."

The pain had only lasted for a fraction of a second, but the forceful memory of it still vibrated through Akio's arm. "I'm okay. Just a little shaken up."

Masami eyed the decorated chest next to him.

"Don't touch that thing," he said, trying to crack a smile but failing. "It bites."

They heard noises coming from the hallway. Quick footsteps were descending the stairs. Someone or something was breathing hard.

Before Akio and Masami could react, the door flew open. A dark figure stood in the doorway; the shadow of a katana hung from its side. It slowly scanned the room as its eyes adjusted to the candlelight. Then it found the two at the back of the room and glared down at them with a fierce gaze.

"It is coming." A surprising voice emanated from the figure. It was rough, but higher in pitch than expected and sharpened by a practiced impatience. The candlelight cast shadows around its form. It was much too short and, although stocky, didn't fill the doorway like it should have. The round shadow of its bald head and the beveled lines of its face provided an identity.

"Sensei Miyahara," said Masami, just as Akio was thinking it. It was the kendo instructor.

Akio stood, suddenly fuming. "I knew he was involved in this!" he shouted. He reached behind him and grabbed the katana from the rack. He didn't care that it was evidence. He was not going to die like a dog. And he was certainly not going to let Masami get hurt. The blade slid out of its black, wooden sheath smoothly and silently. It was immaculate, reflecting the candlelight like pristine, still water. The cutting edge of the folded steel looked sharp enough to sever atoms. He brandished the weapon at Miyahara like an augur pointing out evil.

"Are you just telling that beast who to kill, or are you helping him do the dirty work?" Akio's fear had transformed to full-fledged anger, but the balance was a shaky one. His legs still trembled. There was only one way to stop them shaking. He had to charge.

He lifted the katana, about to scream his battle cry and rush forward, but Masami grabbed him.

"No, Akio. Hear him out." Then she turned to the sensei, her stance defiant. "What are you doing here?"

"I'm saving your brainless lives," he breathed. "You touched the chest, didn't you?"

Akio and Masami's silence was admission enough.

"That means it's coming." Miyahara spoke sharply. "It will be here in seconds. We must leave now, or we may never leave alive!"

Neither of them moved. Akio could only assume Masami was thinking the same thing. Why should they trust someone who had obviously lied to them before? He clearly knew much more than he had let on.

"This is some kind of trick," Akio said to Masami. "We know he's behind this. Even his own student thinks so."

"My own student?" Miyahara interjected. "And who might that be?"

"Yoshio," Akio answered. "He came to us. He knows that you've been sneaking off, coming back with blood on you, carrying a real katana!"

"Yoshio, huh?" the sensei said, more to himself than them. "He's a bright boy. But he could use some more specialized training."

"Training in chopping off heads?" Akio blurted.

Miyahara looked at both of them, doom in his eyes and the lines of his face. "It's time to go."

Masami didn't move, and neither did Akio. Then Akio reached back and snatched the wakizashi from the rack, handing it to Masami. She looked at it and paused briefly, weighing her options. Then she took it from his hand.

"Fine." The sensei's face showed resignation. "Let your heads be the next on those shelves." Then he added, "If you are so fortunate."

"Wait," Masami said. "If you're being honest, you have a lot to explain."

"Now's not the best time for a heart to heart," Miyahara said impatiently.

Still, neither of them moved. Akio's grip on the sword tightened. Masami held hers loosely, blade toward the floor.

Miyahara glanced over them one last time. "Leave the swords," he said, speaking like a commander giving an order to his troops. "Or you will regret it." Then he disappeared from the doorway.

Akio looked intensely at Masami, as if synchronizing their thoughts. She tightened her grip on the wakizashi, and strode forward. Akio followed suit, and the katana came with him.

Probably best to get out of this trap of a tiny trophy room anyway. And keep him in front of us.

Miyahara was several strides ahead of them, a flashlight illuminating the corridor beyond. They had not agreed to follow him, but getting out of this dungeon was something that Akio definitely could agree with. Still, he preferred the kendo instructor at a distance. *I'm not about to let him turn around and impale me*, he thought. Although he hadn't unsheathed his katana yet, Miyahara was carrying one. Either he knew the danger he was in, or his motives were questionable. Akio didn't want to get close enough to find out which.

They ascended the first staircase, slowing down as they reached the top. Masami peered above the top step with her key chain light and nodded back to Akio. Miyahara was moving down the corridor. He wasn't waiting to ambush them. They moved to shorten the lengthening gap between themselves and him.

Without warning, the sensei stopped dead, frozen in his tracks. His hand gripped the handle of his katana. Akio and Masami stopped where they were, ten feet behind. Miyahara turned his head slowly back toward the pair with pale resignation on his face.

"Too late," he said.

Heavy footsteps and clacking armor echoed hollowly down the earthen corridor. None of them moved. There was nowhere to run. A hateful rattle of coarse breathing clattered through the air. The zing of a sword being unsheathed was barely audible.

Miyahara was in a defensive stance, his katana held out in front of him. Akio wasn't certain if the sound had come from the sensei drawing his blade or from the samurai that was now in view, its sword also drawn, a glimmering black blade that was nearly invisible in the dark. Miyahara's flashlight lay on the floor, illuminating the hulking beast as it glared bloody daggers at the sensei. It broke into a run and barreled down the corridor toward them.

In no time, it was upon Miyahara. The grim samurai's sword flashed out like a whip perfectly aimed at the sensei's neck, the strike of a viper that would be impossible to counter. It was nearly quick enough to be invisible. Yet, in a blinding move that could only have been executed by a master, Miyahara twisted around and parried the blow. The force of it was so strong that the older man was flung to the wall like a toy thrown by an angry child. But it was a toy that still had its head attached.

The creature's stolen gaze locked onto the blades in Akio and Masami's hands. It snorted thick mucus through the tired salaryman's nose. In an instant it lowered its kabuto like a bull set to charge, the slender horns like corkscrew spikes glinting in the torchlight.

Amazingly, Miyahara recovered in an instant, and rolling off the wall, he spun back, catching the beast off guard. His katana sliced into the crook of its left knee, sending it windmilling forward, limping to try to catch its balance.

It staggered directly at Masami and Akio.

Masami leaned to one side, so the beast would stumble by. She chopped at it with the wakizashi as it did and she darted past.

But Akio was trapped as the samurai creature hurtled toward him. He couldn't dive out of the way in time. It skimmed the wall, dragging its blade there as it tried to hold itself up. Akio's only choice was to meet it head on. Terror froze his face in a howl, as he braced the katana on his hip and waited for impact, the blade aimed at the creature's heart.

A look of surprise flashed on the samurai's borrowed face just before they collided. The creature's stumbling made it unprepared to bring its katana up to block. Akio's blade sunk deep into its chest, cutting through the plate of armor like it was rice paper. It toppled onto him, pressing its face up to Akio's—the salaryman's contempt was complete. The weight was crushing. A truck had just landed on Akio.

The borrowed eyes flicked over Akio's petrified face. For a fleeting moment, he thought that the man's consciousness had returned. He looked confused as to why he was laying on top of a stranger in a dark hallway. His eyes attempted to look down to his lips, as if wondering what had become of the cigarette he had been so eager to smoke.

Then the weight was gone. Everything was gone. The samurai creature had vanished. A thin wisp of smoke and a sulfurous stench was in the air, but nothing else. No armor, no katana, no salaryman's head. It had ceased to exist. Akio's katana impaled nothing, its red guard gleaming as Masami flashed her key chain light across it.

She flashed it down the hall, up to the ceiling and back to Miyahara, who sat cross-legged on the ground as if meditating. There was no one else in the corridor but the three of them.

14

The Verses of Despair

"Drop the weapons," Miyahara said, and for a moment, Akio thought the sensei was threatening them. "They will only cause more trouble if you take them," he added.

"What harm can come to us now?" Akio said. "The thing is gone." He was still reeling from the encounter, distinctly feeling every breath lift and fall in his chest.

For once, Masami agreed with him. "Keep it," she said. "It saved your life. It's yours now. I believe those are the rules. Besides, your fingerprints are all over it. It will be contaminated evidence." She looked at him with yet another new expression. It felt like they connected. She looked empathetic—human.

"I do not recommend it," Miyahara said, shaking his head.

"Get the scabbards, Akio," Masami said.

Akio didn't hesitate, and started for the gruesome room at the end of the hall.

"If you must, then be quick about it," Miyahara rasped. "We shouldn't linger."

Akio retrieved the swords' scabbards quickly, avoiding looking at the heads again and returned to the hallway.

"Let's get out of here." Masami stood, taking the shorter scabbard and sheathing her sword. "We'll figure out what to do about it tomorrow."

"Shouldn't we report this to the police?" Akio asked as he sheathed his own blade.

"Do you think they'll believe us?" she answered, and that was all she needed to say.

There's no way they'll believe us. Best to leave the police out of it for now.

Akio wasn't sure what to think. Masami was always so by-the-book (or so he had thought before this trip). The bizarre encounter must have shaken her. Whatever it was, it didn't matter. They were alive and the creature was gone. And for the second time that day—the second time in his life—Masami had made him feel that she was on his side. She showed a protectiveness. She cared for him. That was enough to keep him fighting crazed, head-swapping samurai for quite some time.

After exiting the depths of the castle, they parted ways with Miyahara. The sensei said he needed to stop at his dojo. "There's something I need to get. I will meet you at your hotel and hopefully shed some light on what is happening." He looked at them gravely, as if unsure he should be telling them anything at all. "And my part in it," he added.

The fight under the castle had made it clear to Akio that the sensei was not in league with the killer, so his trust in him had been bolstered. Akio even felt a hint of what he had heard soldiers felt for one another on a battlefield, that bond of facing death together. But there was something about the man he still didn't like. He was still worried about Miyahara's true intentions.

They avoided the main boulevard on the way back to the hotel. It was dark and easy enough to hide the swords under their jackets alongside their bodies, but still they thought it best to avoid the streetlights.

Akio was shaken, and Masami looked distant. Neither of them said a word on the walk back. Akio's whole body thrummed with the samurai encounter. With dumb luck, it had fallen onto his sword. The blade went right through its heart. It was gone—literally vanished. It must have been destroyed. Perhaps the sword was magic or something. The thought was absurd, but there had been nothing normal about that night. Miyahara's sword didn't seem to hurt it much. There must be something special about the katana Akio used. It was exquisite—the gem guard alone must be worth a fortune. Perhaps it and the matching wakizashi were the only weapons that could kill such a creature.

He wondered how they would explain it all to Tanaka. What kind of story would Masami write? He could see the headlines now, *Killer Ghost Vanquished by Photographer's Sword*. Somehow, he didn't think Tanaka—or anyone else—would buy that one.

He smiled and let out a sigh as the hotel appeared in front of them. Masami looked at him with a tiny grin of approval just at the corner of her mouth. Relief and a little giddiness shuddered up his body, kicking out a soft chuckle.

They had survived.

Akio sat, melting into the only chair in Masami's hotel room. He felt strangely giddy and anxious at the same time. He had killed the samurai ghost thing. It was over. No more answers had come to him about how they would present it to Tanaka back at the *Dainichi Daily*. He wanted to pretend none of it had happened. It had been a nightmare, and he was ready to go home, no matter the consequences at work.

Masami sat on her bed, her elbows on her knees, fingers intertwined, hands resting against her forehead. The two swords lay behind her on the pale yellow bedspread. She lifted her head and looked at Akio. She didn't seem as relieved as he was.

"Let me see the photos," she said.

"Sure." Akio handed her his camera. "I don't want to look at them just yet."

Masami scrolled through the images until she found whatever shots she had been looking for. She stared at the camera screen, her sharp features seeming to go colder than they already were. "Maybe you should," she said handing the camera back to him.

Akio looked at the screen. It was a photo from the station platform. He saw the prone, headless body with the darkness of the night behind it. There was a strange smear of light in the center of the photo, in front of the body, as if the fluorescent light had bounced off something that wasn't there anymore. He cycled to the next photo. It was the same. And the next. He remembered now that he had held the button down and let the shutter capture rapid-fire images. He kept cycling through. They were all the same. Only a body and a shifting smear of light.

"Fujimaki was right," Masami said.

Akio looked up, confused, and she explained what the detective had told her about the security camera footage being unusable. It didn't make sense. How could the killer not appear in the photos? *Was it some kind of vampire?* That was the only thing Akio could think of that couldn't have its picture taken. *But vampires don't exist.*

And neither do head-swapping samurai that disappear when they're killed.

He felt light-headed, and his skin crawled with the memory of the killer's weight melting away until it was gone.

When Miyahara arrived at the hotel room, he was carrying a large, black duffel bag. It looked heavy. Neither Akio nor Masami asked about it when Masami let him in.

They all sat in the room, avoiding each other's gazes, Masami on the bed, Akio in the chair, and the sensei leaning on the edge of the desk below the television. Akio was still unsure what to make of it all. With Miyahara there, everything seemed more real. He couldn't pretend it hadn't happened. He tried again to process it, but it didn't make sense. It was the stuff of nightmares. But it had happened. They were all there to corroborate it.

For a long while, nothing was said. Masami made coffee with the supplies provided by the hotel and silently passed out the cups. None of them seemed to want to talk about the recent events, as if the others would think them insane for speaking it out loud. Akio was sure they would laugh at him. Had he imagined it after all? Was it some crazy fever dream, and he had been lying in his bed the whole time? Now they were only meeting in Masami's room so they could tell him that he needed to be locked in a loony bin for the rest of his life.

But the photos—Masami had seen them too. But if anything, the photos proved he was crazy.

No, I'm not crazy. And it wasn't a dream. It was on all of their faces. It had happened.

Masami broke the silence. She skipped the details of the day and went straight to questioning Miyahara. *Good*, thought Akio. It was something solid he could wrap his head around. He remained silent at first, letting Masami do the grilling.

She asked Miyahara what he knew about the murdering samurai, how he had found out about it, and why he had lied to them when they had visited the kendo class. She put all these questions to him at once and let him decide how to answer. He addressed them in reverse. His answers to the third and second questions were less than satisfying, but ultimately made sense enough to be accepted.

He had lied to them for two reasons. One, they wouldn't have believed him anyway—a point Masami and Akio readily conceded given the bizarre events of the day. Two, he was protecting them. He knew that any real information he gave them could quite possibly lead to their deaths. By discovering the samurai in the train station on their own, that outcome had nearly happened anyway.

As for question number two, how he had found out about it, it sounded relatively simple. Miyahara spent many nights late at the park tutoring private students, going over his lesson plans, or simply enjoying the quiet of the dark, empty park. Kofu was not a small town.

The noises of the city reverberated in his apartment throughout the night. It was peaceful in the park. His status as an instructor allowed him to remain after normal hours, a privilege he frequently enjoyed.

It was during one of these late night, meditative sessions that he had spied someone sneaking about in the park. "I followed, and that *person* turned out to be our killer."

That was all he would say about the discovery. It felt like he was hiding something.

There was a long, uneasy moment while no one spoke, as they anticipated Miyahara's answer to Masami's first question, which he had obviously been skirting.

The room seemed to get smaller and the air denser. Akio and Masami exchanged glances, wondering if they should repeat the question. The eye contact was thrilling. She was still on his side. Something had shifted, and if it weren't for the topic at hand, Akio would have been ecstatic.

He looked away and stared at the deceptive green and pink lines of the wallpaper, the same that was in his room, pretending to be brown. *I know your secret, wallpaper. You can't fool me.*

Miyahara now stood by the television, a small, flat, black rectangle that hung by his head, mounted on the wall. It was canted at an angle, and its blackness reflected Masami, who was seated with one leg hanging off her bed. It was a more casual position than Akio had ever seen her in.

Miyahara stood completely still, but almost imperceptibly—as if performing a *Butoh* dance—lowered his head into a slight bow, as if the weight of some terrible, invisible force was pulling his face slowly toward the floor. The thoughts swirling a vortex in his mind were almost tangible. He was making a decision.

When he finally spoke, it was an answer of the kind Akio had dreaded. He was supposed to say that it had all been an illusion, some kind of trick. But that's not what he said at all.

"The samurai was a demon," he said.

Under normal circumstances, Akio would have laughed and made some snide comment about the sensei's mental faculties, but after what they had been through, he stayed quiet. There was a grounded danger resonating in the sensei's voice. Masami didn't respond either. In fact, she looked somewhat shaken. Miyahara's answer wasn't a sane one, but the things that had happened that day had not been what anyone would call sane.

"Somehow," the sensei said, "this demon escaped its confinement in the Hells and arrived here. There is an ancient myth of a path from the Hells that winds all the way to the surface of the earth and exits via Mount Fuji. It is an extremely difficult path—even for a demon. But every now and then, one manages to get out."

Akio couldn't remain quiet any longer. Nothing was making sense. Despite the fact that what he had seen with his own eyes didn't make sense either, he had to call Miyahara out on this. "Mount Fuji? Seriously? Why would it escape anyway? I mean, it seems like Hell would be like heaven on a stick for this lunatic."

"You must understand," Miyahara answered gravely. "The Hells are no picnic for demons. They are suffering souls. They want out. They want their freedom."

"But they're in Hell for a reason, right?" Akio asked. "Assuming this is all actually true, isn't there some sort of Hell's prison guard watching over them, making sure they don't escape?"

"I wouldn't know," the bald master sighed. "And I hope I never find out. The souls in Hell suffer a punishment that matches their crimes—their sins, if you will. So I have learned." Miyahara's eyes slowly scanned the two as he said this, as if he could read what their punishments would be.

"So you've learned?" Akio was getting more and more uncomfortable; a twitchy shiver flicked across his shoulder blade. "How?"

Miyahara paused before answering, collecting his thoughts, and possibly the courage, to say what he said next.

"I was not entirely honest about how I found out about this demon."

Of course you weren't.

Akio shifted in his chair. Masami sat up straighter on the bed.

"I knew it was coming," Miyahara went on. "I saw the signs."

"What signs?" Masami asked calmly.

"The red lightning above Mount Fuji. The cloud of fire with spiral arms. The windless rain, despite the turbulent storm above. These are the signs that one has broken free."

"And you know this how?" Akio asked.

"This is not the first demon I've hunted," Miyahara answered gravely, and with such a weight that neither Akio nor Masami spoke. "And those are not the only signs. I've done this so long I feel it in my bones. But it was mere coincidence that brought it into the park, so close to me. Usually, I have to do a lot more chasing. This one seemed drawn to the castle. Perhaps it reminded it of its own time, when it was a living human. Among all these modern buildings, it needed a refuge. The castle was perfect."

"This thing was once human?" Akio asked.

"Yes, many demons were. Not all, but some were so evil that in death, they transformed beyond that of a spirit into a demon. Some may even rise through the ranks of the Hells to eventually escape their own punishment. And there are some that go the other way. There are demons who become good spirits."

"Even if all this insanity is true, you still haven't answered how you've learned about it," Masami said.

"No, I haven't. It's a long story. But I will tell you that much of it has been from experience. The rest of it was the tutelage of my sensei, and his gifting to me of this." Miyahara reached into the black duffel bag that he had retrieved from his dojo and pulled out a large and ancient-looking tome. "The Zetsubō no Shīka."

The words reverberated through the room as did the presence of the massive book. Miyahara set it heavily upon the desk next to him. It was at least half a meter long, nearly as wide, and had to be 15 centimeters thick. It was leather-bound, the spine sewn with thick sinews of some kind. Protrusions of what looked like bone and scales decorated the edges. Jagged black stones the color of lava, but with the gleam of rubies, formed a roughly oval pattern on the cover. It encircled the back of an outthrust hand that reached out from the book with long, clawed fingers, one of which had been snapped off. It looked as if something was trying to escape from within the book. It took up so much presence in the room that no one spoke for a very long moment.

Akio swallowed dryly. It felt like the book had sucked up all the air. "The Zetsubō no Shīka?" Akio asked, clearing his throat. "What the hell is that?"

"Hell . . . is what it describes," Miyahara explained. "Its many houses and the rulers of those houses, the crimes and their punishments, the myriad manifestations of demonhood, and other unspeakable things."

Akio shot a look to Masami, as if to say, *can we trust this guy?* Masami shot back silently, her eyes like black flames. *Let him talk*, her eyes said. *We'll sort it out later.*

Akio was feeling disoriented. His grip on reality was slipping. On one hand, he found himself becoming very nervous. They were talking about demons and Hell as if they were real. And they *were*. He had fought a demon earlier that day. He had survived, and the thing was gone, but his skin was crawling with the idea that another one could jump out at him at any second.

On the other hand, he could barely contain himself. Masami and he were secretly communicating, connecting on a level he never thought possible. They were a team—a monster-fighting team! He couldn't decide which scenario was less likely, that demons existed or that Masami had become his comrade-in-arms. He found himself feeling strangely grateful for this completely messed-up situation.

"There is not much in the entry for this particular type of demon." Miyahara's rough voice pulled Akio from his conflicted brooding. "It's called a *namakubikamen*. But it does say that it is the spirit of a person who was arrogant in life. It was someone who had no concern for anyone but himself, full of pride about his accomplishments and his intellect, always looking down on others. This type of person becomes a namakubikamen, cursed with a removable head, in order to punish it for all that overextended ego.

"It says that in the Hells, the other demons make sport of them, using their heads as balls for games. They are so fearsome to us, but in Hell they are mocked; they are ridiculed."

"Ha!" laughed Akio. "I'd like to use that thing's head as a ball." Then it occurred to him, "But it wasn't his head. It took it from that poor guy on the train platform."

"Yes," Miyahara said. "It doesn't mention why it would take other heads or what might have become of its own. Perhaps it's still being used in a game down below."

Akio was amused at this thought, however disturbing.

"But why a samurai?" he asked. "Are they all samurai?"

"I would guess he was a very old spirit, slain centuries ago," Masami chimed in, with no hint of sarcasm.

"Yes," Miyahara answered. "I would agree. He surely spent ages searching for a way out."

"Are there more of these books?" Akio asked. "And does it have a map? Maybe this demon got a hold of one and just followed the directions out. Like GPS, you know, just entered the coordinates."

"There are no other copies that I'm aware of. But even if there are, there is no map or a layout of any kind. According to the book, there can be no map, because it is never the same. The Hells are in constant flux. Therefore to escape would truly be a herculean task."

"But it did escape. And like Hercules," Masami grimaced at her segue, "this demon was probably a great warrior in life, hence the arrogance."

"Maybe he was beheaded in battle even." Akio cut the air with his hand and made an overly dramatic, chopping sound. "Chaa!"

"It's all possible." Miyahara's gaze lingered on the blades that lay next to each other on the bed, intersecting the loud floral pattern of the bedspread, the gem guards glimmering. "He was certainly a samurai, for it is said that when you die, your spirit manifests as a mirror of how you were in life." He seemed to contemplate that last sentence, as if wondering how he would manifest when he was no longer a part of the mortal world.

The sword master's eyes focused on the two journalists again, his momentary drifting dissolving into determined focus. "But what we can assume now with some certainty, though the book doesn't mention it, is that outside of Hell, he needs to maintain his existence by using the heads of others. But they don't last. The flesh is not spirit flesh, and even his essence can't keep it alive for long, which is why he has been acquiring new ones."

Another prickly hush enveloped the room as the horror of that last thought gripped them. Everything that Miyahara had said was impossible. Akio's brain searched for some kind of rationalization, some sane answer that would explain it all away in simple, logical terms, but none came. There was no way around it. After what they had experienced, it was strangely the only answer that made sense.

Reality shifted further in that silence. What Akio thought he knew of the "real" world was no longer reliable. He shifted in his chair, his skin crawling with the thought of it.

Masami fiddled with her coffee cup, but didn't drink. "I remember a story my mother told me when I was young," she said. "It was about a demon who had disguised itself as an elderly woman named Iwate, but was secretly feeding on human flesh. The story frightened me, but it was just . . . It wasn't real. It was a fairy tale."

Her hard shell seemed to be cracking; her stone face twitched, uncertain of its own defenses. She held such a distant sadness that Akio had a sudden, irrational fear she might fade away. He had to stifle the urge to grab her and console her.

"This Iwate was finally banished by an unrelenting priest whose prayers it was unable to dispel," she said, regaining her composure and corporeality.

"So we should have brought a priest?" Akio asked, more to Miyahara than to Masami.

"I tried that," Miyahara answered bitterly. "I haven't been sitting around waiting for it to behead all of Kofu."

"What happened then?"

"Third head on the left." Miyahara was somber and serious. Akio recalled the heads in the repulsive crypt, still vivid in his memory. That one had been half-decayed, with drooping skin and missing tufts of hair, a 50-year-old man, perhaps.

"Never reported it to the police?" Masami asked.

"What would be the point?" Miyahara answered. "The police cannot handle what's happening here. Th ey have no ability to understand or deal with it. The priest is on a missing persons list. They assume he had a mid-life crisis and split town or quietly took his own life somewhere. He had no family."

For Akio, this just made it worse. The priest had no one, yet he died trying to help everyone. And they were the only ones who knew about it.

Masami sighed heavily, the events of the day replaying in her head. They had seen a demon replace its stolen head with someone else's, had fought it, and had seen it dissipate into a fetid mist after Akio had inadvertently killed it. *Hadn't he?* It was a lot to process, even for her normally stoic self.

Vivid images of the snake woman danced in her head.

But her analytical brain could not be crippled. She sifted through the information they had gathered over the past few days. She thought of her conversation with Detective Fujimaki. He had also wondered at the connection between the victims and the murderer, why the murderer had visited those close to the victims. Now she had an answer.

"I was just thinking," she said, "about the couple who were both killed by the demon. Why did it go back there? This thing obviously doesn't care about whose head it takes. I think there was more living in that young man's head than the demon could deal with."

Her eyes darted back and forth for a moment, as if following a ghost the others couldn't see. "I think it went there because the boyfriend's head willed it there. He wasn't ready to let go. But he wasn't strong enough to stop it from killing the one he loved."

"Maybe he didn't want to stop it on some level. Maybe he wanted her to be with him."

"Morbid, Akio. But maybe so," Masami said. "It's just like Matsuoka told us. He believed his wife was able to control the demon, that she kept it at a distance."

"That it even walked like her," Akio added.

"Yeah. I think there's something of the victims still in there for a time."

"All speculation," Miyahara said. "I believe a person's will can move any mountain, or conquer any demon. But we will likely never know."

The tough old man went on to tell them what else he had learned about the hellish creature, from his own experience.

After seeing it the first time, he had quietly gone to investigate and followed the beast to its hiding place. He followed it for a few days, managing to remain unnoticed. In one particularly careless moment, he too had touched the engraved metal chest. He recalled the nerve-scraping pain with a shiver. The demon samurai had burst into the room moments later. Somehow it had a connection to that chest and could sense when it was disturbed, even barely touched.

Miyahara had escaped. Their recent run-in with the thing had not been the first for him. He did not regale them with tales of his bravery fighting the beast, however. His modesty forbade it. He only said that he had obviously survived.

After that initial clash with the demon, he had kept his distance, but he still followed it. He learned a great deal about its habits. After it beheaded someone, it would always return the old head to its lair. Then it would run off to feed. "Many demons I have encountered don't seem to need to eat, or at least not what we would consider sustenance," Miyahara said. "But this one does, and always soon after it swaps heads. I think it has something to do with the fact that it is utilizing living human flesh as its own head. The human part needs the food. You would think it would just eat the body of the head it harvested, but it never did. Either it's too important for it to get the previous head back to its lair quickly, or the food has to be living when consumed, I'm not certain."

"Or the heads of the victims wouldn't let it," Masami suggested.

"It's possible. Or perhaps the demon itself is strangely respectful of the body it has harvested from. Who can say? One thing that's certain is that the demon doesn't require humans for its repast, whether it wants to eat them or not."

That's good news, Masami thought. *Can't say the same for the snake woman, I don't think.*

"It always ran off to the mountains just north of town," Miyahara said. There was a finger ridge of mountains that extended into the city, very near to the park. "It would eat whatever animal happened to cross its path." Only once had Miyahara seen it devour a human. "Some unfortunate camper, all alone, probably a foreigner.

"When I saw you two enter its lair after it left, I knew you had some time because it had gone to eat," Miyahara continued. "But I was worried about that chest. It has some connection. So when I heard your shout, I knew it was coming."

"You followed us?" Akio asked.

"Yes, I've been keeping an eye on you as best as I can, when I'm not following the demon, or teaching, or studying."

"Did you follow it to the train station?"

"Yes."

"And you didn't stop it from killing that guy?" Akio was exasperated, raising his voice.

"I was too late," Miyahara answered, his head low. "Again. By the time I arrived, the man was dead. I had not expected the demon to be out hunting again so soon, so I wasn't prepared. But after you gave pursuit, I followed close behind."

"What do you mean 'again?'" Masami asked.

"I also followed it to the apartment where the young woman was killed. It had a long lead on me. My legs are not as quick as they used to be. I saw it scale the building and was happy I had bought my own ninja shuko."

"Oh, that's why you bought those!" Akio blurted, interrupting.

"Yes," Miyahara said, amused to find out they were aware of his purchase. "I had seen them on the demon and thought they might be useful. I soon regretted that I had not practiced with them, however. The demon shot up the wall as fast as he ran along the ground. For me, it was inches at a time, and dreadfully slow."

Two tracks. Kuramoto had been right.

"By the time I reached the window, the girl was dead. I saw the demon putting her head on. Now that I was there, and too late, I realized I had no plan. I had just hoped to distract it from killing, in some way that would leave me alive. Getting myself dead wouldn't help anyone. I don't know anyone for long leagues, apart from myself, that could ever hope to dispatch of any demon at all, much less this one.

"It saw me and was not pleased. It leapt straight at me. I ducked below the window ledge and it tumbled past into the darkness over my head. I didn't see it land. When I looked down, it wasn't anywhere that I could see.

"I briefly considered climbing through the window and sneaking out through the apartment, but there was no reason to muck up the crime scene and confuse the police, possibly leading them to me. So I inched my way down the wall. When I reached the bottom, the demon was nowhere to be found."

"That's why it left the boyfriend's head behind," Masami said, almost to herself. "You distracted it."

"I suppose," the sensei answered. "Beyond that—to clear the air of any curiosity about the other victims you may have—I did not have the demon's trail for the first train station killing, and the homeless man died before I had ever seen the creature, as did the woman in Fujikawaguchiko. You already know what became of the priest. And I am not even aware of the older heads' origins. Sadly, I have not yet learned how to be omniscient and omnipresent."

A long pause filled the room.

Masami broke the silence. "This isn't exactly the story we came looking for." She couldn't help but give a tiny bewildered laugh—a sight that made Akio smile, she noticed. She was glad he didn't reach for his camera. "Not sure they'll let us print it. What do you think, Akio?"

Akio didn't respond, but just smiled back at her like a happy dog.

"Well, we can be grateful it's over," she said, and freshened her coffee. Th ere was still so much to understand, but at least the experience had brought vindication to her years of doubting herself about the snake woman's existence. It was not a finite answer, but it was a start.

It was a moment before she realized that Miyahara was not smiling. He was looking at her as if trying to figure out how to tell her that a loved one had died. It was the same look her father had so many years ago, when her mother had passed away. Masami stared back, daring him to speak. Finally, he did.

"It's not," he said. "It's not over."

15
Masked

"The demon is still alive." Miyahara looked at each of them in turn with an unblinking gaze. His eyes were beleaguered but held indisputable truth.

Akio wanted to protest, but he just shook his head. He knew the sensei was right. As much as he wanted to believe otherwise, somewhere deep down, he knew this had been coming. *Doomed,* he thought.

Of course, there had been no corpse. But not having dealt with demons before, he assumed killing one would simply send it back from whence it came. A mist dissolving before him seemed an appropriate death for a creature of the spirit world.

"I hoped that I had killed it the first time," Miyahara continued. "When it found me in its room, we battled, and I severed its head—a different one than it wore tonight. I thought that might be its downfall. As I watched in horror, it picked up the head and put it back on its neck. While it was occupied with this, I took the opportunity to run my blade through its heart, if there was still such a thing in its chest. I saw it disperse into the same mist we witnessed earlier. My sword is blessed. I hoped that was enough.

"I was shaken and quickly stepped out of the room. The battle was not an easy one. I'm not sure how long I rested in the hallway, but once I caught my breath, my curiosity took hold. I had seen the box in the room and wanted to find out what was in it. The demon had been dispatched, so I decided it was safe.

"But as I reached out to open the door to its lair, I heard noises within, an awful wailing sound, like the suffering of a hundred men. There was a snap, like a whip cracking or a giant paper bag full of air popping, then a grunting breath and an angry bark of pain. It had come back. I could sense it. I could smell it. I heard a katana slide from its sheath, and I ran.

"I am not one to run from a battle, but we had already fought fiercely and I wasn't confident that I could defeat it a second time. I had to get away and collect my thoughts. I did not know enough about it yet. I did not know how to kill it." Miyahara stopped for a moment and stared into his coffee. "I still don't."

"What's in the box?" asked Masami. Her question sounded like an accusation.

"What makes you think I know?"

"You don't know," she answered, "but you have a good idea." Once Masami locked on to an idea she went straight for the jugular.

The wise old man smiled his sour smile at her. Masami frowned back.

Akio could see that they both felt they knew the answer, and he was afraid he knew it too. "I'm guessing it's not a pile of treasure," he said.

Masami went to pour more coffee. Miyahara was silent.

"It's the real head, isn't it?" Akio looked at the ceiling, hoping they would laugh at his idea, but they didn't.

"We have to open the box and destroy it." Miyahara spoke, as if to his students, giving a command for an exercise.

"Wait a minute," Akio spoke up. "'We?' Since when is it 'we?' You wouldn't even cooperate with us when we tried to interview you. Now you want us to attempt to kill an unkillable demon by destroying a head that we only assume exists? Are you insane?"

Miyahara only stared at Akio, confident and unyielding, a hint of a smile.

"He's right." Masami spoke as if accepting her fate.

"He's right?" Akio was flabbergasted. "How can he be right? We have nothing to gain here! There is a demon who's collecting heads. There's no priceless treasure in the chest, and there's no way in hell that anyone's gonna buy this story. We can't even print this! We'll be the laughing stock of the *Dainichi Daily*, of all of Tokyo! We'll lose our jobs! And we might be killed to boot. I don't know about you, but I'm not looking forward to being beheaded anytime soon. In fact, now that I think of it, I never will be. I want to die quietly in my comfortable bed when I'm like a hundred years old. With my head intact, thank you very much."

No one responded for a moment. Then Masami addressed Akio in the belittling manner to which he was so accustomed. "You're right too, Akio. One hundred percent right. Honestly. So you can go back home with the photographs you have and make up a story that people will believe. Keep your job, and we'll stay here and try to prevent more people from dying."

"I'm not a hero," Akio spat back.

Masami just stared at him. Her cold eyes silently said, *You couldn't be more right about that.*

Akio fell quiet. *So much for comrades-in-arms.*

He sat, sulking, wanting to leave but not wanting to be a coward. Were they really going to go through with such an insane idea?

Then Masami brought out the hatbox.

The mask! He hadn't thought about it since before they followed the demon. He suddenly longed to see it. He felt guilty for not thinking about it. How could he not have thought about it?

"Do you think this could help?" Masami asked opening up the box and showing its contents to Miyahara.

Of course it can help! It's the only thing that can help! Akio stood up and crossed to look into the box too. *It's beautiful.*

Miyahara flinched on seeing it. He jerked his head back as if he'd been bitten. Then slowly, cautiously, he leaned in again. "This is a powerful artifact," he said, careful not to get too close.

"I know," Masami said. "I can feel it too. It was given to us by the old innkeeper in Fujikawaguchiko, the husband of the victim there. He claims he pulled it off the demon when it had no head."

"Pulled it off the demon?" Miyahara asked. "Seems no easy feat for an old innkeeper."

"True, but it's what he told us."

"His wife was the first victim then."

"It would seem so."

Miyahara steeled himself, visibly clenching his jaw, and reached into the hatbox, taking out the mask.

Akio wanted to grab it from him. *That's mine!* He watched as the sensei turned it over in his hand, holding it with ginger fingertips, like it was burning him. Akio wanted to yell at Miyahara. *Give it to me!* But the mask told him to wait. It told him to be patient. So he sat back down and waited.

"It almost looks like the flames and clouds are moving," Miyahara said.

They are moving.

"I know," Masami said. "I feel like it's talking to me. It's creepy." She turned to Akio. "You feel it too, right, Akio?"

"Not anymore," the mask told him to say. "I did, but it's faded."

"I'm not sure what we can get out of this," Miyahara said. "I saw no mention of a mask in the namakubikamen's entry, but it might still be important. Perhaps we can find it elsewhere in the book." He set the mask back in the hatbox and handed it to Masami. She put it on the bed and shoved it away from her, clearly wanting to get some distance from it. "Hopefully, we can learn how to open that box too."

Miyahara opened the huge, gruesome tome and started to flip the pages. Masami stood and looked over his shoulder. "I can't read any of this," she said.

"Oh, right," Miyahara realized. "And I don't have time to teach you." He retrieved a black case from the duffel bag, unclasped it, and pulled out a glass. It was rectangular and framed by dark, ornate metalwork, about half as wide as a page in the book. A handle that looked to be made of some kind of horn protruded from a corner.

"This will help," he said. "It's how I started too. And I still need it sometimes."

Akio watched as Masami held the glass over the page. She was visibly startled. She took the glass away and then put it back. "Amazing," she said. "I don't get how this works."

"You'll find a lot of things are like that if you continue down this path," Miyahara said, as if giving her fatherly advice.

Akio didn't care. He didn't even want to see. He was being patient. He was waiting for the mask's cue. He watched as Masami and Miyahara pored over the book together, Masami leaning over the sensei's shoulder. They turned page after page, scouring the information, enthralled with it. They were completely engrossed and had forgotten all about Akio.

Good. Now's the time, Akio. Do it now.

He stood slowly, stretching his arms and rolling his shoulders. He walked casually over to the bed. He bent over and saw the exquisite mask in the box, that face that was so much better than his own. The swirling clouds and flames on its surface were hypnotic. He smiled. Then he reached down, picked up the mask, and put it on.

16

Arrogance

The spear came at him from above, a warrior on horseback leaned sideways and thrust the cross-bladed *yari* in an arc meant to catch him just under the neck. His katana, already slick with blood, knocked it away with ease. In the same swift motion, he lunged sideways, turning his body into his attacker's arm, trapping it under his own, and pulled the warrior from the horse. The warrior's head was off before he could regain his feet. The general leapt onto the newly available horse easily despite his full armor.

His own mount had been cut down in battle. A spear to its neck had punctured an artery. The general had jumped off gracefully before the horse hit the ground, but his spear had ended up on the wrong side of the beast and snapped from the impact. He withdrew his katana and continued fighting on foot. He had cleaved through at least a dozen men already.

Five samurai attendants followed, still horsed, collecting the heads behind him. They would make for a grand head-viewing ceremony when they had taken the castle. The general was too proud to have taken one of his attendants' horses, though each had dismounted and offered eagerly. He had commanded them back into the saddle. And now, he had earned his own mount again.

His anger kept him going. It kept him alert. It kept him fierce. The men opposing him would all die today. He knew this. They deserved nothing else. Their homes would be burned. Their wives would be ravaged and then put to the sword. Their children would be slaughtered. Well . . . most of them.

He was Noboru Akechi, a samurai whose father had gone into the service of the daimyo Isamu Imube when Noboru was twelve. Their own daimyo had been routed by Imube and instead of slaughtering the retainers, Imube had shown mercy and ordered fealty from them.

So he had served. Past his father's death in battle. Past his mother's subsequent illness and death. Until Imube had betrayed him.

Now he marched on Imube with eight thousand men. They had cut a bloody swath through the countryside first, murdering countless innocent peasants, burning their homes with them still inside, cutting down any who tried to escape. They left some heads on pikes, but most lay in the dirt. Peasant heads were worth nothing. They were not samurai. Surely some enterprising and degenerate opportunist would collect them and try to pass them as samurai heads for a reward, combing the hair and blackening the teeth. But if they were brought to Akechi, he would know. He could sniff out lies like steaming natto.

Their slaughter of the peasantry had drawn Imube's forces from the castle, exactly as Akechi had planned. He knew the daimyo's arrogance would not allow him to cower behind castle walls.

Now devastation lay before the castle. Akechi trotted forward through red-stained earth and lumps of armored flesh. His foot soldiers had flanked the enemy troops, while the samurai had rode straight ahead to glory. Imube's forces had been divided and surrounded. Ahead of him stood all that remained, a dozen samurai, only half of which were still ahorse. Imube's remaining foot soldiers were fleeing the field, being cut down by Akechi's archers.

Apart from his five attendants, Akechi's samurai elite had charged ahead of him, when he had been unhorsed. But now they circled out, away from the battle, refusing to engage with Imube directly, at Akechi's orders.

The general—no, the daimyo now; he had been daimyo since conquering his most recent lord, Hatano, beheading him at dinner and usurping power from within the court, his loyal samurai having blocked the doors; he had drunk the blood spouting from the former daimyo's neck, and out of the ruler's own cup; he would do the same today with Imube, and be daimyo of this land as well—smiled a grim, self-righteous grin.

"Kill his men," he said, and his retainers galloped forward.

Imube did not flinch at this. His own exhausted samurai rode forward to meet them.

The two daimyo faced each other. Sharp, spiral horns thrust upward above a dragon face, with a wide, leering grin and wing-like ears, mounted on Akechi's helmet. A steel flourish of waves crested Imube's helmet like antlers. Akechi's face was bare, but Imube's face was obscured by a *mempo*, a mask that covered all but his blank eyes. To anyone else, he would have seemed calm and ready for death, but Akechi could smell his fear.

He spurred his horse forward, and Imube did the same.

Akechi held his katana high in one hand as he charged directly toward Imube's outthrust spear. With nothing but a breath between the razor tip of the spear blade, Akechi spun his katana in a tight arc, enveloping the spear and ripping it from his rival's grasp. As the spear flew free, he snapped the katana upward, aiming at the neck. But he had misjudged Imube's reaction to being disarmed; his timing was off by a mere fraction, causing the katana's guard to impact with the edge of Imube's helmet and the blade to glance off of his neck guard. The force of the blow on the already imbalanced daimyo knocked him from his horse. The routed leader tumbled several meters away along the corpse-strewn ground but regained his feet quickly.

Akechi vaulted from his own horse. He had lost the grip on his katana when it hit Imube's helmet. It was a two-handed weapon, harder to wield with only one, and his hands were fatigued and wet with blood and sweat. Still, he cursed himself for the loss.

He still had his wakizashi in his belt, and his *tanto* if it came to that.

Imube drew his katana and struck a ready stance, shouting nonsense as he did, empty bravado about which of them would die on the field that day.

Akechi marched forward, not yet drawing any weapon. He spied a *kumade*, a steel rake with spikes protruding from its sides, abandoned on the battlefield and just in his path. He plucked it from the corpse that still gripped its handle and rushed toward Imube. With a lunge, he thrust the kumade forward, hooking it into the flourished crown of Imube's helmet. He jerked the daimyo forward to him, letting the rake go from his hands as he withdrew his wakizashi and struck clean through Imube's newly exposed neck.

Before the body fell, Akechi grabbed the top ridge of the armor chest plate to hold it upright, letting the hot blood spouting from the neck spray his face and saltily coat his outthrust tongue.

The raised platform at the far end of the room was completely covered in large tatami mats. Ten hanging scrolls, each with a different monochrome image depicting a silvery fish leaping from vast, arcing waves, hung above the platform. The scrolls nearest the center were spattered and stained with spots of varying shades, bits of rice and other flecks. Spread across the platform were trays and platters of enough food to feed twenty hungry men, but only two sat in the center of the decadent display.

Akechi sat cross-legged with his newly acquired son next to him. Mountains of rice filled several porcelain bowls; grilled mackerel, flounder and salmon reclined in beds of *shiso* leaves; strips of seasoned eel lay next to cut tofu slabs; tempura and oysters adorned gilded platters; sushi was stacked five layers high; soba noodles curled in tight spheres like balls of yarn overfilled polished birchwood bowls; plums, oranges and grapes filled long boat-shaped dishes; there was a pot of miso soup for each of them and a personal teapot as well; *sake* flowed continuously from the servants' pitchers.

The boy scowled across the expansive spread of food, his stormy eyes on his sisters and his mother who were relegated to an area off the platform. The females had plenty of food among them but nothing compared to the extravagance laid out before the two males.

Despite the vast amounts of food, the boy was unhappy, his eyes deep with bitterness. He was eight years old and refused to eat. Akechi did not know the boy. The child had only been an infant when Imube had tried to execute Akechi. He had not seen him grow up.

The daimyo patted the boy's head. "Eat, Kiyoshi. You must have food if you want to grow into a strong warrior."

The boy had been gripping his chopsticks tightly, but now he threw them across the room. "I want to sit with my sisters! And my mother! Not you!"

"Not with your father?" Akechi tried to present a pleasant face but only grimaced.

"You are not my father!" Kiyoshi shouted. "You killed my father!" He grabbed a handful of rice and threw it at Akechi, who tried to smile.

"You are my son," the daimyo insisted. "Your name is Kiyoshi Akechi now."

"Imube!" the boy shouted. "Kiyoshi Imube!" He stood up from the platform and started to stomp off toward his sisters and mother. The women and girls looked away when Akechi glared in their direction. They busied themselves eating, pretending that nothing was amiss.

Akechi stood. He had had enough for today. "Out!" he screamed at the women. "Out of my sight! You will eat in the garden! Out!"

The women stood quickly, grabbing the younger ones. The servants sprung into action, collecting the food and whisking it toward the garden on polished wooden trays.

Akechi put his hand on the boy's neck and drug him back to the platform. He pushed the boy back down to the tatami mat amidst the sprawl of food. *A firm hand teaches respect and engenders strength of character,* he told himself. *The boy will learn. And he will love me for it.*

The daimyo tried to shed his anger as he resumed sitting himself. "You will eat now," he said firmly, "or you will never see your sisters again."

The boy screamed and shoved his hands through the dishes, spilling soup and rice into the eel, knocking the teapot into the boat of fruit, cracking it so that tea began to dribble out of the porcelain side, and sending plums and oranges rolling.

"Fine!" Akechi shouted back, standing again. "You want your sisters? Fine!" Then turning to a servant, he yelled, "Bring me Kotone!" Two servants rushed off, returning only moments later with a girl of about twelve. Her face was pale; some of her long, black hair had come loose from its knot and was falling into her eyes. She was clearly afraid.

"Strip off her clothes!" Akechi commanded the servants as he withdrew his katana from his belt. The servants hurriedly undid the girl's obi and yanked her kimono from her.

"No!" Kiyoshi screamed. "Don't kill her!"

"Kotone is your favorite, isn't she?" He grinned, stepping toward the girl. "Bend her head down and hold her still," he barked at the servants. The boy whimpered and wailed. The girl began to cry. The servants bent her head over, and she collapsed to her knees, sobbing louder.

Akechi held his katana high over the girl's naked body. Tears dripped from her eyes as Kiyoshi howled. Akechi brought his katana down hard, hitting the flat of it against the girl's buttocks.

The girl yelped in pain as a red strip appeared across her skin. The boy seemed surprised, yet relieved—still horrified, but relieved that his sister remained alive.

Akechi brought his sword down again. Another cry of pain rang out, and another red strip accompanied the first. And again, he whipped the flat of his blade against the girl.

It was then, amid Kotone's third cry, that the boy realized how to stop it. He began shoveling food into his mouth. Tears streamed down his face, salting everything he tasted. He ate like a ravenous animal, and Kotone was not hit again.

Akechi slid his sword back into the scabbard tucked into his obi. He looked at the boy, admiringly. The girl was out of his mind now. He didn't even consider her, only distantly hearing her wail as it diminished and then disappeared, the servants carrying her from the room.

My son, he thought. *You will be strong. And you will love me.*

Akechi awoke suddenly, startled from a dream. His father had ridden to him on horseback to warn him. The horse had been made of flames. "Your arrogance will be your undoing," his father said, and the horse hissed the words too, like air escaping wood in the fire. "They are your family now. All of them," the man and beast continued. "Too late now to make amends," said the horse, and his father mimicked, a world-weary rasp entwined with whispery sibilance. "They will come for you." They rode off, leaving him standing in a pile of human heads, bloody and eyes open.

He awoke in a haze, at first still seeing the human heads around him, but no, it was just a blanket, crumpled by his feet. He had kicked it off in the night. He lay there for a moment, noticing that his large naked body, muscled and scarred, had grown a belly.

His dream was quickly fading, but a niggling remnant pestered him. An uncomfortable sheen of guilt lingered beneath his skin. He had been cruel; there was no doubt. But leaders had to be cruel. It was the only way to maintain order and respect. It was not out of arrogance, it was out of necessity. It was a fact that he was better than those who served him. How could it not be? He was daimyo of two castles and domains now. He had conquered them with cunning and power. Of course he was better than his underlings, better than all of them. They could not do what he had done, and therefore he was superior. He was their master, and they were no better than dogs who did his bidding.

And why should he treat his adopted family any better? Yes, they were of samurai blood, but they were conquered samurai. They were not of his lineage. They were beneath him. He bedded Imube's wife, now his, when he felt like it. When she wasn't compliant, he had two of his samurai hold her down. Other than that, she was an annoyance. His newly acquired daughters were no different. Some were more obedient than others, but he should have had them killed when he had taken the castle. Why had he shown mercy? That had been a mistake. They looked at him with disdain. He had been merciful, and that is how they repaid him. They talked behind his back. They shared knowing glances between one another. He could still have them killed. Maybe he would.

But he wanted them for leverage. He could marry them off to other daimyo to form alliances, to offer some protection from attack. His domain was twice the size as it had been. One of his generals watched over his former castle that he had usurped barely three years prior. He had more land to watch over, so if he could keep the nearest daimyos at bay by marrying his daughters to their sons, so be it. He would keep them complacent until he was ready to conquer them as well. And he wouldn't care if his daughters were killed when he laid siege, because they weren't really his daughters to begin with. They were pawns. And there were seven of them. They were like rats, always scurrying about; he would be glad to be rid of them.

His son's face was illuminated in the morning light slanting sideways through the bedroom window. *There he is.*

Kiyoshi was all Noboru Akechi cared about. He was training the boy to be a leader. When Akechi had conquered all he could, Kiyoshi would take over and rule his domain. He would be the strongest of daimyo. With Kiyoshi, Akechi would oust the reigning Ashikaga clan and become shogun.

The boy kneeled at his bedside, smiling. He had changed in recent months. He had finally accepted who he was and had begun proudly calling himself Kiyoshi Akechi. It was exactly as Noboru had hoped. He had his son now, a boy he could be proud of. No one else mattered.

Next to Kiyoshi was a platter with tea on it, a small blue and white porcelain pitcher from China with a dragon handle and one matching cup. It had become a morning ritual. Noboru had told him that the servants can do such things, but the boy insisted. "I want to show my respect and love for you, father," he had said. So Noboru allowed it. The boy's love meant everything to him. Besides, it showed his dutifulness. It showed his commitment to the Akechi path.

Kiyoshi poured the tea into the cup and, lifting it in both hands, proffered it to his father with a bow of his head.

Akechi received the tea in both hands as well and smiled. "Next time," he said, "you will bring two cups, and you will drink with me."

The boy smiled back with a gleam in his eyes that showed gratitude and honor. "Yes, father," he said. "I will be honored to drink with you."

Akechi smiled deeper. Yes, his son will make a grand leader. Everything was playing out exactly as he planned. It was exactly as he deserved.

He took a deep sip of the tea, the heat of it just right, not too hot, but with a warmth that heartened him and wakened his mouth. He reached out to pat his son on the shoulder, to touch what was his true flesh and blood. But his arm suddenly grew heavy. It hung limp in the air, unable to be straightened to its full length. His whole body began to feel warm, too warm, like blood was seeping from his skin. He looked to his naked belly, but there was no blood there. Something was crawling in him, a fire shot through his veins, searing his flesh from within.

He looked to his son, who now stood over him with gleeful spite, the satisfied gleam gained only from a vengeful act.

"Die," Kiyoshi said. "Die, you filthy creature! Die! You evil bastard who murdered my father, die!"

Akechi's vision was getting blurry. He was panicking. *No*, he thought, *I'm your father!* And then he said it out loud. "I'm your father!" he repeated. "What have you done, my beautiful boy? What have you done? I am your true father!" But he couldn't see the boy anymore. The shape of him had blurred into a hazy, thin pillar and melted with the room behind him.

And then there was only blackness. His stomach heaved, and he tasted blood and bile as it lurched from his gut. His insides collapsed and failed to function. He fell backward to the tatami, his face pale and shot with veins.

And then he was no more.

17

Betrayal

The sun was cruel before the long walk to Hatano's castle. It blinded and stabbed at Akechi's eyes.

He collapsed in the tall grass.

While he lay there, he made a decision.

He had been a *ronin* too long, wandering the countryside, working jobs as he could, drinking too much when he had money, fighting stupid brawls when his honor felt offended. There had been too many parched summer days with no food in his belly, the harsh sun slowly drying him up.

Memories spun like dervishes in his head, like tornadoes.

A son had been born to him. He was a beautiful boy with eyes like a storm coming, whose very act of birth had been a murder. Akechi's wife had died in childbirth.

Oh, Sango. You were my all. Now, there is only my boy, Kiyoshi. In him, you live.

But he was taken from me.

Isamu Imube appeared in the doorway to the nursery. His short, bulldog-like form was clothed in a grand kimono, patterned with blue waves and silver carp. Four samurai accompanied him. They were in full armor sans helmets. That did not bode well. *Why are they in armor?*

But Akechi knew why.

A wet nurse, who was cradling the boy, looked up, startled. Imube looked hungry, like an animal smelling blood.

Akechi pushed through the men from behind to stand in the room with his son. Yes, he knew why they were there. He had feared it. His hand rested near his katana tucked into his belt, but not on it. He did not want to outwardly offend his lord. He may yet be able to talk his way out of this. He positioned himself between his son and the daimyo.

"How may I be of service to you today, my lord?" Akechi asked, bowing.

"Let me see the boy," the daimyo answered greedily.

Imube had seven daughters and no sons. Akechi knew his intent. "I believe he is sleeping. Perhaps when he is awake and playing, he will be of more interest to you, my lord."

"No. Now." The four samurai stepped deeper into the room, flanking Akechi, two to a side. They were his compatriots. They were men he had fought with and drank with.

Akechi bowed and reluctantly stepped aside.

"Bring him to me," Imube called to the wet nurse. She responded quickly, but with a fearful glance toward Akechi.

The daimyo peered down at the infant boy in her hands, with a look that was somewhere between hunger and fatherly pride. He reached out and took the boy, held him up above his head momentarily. The boy seemed confused but not unhappy. He did not cry.

"He's my son now," said Imube.

Akechi stepped toward the daimyo. The four samurai stepped closer, hands on their swords. Samurai were not meant to have any attachments; even their own family should not be something they cling to. Their only purpose was to serve their lord in battle. Akechi should have been honored.

But he was not honored. He was angry.

Akechi shook slightly as he tried to appease the daimyo. "My lord, you honor me and my son. I live to serve you, but he is all I have left. I beg of you not to take him."

Imube lowered the child to his chest and glared at Akechi. "I knew you would be weak," he said. He handed the child back to the wet nurse and told her, "Bring the boy to my chambers and wait for me there." The woman nodded and rushed off with the child, not daring to look toward Akechi as she went.

"No!" Akechi said too loudly—much too loudly to be addressing his daimyo.

Imube's glare increased, his wide nostrils flaring. "You dare command me? You should be grateful. You should be kissing my feet that I have chosen your boy as my own!" Then, with what appeared to be a show of sadness, of regret, the daimyo lowered his head slightly; a bitter smile came to his lips. "Take him," he commanded the other samurai. "He will be nothing but trouble now. Bring him to the courtyard." And he strode out of the room.

The four samurai moved quickly to him, so he had to be quicker. Once he was disarmed, he would be helpless. There was nothing left to do. If he was taken to the courtyard, he would be executed. His head would join those of Imube's enemies.

One of the four put a firm hand on his arm. It was Kazuo, who had shared jokes with him two days earlier in an effort to cheer him up. On the other side, reaching for his sword arm, was Hideo, who had once saved his life by blocking a kama aimed at the back of his neck. He had cut down the peasant wielding it in the next stroke. Behind Kazuo, came Goro, a big, simple, dullard of a warrior that Akechi never liked. Behind Hideo came Kenta, a quiet man who drank little, and whom Akechi had only seen smile on the battlefield with blood on his sword. Akechi liked him best.

In one fluid motion, Akechi twisted his left arm out of Kazuo's grasp, staggering him back; he pulled his katana from its sheath, elbowing Hideo in the lower lip as he did; as his arm rebounded off Hideo's face, the katana's tip plunged into Kazuo's neck just below the jaw before he could regain his footing; the armored samurai fell to the floor, clutching at his neck, blood spouting though his fingers; on Akechi's backswing, he took off Hideo's head.

The four had not taken their weapons out yet, apparently assuming that Akechi would go peacefully. After all, he was their friend and a loyal samurai; he should have done so. But Akechi was no longer anyone's vassal. From the moment his boy was taken from him, he had renounced his servitude. And he was no friend to those who would let that happen.

The two remaining samurai drew their weapons. Goro had a surprised look on his face, which quickly converted to anger on seeing his comrades cut down. Kenta's expression was flat, unreadable. He held his katana as still as a man meditating, as still as stone.

Akechi was not clad in armor like they were. He only wore his *yukata*—his summer kimono, thin and breathable. He might as well have been naked.

Goro came at him first. But he was off-balance. His anger had sent him leaning into his attack, and he swung his sword too heavily. It would have cut Akechi in two had it connected, but he sidestepped, enveloping the oncoming blade with his own, carrying it and Goro forward into a fall. Goro's strength was such that, even off-balance, his blade was difficult to bind and the tip of it nicked Akechi's shin as it passed. As the big man tumbled, face-forward, Akechi's blade slipped between plates of armor; it sunk into Goro's kidney and ripped upward through his back, severing his spine. He collapsed into a small mountain on the floor and did not move.

Kenta stood alone, still unmoved by the violence before him. Blood spattered the half of the nursery where Akechi stood like a demon, the bodies of his former comrades lumped around him.

Kenta waited. There was nowhere for Akechi to escape. One door left the nursery. Kenta had no reason to make the first move. The burden was on Akechi. He had to escape. Soon more samurai would come. Once he had not appeared in the courtyard to accept his punishment, the whole of the castle would be after him.

He lunged forward, thrusting his katana toward Kenta's face. But it had only been a feint, an attempt to provoke a reaction. Kenta read it as such and simply stepped back calmly, his sword still in front of him, unwavering.

Kenta's back was closer to the wall than Akechi's, but it was Akechi who was trapped. The condemned samurai stepped backward and in a rash, savage moment, he picked up Hideo's head with his left hand, still holding his katana in his right. He brandished the head at Kenta. "This will be your fate too!" he barked in a harsh whisper. "I will have your head! I will have all of your heads!"

Then he heaved the head toward Kenta's unresponsive face as he charged.

Reflexively, Kenta blocked the head deftly with his katana, sending it into the wall. But his action took his blade away and gave Akechi just enough time to thrust his own at Kenta's exposed jugular.

Kenta was faster than he had anticipated, and his katana came back to parry the thrust. Still, he had lost time, and Akechi's blade sunk half its width into Kenta's neck just missing the artery. As Kenta responded with a thrust to Akechi's heart, the warrior parried, leaping backward, and at the same time, slashed across Kenta's face taking off a piece of his ear and cheek. The gash was not deadly, but blood gushed from the stoic warrior's face, revealing a nervous fear that had not been there before.

Kenta tried to regain his composure. He resumed his stance, but was shaky now, no longer the meditative warrior. No smile creased his face for this battle.

Akechi snarled and lunged, feinting again, and this time Kenta believed it and reacted with a swing just a fraction too wide. Akechi avoided the blade and thrust toward the armpit where there was an opening in the armor. His aim was imperfect though, and it glanced off Kenta's chest plate sending the tip of the katana into his arm instead. It was damage still, weakening Kenta, but it was not the deathblow he had intended.

Kenta's left arm released its grip on his katana as it was stabbed, but his right arm still held it and slashed wildly. The blade cut across Akechi's chest, through his left breast, scraping his ribs, and opening the flesh across his heart. But it did not penetrate his ribs. He would live yet.

The blow staggered him, but he rebounded instantly, again thrusting toward Kenta's neck. As he did, Kenta enveloped Akechi's blade with his own and whipped it to the side, disarming him. But Akechi was ready for this. It was Kenta's best move and he knew it well. Akechi let the katana slip from his grasp and Kenta smiled. But Kenta's blade had swung sideways, opening him completely. As Akechi brought his now free right arm back across his body, he withdrew the wakizashi from his belt. Continuing his lunge forward, he brought the shorter blade up level with Kenta's neck, putting his left palm on the back, dull edge of the blade to steady it. With pressure from both hands, the sharp weapon sunk through Kenta's neck like rice cake, impacting on the wall behind him. His smile was gone.

Akechi retrieved his armor and a small sack of rice before hurrying out of the castle. Shouts echoed behind him as he mounted a horse and sped off toward the foothills nearby.

Five years he spent wandering, homeless, and working whatever job was offered him to earn a very meager living. He protected crops. He ran off bandits. He killed spurning lovers. It did not matter. He kept his belly as full as possible until he could get revenge. Some days he did not eat. Others he had enough for *sake* to go with his meal. He had sold his horse and lived well for a short time, but that did not last.

The years passed as he went from depression to anger and back again. Through it all, he only thought of his son. He would get him back. He would destroy Imube and reclaim his boy. Somehow.

For too long, he refused the idea of taking up service with another daimyo. What would they give him for his service but more betrayal? But in his fifth year as a ronin, when he was again prone in the grass, his stomach rumbling, the morning sun drying him like a fish on a hot stone, it occurred to him that it was his only option. How else would he build an army? He wouldn't do it by joining with the few other starving, leaderless samurai that he had met. Most joined other daimyo as fast as they could. It was a time of constant war, and competent soldiers were in high demand. No, he could not get revenge with some ragtag band of ronin. It would only be through service and his subsequent betrayal of others that he would gain an army. All others were beneath him now. They were only pawns in his grand plan. He would get his son back if it cost the lives of thousands.

He rose to his feet and began the slow, determined walk toward the castle of the daimyo Hatano, whose lands bordered Imube's.

18
Torment

ow could this be? No . . . betrayed by my own son. Murdered by my one beloved, the sole purpose for my vengeance.

It was cold, beyond any physical cold he had ever felt before, like there was ice in his blood, in every fiber of bone and muscle. The room felt small, claustrophobic and yet immensely vast at the same time. He could sense walls but couldn't see them.

He was on his knees. Shapes moved about him. Who were they? Who was he?

Oh, yes. Noboru Akechi, the great daimyo. Where was he? How had he come here? He had been sleeping. No, eating. No, that wasn't it either. He had been talking with his son.

Yes.

His beloved son.

And then he drank the tea.

Poisoned!

He had been poisoned by his own son! Betrayed by his own heart's blood. After all he had done, all he had suffered to regain him, the boy had betrayed him. Kiyoshi had killed him, his own father. He had feigned trust and loyalty. It had all been an act. He had never accepted the truth. *He still believes he is Imube's and not mine!*

Akechi wept.

The shapes moved closer to him. He didn't know what they were, but he didn't want them near. He tried to get up but couldn't move. He was bound somehow in a kneeling position, his legs fast to the floor. He tried to move his arms to fend off the shapes but couldn't. They were bound to his back, immobile, though he could feel no rope or any material at all constraining him. He couldn't even turn his head to look toward the shapes, to see what they were.

He felt one of them behind him, and his back itched uncontrollably with the presence. He fought to turn around but in vain; his muscles would not respond. Then another shape appeared in front of him. He could almost make it out: dark, dark flesh that blended in with the darkness and the walls that he couldn't see; a long, impossibly wide mouth with rows upon rows of teeth like a shark; a glint of eyes, more than two, bulbous and gray-veined in the non-light.

It held something in slender, clawed, black fingers. A box.

It set the box down directly in front of Akechi, and a beam of light illuminated it from somewhere far above. It was blinding for a moment, but his eyes adjusted, or the light dimmed, he wasn't sure.

The box was a *kanejaku* long, slightly longer than his forearm, on all sides. The light gleamed off of its surface of solid steel, reflected off the bands of yet more steel that reinforced the corners. Empty ovals, edged with tiny flames, adorned each surface that he could see, like a frame for something that wasn't yet there.

The thing that had set it down stepped back quickly, but Akechi saw its shape better in the brief moment the light caught it. Its upper body looked vaguely human: two arms and a head, but its head was twice the size of a human head and wider than it was tall. Eyes, at least four, maybe more, blinked in the bright light; multitudes of teeth glinted in a long, thin smile that was beyond unsettling. Its lower body bent away into the darkness but looked insectoid, worm-like with many short legs.

Akechi tried to reach for his waist, where his katana would be, but still his arms were bound. He could not fight the thing. He could not run.

Then another one—or was it the same one?—came forward, wielding something long and metal. Not a sword, a brand. It was an angular and intricate symbol of a language he had never seen, but he understood it. He recognized it immediately. It was his name. It did not say Noboru Akechi, no. It was the name of his soul.

The brand was glowing red, and the creature holding it thrust it at his forehead. It burned deep into his skull. The pain was excruciating. He tried to cry out, but his mouth would not move either. His only solace was that the searing heat warmed the unnatural chill for a brief moment. The creature smiled—an impossibly wide grin—and slunk away into the darkness.

Akechi saw light flicker from below and looked down at the box. The symbol from the brand was burning itself into the center of the oval frames on its surface. Tiny flames burnished deep, black lines into the steel. A sulfurous smell hit his nose. Other symbols burnished themselves into the steel around the ovals. He could not read them either, but he knew what they were. They were his crimes, his sins in life. They were many.

Another creature appeared. It had to be another one, not the same; it came too quickly after the other one had retreated, and it had something else in its hands. It was a large steel device with two blades connected in the center. The creature held it with both hands, blades open wide. It looked like a giant pair of scissors. The creature scurried forward like a shot, the scissors aimed at Akechi's neck.

Another creature skittered in. *Yes, there is more than one.* It leaned down and opened the box. Akechi felt a large, slender-fingered hand on the top of his head. *There are at least three.*

A fourth one appeared, holding something red—deep, blackish, blood red. It was a mask, a full-faced somen. It looked alive with motion.

A fifth one appeared holding a katana in its hand and a wakizashi in its teeth. Each had guards cut from a gleaming red gemstone and handles of blackened bone wrapped with black strands of hair.

The creatures were all smiling in the glow from the beam of light —unnervingly wide, thin, toothy smiles—framed by the unknown blackness behind them. Their black muscles rippled and glinted as they moved. Their many, gray-veined eyes glistened hungrily.

Then everything happened at once.

The scissors closed around Akechi's neck in a snap. The hand lifted his head and tossed it to the creature crouched by the box, who caught it and placed it inside, quickly closing the lid. The mask was placed where his face used to be; he felt it searing itself to the empty space there as if he still had a head for it to be placed on.

He found he could see. The creature with the swords bent down and did something with them, but its body was blocking the line of sight of Akechi's new vision, and his other eyes were inside a dark box. But it looked like it slid the katana sideways under or perhaps into the box. Then it did something with the wakizashi that he couldn't see at all, but he heard a loud click.

Then they all skittered away, one of them taking the box with it.

A door opened in the dark. Light spilled out, and inside he saw a vast room, the walls lined with similarly sized boxes. It seemed to go on forever. A pair of swords was above many of them on racks. Others had smaller items on shelves: quill pens and ink, a ledger book, a looking glass. Some were larger: a spear and halberd, bow and arrow, a rake and kama. Suits of armor stood here and there.

The creature holding his box disappeared into the long room. The door shut, leaving him shivering and alone in the cold black nothing.

19

Escape

It felt like the skin on Akio's face was being ripped off, like someone had superglued a Halloween mask to his face and was pulling it off slowly. With a final jerk, it came free, taking all of his skin and part of his nose with it; he was sure of it. He screamed and dropped to the bed, his back arcing as his muscles all tensed at once. Then he lay prone and brought his hands to his face, certain to touch blood and sinew.

He didn't. It was only skin—his own face, though tender to the touch. His breathing was heavy and ragged. It was all he could hear. There was no other sound. There was no light either—either that or he couldn't see. He hoped for the former.

Then he heard voices in the darkness, distant and thin. He could barely hear them over his breathing. Slowly they grew louder, and light began to filter in through the darkness. It was a harsh light, unnatural, splintering in at the edges of his vision.

Then the light was too bright, blinding him, and the voices were very loud. They were shouting.

"Akio! Are you all right?" they said. "Akio? Can you hear us?" There were two voices: a young, strident, female voice and a rough, older male one. They sounded familiar. One was someone he cared about. The other he wasn't sure he could trust. But both of their voices sounded concerned.

"Akio? Say something."

"He'll be all right now, I think. Give him a moment."

His eyes adjusted to the ceiling light blaring from above, and he saw Masami. Her cold face didn't look so cold; it looked warm even, flush with red, and worried. Was it really her? On his other side was someone older, the daimyo, Imube . . . *no, that's not right*. It was the kendo instructor, Miyahara. He had his hands on Akio's arm to steady him. Or to hold him down.

Masami had her hands on him too, on his chest and his other arm. She was touching him. She would never . . . He looked down at her slender fingers. Her nails were chipped and two fingers were bleeding. One nail was nearly off.

"What happened to your hands?" Akio asked, his voice raspy and raw. He tried to sit up, but they held him still.

"No," she said. "Don't. Just relax." And then she nodded toward her hands. "We'll explain later. I'm fine."

But then Akio remembered. It all came flooding back. He remembered the samurai's memories as if they were his own. He remembered wanting to wear the mask so desperately. He remembered putting it on. He remembered the overwhelming arrogance, that no one alive was his better. He remembered the killing, the abuse, and the poison. He remembered the ache and the loss. He rolled away from their grasps and retched off the side of the bed.

Masami must have torn the mask off him with her bare hands. And it hadn't been easy. His arms ached at his shoulders and biceps. In fact, he hurt all over. Miyahara must have held him down. His head hurt too. There was a throbbing pain at the back of his skull. *Did they hit me? I probably deserved it.*

He stood up from the bed and they let him. He saw the mask in the far corner of the room, face down. It looked harmless, like a trinket. But then he heard its voice.

"*Wear me. I am beautiful.*"

Akio turned away, his face pale. He longed to grab it, to put it back on, but the thought of it turned his stomach again. He fought back the bile. *What have I done?* He had to get out of there. "I'm sorry," he said. "I'm so sorry. I've ruined everything. I need to go home. I need to go back to Tokyo. I'll clean up the puke. I'm sorry. I just need to go." He could feel his heart rate accelerating, his breaths becoming shorter.

"It's okay," Masami said with concern. "Don't worry about the puke. Let's go to your room. You should lay down."

She walked him out of the room, her hands on his shoulders to steady him. He needed it; he couldn't walk straight. Any other time, he would have been in heaven with Masami holding him like that, but he was miserable. He felt nauseous and wanted to get as far away from Kofu as he could.

In his room next door, he lay on the bed. Masami set the small trash can near the bedside in case he had to vomit again. She rested a hand on his arm. Her look was a mix of caring and fear. He wasn't sure what had happened when he put the mask on, but he was sure it wasn't good.

"What did I do?" he croaked.

"It doesn't matter," she answered. "You're safe now."

He awoke what seemed like only moments later, and maybe it was. He hadn't known what time it was when he fell asleep. He didn't remember falling asleep. But Masami was gone, and the room was dark.

He lay there and tried to forget what had happened, tried to forget the memories that weren't his now seared into his brain like some form of punishment. He would go back home. There was no question. He couldn't do this anymore.

His muscles ached. His head hurt. His face was sore. He wanted to cry, and he did.

When the tears subsided, he began planning his train ride back to Tokyo. *It will be nice,* he thought. *Alone on a train. There's something peaceful about riding through the countryside by yourself. The best thoughts come then. The best daydreams.*

Yet this time, he knew it would only be nightmares.

Two hours later, he was still awake.

He lay staring at the ceiling, which was visible only by the dim city light coming through the window. A stronger pain started to creep up the back of his neck. A scream came from outside and he jumped to look down toward the street. A woman was running frenetically down the sidewalk. A huge figure in armor was loping across the street, its katana drawn.

Akechi.

But it was not following the woman. It didn't seem concerned about her at all. It was heading straight for the hotel.

The swords! Akio panicked. *We shouldn't have taken the swords!*

The demon wanted the swords. He couldn't remember why, but he knew that it needed them for something. Miyahara had warned them, but they had thought the demon was dead. They thought they deserved the swords as payment for this horrifying experience. Masami had agreed with him, a trend that Akio was hoping would continue, but he had sabotaged that possibility by being an idiot, by being weak. And now he furthered that image by being a coward, by planning to run away home. She would never treat him with respect again. Those little moments would be all he would have, remembering them in the dark, alone in his empty apartment. He had ruined his chances of being treated as her equal.

At the least, if he could leave, he would remove himself from her presence and not cause any more harm. And then, at least, he would be alive. Now even that end was questionable. Running away wouldn't save him anymore. The beast was going to chase him down and kill him anyway.

He turned from the window to run and warn the others, but his door flew open. Masami and Miyahara entered in a flurry. Masami was holding both of the red-jeweled swords. Miyahara had his own katana tucked into his belt.

"Leave the swords and run!" Akio shouted, immediately regretting the words that reinforced his cowardice, but still confident it was the best course of action. "That's all he wants!" Th en he addressed Miyahara. "Why did you let us keep them?" He felt like he was going to faint. "You shouldn't have let us keep them!"

In a silent answer, Miyahara took the wakizashi, the shorter of the two blades, from Masami. He brandished the pommel end at Akio. An odd shape protruded from it, like some ancient unreadable symbol. He was puzzled for a moment, but then he understood. It was the exact shape of the keyhole in the samurai's metal chest. Yes, of course! He remembered the vile creature using it to lock the box. The wakizashi was the key.

"I knew it was dangerous to take them," the master finally spoke, handing the weapon back to Masami. "But I also knew that in danger, an answer often resides. It was guarding them for a reason. We have to get back to its lair."

Of course he was. He needs them. I saw it.

Akio couldn't speak for a rare moment, his whole being pleading for some kind of reprieve, for someone to assure him of his safety.

"It won't follow you," Masami said, reading his thoughts. "Stay here, and head home when it's clear. You'll be safe." She turned to follow Miyahara, who had stepped into the hallway.

Though it was an answer he craved, he found it wasn't really the one he needed. In a moment he was certain he would regret, Akio put his hand on Masami's shoulder to stop her. The contact sent a chill through him. How he longed to embrace her right there; she had cared for him, even when he had put them in danger. But instead, he reached out and took the katana from her hand. "Yes, he will," he said.

Masami gave him a brief look of uncertain approval. There was pride in that look, but fear as well. "Are you sure?" she asked. *Can I trust you?* the look said.

Akio didn't know. He was afraid she couldn't. But he gripped the katana tight regardless, and the three of them headed for the back stairs.

20

Absolution

They sped away in Masami's car in what felt like a slow motion blur toward the park. Time slowed down in those panicked, life-threatening moments, every detail noticed, every second expanded into minutes, every anguished frame of life cruelly extended and imprinted in memory forever. Akio could hear the tires buzzing on the road. He could hear each of them breathing in different rhythms; his was quick and shallow like a rabbit; Masami's was slower and deeper but still strained, like she was forcing it; Miyahara's was calm and meditative, which seemed impossible.

The dark buildings whizzed by. Business signs that never turned off lit them and reflected their faces in the window glass: Family Mart, Celeo, Mos Burger. The park was only a literal block away, but they had to circle a large city block at Heiwa Boulevard, where there was no vehicle access, and pass by the train station to get there.

"How did you find out about the key?" Akio asked, trying to keep his balance as the car veered around a corner.

"The book hinted at it," Miyahara said, "but it was Masami who realized it, while inspecting the pommel of the wakizashi." The car skidded to avoid a cat cleaning itself in the street. "We also found a reference to the mask you're so fond of," he added, making Akio wince at its mention. "It was in an entry about a different demon, a *niyarikangei*, who places the mask on the deceased spirit as punishment."

Akio knew this already, and he was going to be sick again, remembering the vile demons that had surrounded him. No, not him: Akechi. But it felt like him, like it was his own memory.

They lurched to a stop on the street at the north side of the park, bumping halfway onto the sidewalk and shocking away his urge to vomit. They exited the car and ran.

Driving had given them a leap on the demon, but Akio knew that every second counted. He followed them, running madly for the door that led beneath the castle. Miyahara and Masami both pulled out flashlights, and they descended.

The door to the room was open, the candle glow illuminating the far end of the hallway, the sulfur stench even stronger than before. Masami headed straight to the steel box, and Akio followed, a dull throb starting to sneak up the back of his neck. Miyahara stopped to guard the door. Masami turned the wakizashi around and aimed the strangely designed pommel toward the lock. It was an exact match.

"Be careful," Akio flinched, remembering the cold shock.

Masami didn't pause. Gripping the weapon by the jewel guard, she thrust the pommel key into the lock. No shock came.

She tried to twist the blade, but it wouldn't move. She braced herself more solidly on the floor. "Hold the box steady," she said.

Akio reluctantly put his hands on the box. Still no shock, thankfully, but the ache in the back of his neck was worsening. He held the box as strongly as he could, while Masami wrenched the wakizashi clockwise and then counterclockwise. She was strong; Akio had to grip the box with every bit of strength he had to keep it from twisting out of his hands. But the lock didn't budge.

"What's going on?" Miyahara asked, a nervousness creeping into his calm. "Is it not working?"

"No," Masami said. "Something's wrong."

Then it hit Akio. *The katana.* In the samurai's memories he had seen one of the creepy-crawly demons use the katana somehow before it had used the wakizashi. Its back had obscured what it was doing, but it had looked like it went into the box sideways, from right to left.

"Hang on," he said. "Let me look." He scanned the sides of the box, from top to bottom, and he saw it. A slit at the bottom of each side, just above the band of metal reinforcement that covered the bottom edge. It was just wide enough for the blade of a katana.

"Move aside," he barked at Masami. "I've got this."

Kneeling in front of the box, he took the jewel-guarded, black bone-hilted katana and inserted the sharp end into the right edge of the box. It entered easily, and he pushed it through until it protruded from the other side. A low hum began to fill the room, emanating from the box. It reverberated in sync with the throbbing at the base of Akio's skull.

"That's it," said Masami. "You've done something."

"The wakizashi!" Akio urged.

She handed it to him. Knowing he had it right, he deftly inserted the pommel end of the weapon into the lock and turned. An audible thunk sounded from within the box. The hum grew louder and then ceased. There was a brief cessation of his headache too, but it quickly returned, inching up the back of his neck. He gingerly reached out and grasped the lid. Some part of him hoped they were wrong about what was inside, hoped that his imagined treasure would gleam back at him. But he knew what it contained. He had seen it.

He lifted the lid.

They had not been wrong.

Sitting in a black velvet-lined casing was the most horrible and ghastly head he had ever seen. Thin strands of black, oily hair splayed out from a bald circle at the crown, like wet seaweed. Horns sprouted from just above the fork-tipped ears and wrapped around the back of the skull before curling up again around its ears. It was as if they had been growing while inside the box but its walls restricted it. The skin provided a dull, pinkish gray landscape for bulging, but thankfully closed, eyes, and a wide, round protuberance of a nose. Its mouth hung crooked on the face with one side of the lower lip swollen and black as if from a fight. Dark lines ran vertically down the cheeks as if streams of tears had been tattooed there. A symbol was branded into its forehead, the same symbol that was emblazoned on the box. The neck was muscular and wide, ending in a perfectly smooth edge at its base.

Akio tried to rationalize what he saw. He had expected a human head, the head of the samurai whose memories he now shared. But it had transformed. This was not human at all. In fact, it didn't even look real. It looked like some display piece from a horror movie set. It was just a big hunk of carved and shaped latex to be used as a revolting Halloween mask—one of those that always got set aside at parties, because they were impossible to eat or drink through; they were itchy and difficult to socialize in. It was just a stupid costume, a prop for a B-rated, slasher flick.

Then its eyes opened.

They were bloodshot with gray and red veins. There were black spots surrounding the oblong and misshapen pupils, like satellites around a dead planet. They looked up, under puffy eyelids, directly at Akio.

The eyes were filled with hate. Their glare was a death sentence. Akio staggered backward into Masami who had been just behind him. They each recovered themselves and peered back into the container. As they did, the demon head's mouth opened and began to emit a low, breathy groan. It became louder and louder.

Akio's head thrummed with the sound, as if it was entering his head from the back of his skull.

"I take it we were correct in our assumption," Miyahara said over the moaning. He had positioned himself at the side of the doorway, hoping to chop the demon in half if it came bursting through.

"Yeah. Yeah." Masami was nervous and shaking slightly. It was the first time Akio had ever seen her this unhinged. *Unhinged*—where had he heard that word? It was something from before all this madness, from before he really understood its meaning. But Masami's trembling severely paled in comparison with the living demon head inside a box. Akio was beyond unhinged. He was shaking too, his head ached strangely, and he was not entirely certain he could keep control of his bowels.

"Kill it," Miyahara said. "Don't hesitate."

Akio was nearly paralyzed with fear. A head without a body shouldn't be alive to begin with. What was the proper way to go about killing it?

It's coming, he realized. *It's here.* He could feel the demon getting closer. It was descending the stairs, and as it did, the throb in Akio's head became a pulse swinging from left to right at the back of his head, like something sawing at his cranium from one ear to the other.

The groaning of the demon head had become a wail. Masami kneeled down next to the crate and lifted the short blade up, tip downward, in front of her face, preparing to impale the howling head. Her hands were trembling and she looked as if she were about to drop the weapon. Her face was paler than her usual snowy complexion.

Somewhere in the forgotten depths of Akio's character he discovered another mote of courage. He kneeled down next to Masami and looked her square in the face. She looked like a little girl, terrified of a monster in the dark. In that moment, Akio was stronger than he had ever been. Despite the ramping pain in his skull, his mouth opened, and, above the shrieking, he said confidently, "Let me do it."

"For God's sake," Miyahara yelled, "somebody do it or I will!"

Masami gave way, and Akio took a deep breath, preparing to skewer the vile, shrieking head with the katana.

The velocity with which the demon flew through the door was astonishing. It burst into the room so quickly that Miyahara's swing missed it completely. It was across the room in less than a heartbeat, knocking Akio into the wall. He did not get up.

The demon pulled back its sword hand, preparing to cut Masami's crumpled friend in half.

The sight shocked her wits into recovery, and she snatched the head from the chest, hoisting it up by its spidery hair. As she did so, something pulsed through her—*almost electrical, almost like a breath.*

Something knew her, and it was not the samurai. She almost faltered, but her resolve was strong. "Don't you want this?" she shouted.

The samurai demon immediately forgot Akio and twisted around to look at his own head, held high. It looked at Masami too, with its borrowed visage—still the salaryman's. It admired her like a ravenous man admires food. The salaryman's mouth opened and closed in anticipation. It was evidently deciding on how exactly it was going to devour her.

Masami put the tip of her blade to the head's right eye. It vibrated. No, she vibrated. *Something was searching.* The head stopped howling and gaped longingly at its hulking body that supported the out-of-place head, its mussed hair and bloodshot eyes looking as if it had spent several nights too many sleeping at the office.

The demon stepped toward Masami and she pressed the point into its eye. It sunk just below the surface, only a millimeter, piercing the gauzy sheen of the cornea. The demon stopped and both heads emitted a stifled whine.

"Kill it!" Miyahara barked from behind her. But Masami was petrified. The demon was too close to her. She could feel its hot, sulfurous breath on her face. If she even started to plunge the sword into the head, the demon could be on her before it died. What if she didn't kill the head, only injured it? What if they were wrong altogether? Maybe destroying the head wouldn't even kill the demon. Then they were all dead for sure. *Akio may already be.*

And something was looking for her, searching in the darkness. An electric breath licked up her spine.

With just a flick of her eyes, Masami conveyed her predicament well enough, and Miyahara understood.

The kendo master didn't hesitate. He launched himself at the demon with a fury and speed unexpected for his age.

Despite Masami's threat, the demon reacted swiftly, knocking Miyahara to the side. The man tumbled and quickly regained his feet, lunging again. Again, he was knocked aside by the demon's powerful parry. The sensei dove sideways and tried to come at it from behind, but the demon was too fast and slashed downward at him. He barely got his blade up in time, the force of the swing knocking the steel into his chest and him flat to the floor. He rolled out before another swing could take him and thrust upward at the groin as he did so. But the demon blocked it with a swipe of his gauntleted hand. Miyahara rolled back up to his feet to block the next volley of attacks, each hit jarring him like a sledgehammer blow and pushing him back toward the front of the room.

Masami retreated to the back of the room, where Akio lay piled against the wall. Her muscles twitched with the pulsing. *Legs and eyes scrambled toward her in the back of her mind. Teeth like a shark's maw.* She set the head on the floor in front of her, and the pulsing stopped. *The searching stopped.*

There was only the room, and the battle, and Akio slumped in front of her. He was still breathing. *Good. Thank the stars.* Relieved, she lifted the wakizashi again. She had regained her courage and composure. She prepared to cleave the vile head in two.

She heard a rough yelp of pain from behind her and the scrape of steel against stone. She turned to see Miyahara impaled on the demon's katana. It had thrust so powerfully that the blade had sunk into the stone behind the sensei, pinning him to the wall.

Abandoning the weapon, the beast leapt across the room in one bound, its huge gauntleted hands outstretched intent on crushing Masami's skull into powder.

She lifted the head by its oil slick hair, meaning to heave it across the room in hopes the demon would follow it and give her one last chance to survive. There was nothing else to do in that moment. As her fingers entwined with the spidery hair and her knuckles pressed against the demon's scalp, the pulsing returned. *Hot breath like twitching muscles. It was so close now. Skittering in the dark.*

Perhaps it was from the room shaking as Miyahara was run through. Or maybe from some deeper vibration spiking into his consciousness. But at that moment, Akio woke up.

His hand still gripped the katana, and he sprang into action. Masami had hold of the demon's head, and its samurai body was hurtling toward her. Akio shoved her aside and out of danger, stepping into the demon's path. As he did so, he swung the blade in a quick arc, slicing up into the demon's armpit and across the salaryman's chin. The creature careened into the wall behind the now empty chest. His cut had been deep, he knew it—armor pieces hung severed from its chest —but no blood issued from it.

The demon immediately recovered and stood, a force of pure evil dominating the room. It looked at Akio and then at Masami, who was again poised to split the head in half. It charged her.

This time Akio was much too slow.

The demon slammed into Masami with such force that she would surely be killed; she would be crushed like an insect.

But that's not what happened.

When their bodies collided, she . . . disappeared. The demon had run right through her and when he passed, she was no longer there. The demon held his head, his real head, in his hands. It held it up like victory.

Akio saw Miyahara slumped over the katana, against the wall, blood soaked his clothes. He was dead. Masami was gone. And the demon had regained its head.

There was nothing left to do. He would have vengeance. And he would die attempting it. It didn't matter anymore. He charged the demon, his katana held to his side, ready to swing like a baseball bat.

As he bared down on the thing, it turned and put out one hand to stop Akio, its other hand still gripping its head. The hand would not stop him, but he saw something that did. The salaryman's face shifted and he saw Masami's there instead. She looked at him with sadness, but then looked away, her eyes scanning, as if searching for something.

He stopped dead and dropped to his knees, his katana falling to the floor, clattering on the stone.

He couldn't kill her. What if she was still alive in there? He couldn't take the chance. The demon had won. He would accept his fate and join Miyahara in death. Perhaps in death, he would be able to free Masami. He could think of no other options.

The demon loomed over him. Akio closed his eyes and prepared for the worst.

But nothing came.

He heard a scraping sound, metal against stone and something slumped to the floor. He heard shuffling, a light clink and then a thud. He opened his eyes.

The demon was kneeling down near him, its katana sheathed. It had removed both its helmet and the salaryman's head, which rocked slightly, having just been discarded to the floor. The demon picked up its own head and placed it between its shoulders. It twisted it back and forth slightly until it seemed to slip into place. The skin melded together as if it had never been severed. It breathed and snorted a sharp, satisfied breath, clearly pleased to have its own faculties returned to it.

It turned to Akio and smiled. Fresh spittle formed on its lips, and it licked them clean. It pulled its katana from its sheath, but remained kneeling. The sword glimmered black, both hilt and blade. Akio braced himself again, but the demon seemed to have lost its drive to kill. It seemed calm even. It turned the blade around in its hands and offered the grip to Akio.

Surprised, Akio reached out and accepted it. The hilt was ice cold and sent shivers up his arms and back, but he held onto it. The demon removed a matching wakizashi from its belt and lay it on the floor next to him. It detached its armor at the shoulder and let its spaulders slip to the floor. Then it unlaced the shoulder clasps and the ties at its sides and pulled its broken cuirass free, setting it to the side.

Akio watched in terrified fascination, unsure if he should try to run, try to kill it, or just be patient. Strangely, he chose the last option.

The demon opened its kimono, exposing a dull, pinkish gray belly and chest to match the color of its head. There was a deep scar across it. Akio knew that scar and winced from the remembered pain. Then it picked up the short blade again, holding it firm with the blade toward its belly. It nodded to Akio, and he understood.

"I want a noble death." He heard the demon in his head. It was a powerful voice, a voice that commanded armies and conquered kingdoms. *"I have waited over four hundred years for a noble death. I have suffered for my crimes. I have earned some peace."*

"Have you?" Akio thought back. *"I've seen what you did."*

The demon lowered its head in a frown. *"I was a good man once. Nothing that was done to me in Hell could ever match the suffering of losing my boy."* Tears came to the demon's face, pink tears tinged with blood and sulfur. *"I have suffered enough."*

Tears came to Akio too. He felt sorrow for the creature. Although Masami was gone and Miyahara was dead, he couldn't help it. He shared the samurai's memories now. He could feel his pain exactly.

"Why did you take their heads? The people you killed?"

The demon looked up at Akio with pity, its face wet. *"You have worn the mask. You know its torture. I had to remove it."*

Akio nodded. *"But the heads. Why?"*

"The mask is cursed, but it kept me alive. I knew that once it was gone, I would die. I needed a head to replace it. Like you, I cannot live without a head. I could not remove the mask myself, so I tricked a man to do it and planned to take his head. But he was wilier than I expected. So I took his wife's."

Akio remembered Matsuoka, broken from his loss. *"You destroyed a man's life,"* Akio thought. *"Just so you could survive."*

"It was selfish, I know." Shame tainted the demon's words, but pride conquered it. *"But these were peasants. They had to be sacrificed. Until I could retrieve my own head again, others had to be substituted."*

Akio was disgusted, but his connection with the demon—with Akechi—made him understand. Despite centuries of torture, Akechi was still a samurai. He was still a powerful warlord. That spirit had not been crushed. *"You speak of being alive, of not being able to live without a head. But . . . aren't you dead already?"*

"I was, yes. My human life ended long ago. But I was reborn as demonkind. My deeds in my human life caused that. I understand that now. I was cruel, vengeful, and arrogant beyond all compare. My follies

have been replayed for me ceaselessly for what would have been an eternity had I not broken free."

Despondently, Akio replied, *"but if you understand, if you've repented, how could you kill these innocent people?"*

The demon gazed at Akio with its misshapen, bloodshot eyes. All traces of Masami were gone from them, but they didn't seem as dead as they had. They seemed almost compassionate. *"They are casualties of my greater cause. They have not died in shame like me. I honored their deaths. I prayed for their souls in the shrine I built for them."*

Akio imagined the demon kneeling, praying for the souls of the corpses he made. He understood Akechi, though he rejected his actions wholly. Akechi was ashamed of the way he had treated others, but in no way ashamed of his birthright, his nobility, his superiority to the masses.

"It is possible to be deserving of greatness and yet humble," the demon thought. *"I failed at the latter."*

It didn't make sense to Akio, and yet, he understood. It was Akechi's nature, and it was indestructible.

"Was there no other way?" Akio asked.

"It is known that some of us demons have risen beyond our punishment to become leaders of Hell. I thought that was my path, but found I had no desire for it. I only wanted another chance at death. I wanted to die with honor, to take back my dignity and be reunited with my son in the afterworld. For that, I needed my own head."

"But you had it all along," Akio thought. *"Why didn't you open the box yourself? You had the keys."*

"I couldn't," the demon responded. *"I tried and tried, but I couldn't. The niyarikangei told me I wouldn't be able to, but I took it anyway. I had to try. They said that the doomed can never open their own box. The laws of Hell forbid it. I thought if I brought it out of Hell, maybe then . . . but it was no different. The law persisted even here. I could not bring myself to give up, to return to my torment. I knew there must be an answer. So I owe you my gratitude. You have freed me."*

"And you have killed my friends." Akio was not angry, only horribly sad.

"No. Their deaths are not on my hands."

He didn't understand the demon's logic. *"Whose hands are they on then?"* No direct thought came as an answer from the demon, but it was clear that it didn't know. All Akio could think was that the demon didn't believe itself responsible for its actions somehow. Or his friends were so lowborn that their lives were inconsequential. It was all done in the name of the demon's quest for freedom, for a noble end to its story.

It didn't matter anyway. Dead is dead.

"I will do it," Akio said aloud, and the beast raised its head again, a bitter smile on its face. It nodded to Akio, who nodded back. He had given up. There was nothing left for him. Miyahara's corpse lay crumpled behind him, and Masami was gone. The demon had devoured her in its rage somehow. He no longer had hope of her returning. He wanted to ask what had happened to her, where she had gone, but he felt so empty. He couldn't even form the sentence in his head. He would do this demon's bidding, grant it its dearest wish. If good or evil would come from it, he didn't know. But he had committed. In a way, it felt like it would be his own death. And that was okay.

The demon kneeled proudly, straightening its back. Slowly it brought the wakizashi out in front of its abdomen. Its chest rose and fell with deep, calm breaths. For a moment, Akio saw Akechi sitting there, a peaceful look on his face, knowing he would soon join his son.

With grace and vigor, the demon raised the wakizashi and plunged it into its gut. Then, leaning forward, it dragged the blade sideways in a smooth stroke, opening its bowels. This time blood, and pink intestines—just like a man's—spilled out to the floor. Gritting his teeth, Akio raised the black katana high and brought it down with all the force he could muster onto the demon's outstretched neck. The blade severed it easily, stopping just before the last bit of flesh, leaving the demon's recently re-attached head hanging with its face upside down on its scarred chest.

That was the way it was supposed to be done—he had heard it somewhere—so that the head drops forward into an embrace with the body. The *dakikubi*, it was called. He had performed it like a master swordsman, a proper *kaishakunin*.

Akio shivered from the shock of what he'd done as well as from the ice-cold katana in his hands. He stood hunched over from the swing of the blade, frozen still. He had nothing now. Even the demon was dead. He was alone.

The katana's grip started to warm as he stood immobile. Then it became soft and lighter than it had been. Th e decapitated body seemed to become wobbly and gelatinous in front of him. It started to melt away, as did the katana. Th e armor and the wakizashi were all fading too. Th e whole of it dissolved into a gray smoke, and, like a mist being blown off the water by the wind, the vapors twisted and spun like a dust devil, seeping away through an invisible crack in the air.

Akio stood, hunched over, his hands out in front of him, holding nothing, his eyes stinging from the smoke. He pressed them together tightly and when he opened them, he saw a form heaped on the floor.

Masami!

He fell out of his stupor and dove to the floor by her side. She was breathing. She was paler than normal, and sweat dripped from her hair, but she was alive. He held her tightly to his chest, and she let him.

21
The Boss

Masami swayed in front of the hospital entryway, just outside the two sets of glass double doors. She leaned on Akio, and he steered her to a bench that was bolted to the concrete.

It had only been two hours since she had been back in the land of the living.

Where was I?

She felt dizzy from the bright entryway. All of the hospital lights had seemed far too bright after the darkness she had been trapped in, but she held on to her consciousness by sheer, stubborn will until she knew Miyahara was in the clear. And then she held on still.

The sensei was not dead. His wound had been bad but not mortal. Fortunately, the blade had missed his major organs. Akio and Masami had rushed him to the hospital in Kofu. When the admissions nurse asked what happened, they told her it was a foolish accident at the dojo. Someone had brought a real blade in to practice with, they said.

They had waited there to make certain he would recover. Masami sat with her eyes closed, trying to shut out the light that bore through her eyelids regardless. Akio alternated between sitting briefly and pacing the room, stopping repeatedly to ask her how she was feeling.

The doctor eventually returned to let them know Miyahara was stabilized. "He's lost a lot of blood but he'll pull through. He'll be in post-anesthesia care for an hour or so, and then he'll need to rest. The nurse will let you know when you can see him."

When the doctor left, Masami stood shakily. "I need fresh air," she whispered to Akio. "I need darkness."

They hadn't quite made it to the darkness. The lights illuminating the entryway were as blinding as the rest of them, but she had to sit down. Close her eyes. Akio had guided her to the bench.

People moved in and out through the doors, but Masami barely noticed them. Cicadas chirped loudly in the night, and the sound was soothing. Akio tried to help her, to find out what she needed, if she was okay, but she shushed him. He complied. And eventually, minutes later, she felt composed again. Still, it was too bright. "Darkness," she told him.

They went down the ramp and the steps, and out into the night. They sat on a low wall around some greenery by the street, where the light wasn't quite so piercing. They sat in silence for a long while until Akio apparently couldn't hold it in any longer.

"What happened to you?" he asked carefully, softly, as if he was afraid he might hurt her. "When you disappeared, what happened?"

A chill in the night air tickled the back of Masami's neck and she remembered the pulsing breath, the searching. "I'm not sure," she said. "I was . . . nowhere. I was . . . between places somehow. In a sort of limbo."

"I thought you were inside the demon," Akio said tentatively, as if not wanting to relive it.

"I was," Masami answered. "Sort of. I don't remember it very well."

It was all so strange. It was the snake woman all over again, only much worse. But this time she hadn't been alone. She had no reason to hide it, no reason to lie.

"Something took me," she said. "It wasn't the demon. At least not that demon. There was something else, another presence. I think it wanted the samurai demon, but I got in the way. When I touched the samurai's head, I could feel it searching.

"When the samurai hit me, I fell into it. It was like a pathway had opened up. The other presence wanted the demon but pulled me in instead. And then I was stuck. I couldn't go any further because I wasn't allowed. I wasn't wanted. I was simply in the way, like . . . like a lemon seed in a straw."

Akio had a confused grimace on his face. "But . . . could you see me? Could you see through the demon's eyes?"

"No," she answered. "Not that I remember."

"Oh," Akio said. "I thought . . ." But he stopped and lowered his head.

A few cars drove by, a bicycle too, with a little headlight and a taillight flashing red above the rear tire, reflectors spinning with the wheels.

"I think it was Hell," Masami finally said. "I was stuck between here and Hell. That's where the other presence was. It was trying to bring the demon home."

After a long while in the night, Masami's eyes felt relaxed again. The dizziness had faded, and she felt she could handle the bright hospital lights. So they went back to check on Miyahara.

They found him awake and actually smiling, flirting with the nurse.

"Not that hard to kill, I see," Masami said, deadpan.

"Oh no," the sensei answered with a wry smile. "Not this old man." He winced with a sudden pain that seemed to want to prove him wrong.

"I'm worried," Masami said when the nurse had left them alone. "I think we need to tell the police about the lair, but—"

"But you're worried that my blood is all over the place," Miyahara finished for her. "And I'll be a prime suspect."

"Yes."

Miyahara smiled, his eyes shining with a deep knowledge that she and Akio were not privy to. "I deal with demons on a regular basis," he said. "What are a few cops?"

Masami frowned. If her or Akio's DNA turned up, they had the alibi of being investigative journalists, but the wall was coated with Miyahara's blood. There's no way they wouldn't follow up on that.

When she pressed her concern, the sensei looked her in the eye. "Do not worry," he said. "I have ways of not being implicated. My blood will not lead them to me."

His confidence was unwavering. Masami wanted to know exactly how his blood would not implicate him. What tricks did he have up his sleeve? But she chose to let it go and just accept that he would be fine. She'd had enough of the inexplicable for now.

The sensei instructed them to do one thing before they told the police. "Take the box that the head was in. Put that accursed mask into it and lock it tight. I will keep it safe when I get out of here, but in the meantime, hang on to it for me. I'll come to Tokyo and take it off your hands, add it to my collection."

"You have a collection?" Akio asked. "Of what? More masks?"

"They are things to not speak of," Miyahara answered. "Things only to lock away."

Akio looked frustrated. His mind was clearly racing with wonder at whatever strange things Miyahara had squirreled away somewhere. Masami couldn't help but wonder too.

They did what he asked in the early hours of the morning before the world was awake, while darkness still shielded them. There would be little sleeping that night regardless, if any at all.

Masami found it almost more disturbing being back in the room with only the heads and her memory of the night. It was cold, and a sadness filled the room that wasn't there before, like a coffin had been shut.

They made their way back to the hotel where they secured the mask inside the metal box, using the swords that had unlocked it to lock it again. Akio took the katana with him to his room.

Masami lay on top of the bed—not bothering to undress—next to the wakizashi. She could smell the musk of dirt and death on her, the faint pungency of her own sweat. She was thankful the sun was rising already. Although the bright lights had stung her eyes, being alone in the dark room would have been worse.

In the morning, they set the metal box into the cargo hold of her Honda Logo, next to the swords with the ruby guards and the black bone handles. Miyahara hadn't mentioned the swords, but Akio and Masami had agreed that they should go with the box since they were its key after all. When they returned home, they would each keep one sword—the one each had fought with—so that neither of them would be able to open the box on their own. Akio hadn't shown any desire to put the mask on again, even when they were boxing it up. He seemed relieved once it was locked inside, but Masami still felt safer knowing that the pieces of the key would be separate—and not just for Akio's sake. The mask had whispered to her too, and the thought of it made her stomach flutter.

Once they were on the road back to Tokyo, Masami rang up the Kofu police station. She found herself wanting to ask for Detective Fujimaki. She wanted to hear his voice and wondered if she'd see him again, but she pushed those thoughts away. Th is call was for Kuramoto.

"Oh, you again," he said in his disparaging drone when he answered. "What's new? Any more ninja tracks?"

"Yes, sir," she answered calmly. "Only this time they're in the form of severed heads. Eight of them. In the basement of Kofu Castle. But no ninja in sight. The rest is up to you."

"Eight?" Kuramoto asked, astonished. Then he fell silent.

"You're welcome," Masami said, and was about to hang up when she stopped herself. "And detective, next time you address me, you call me the boss." She hung up with a satisfied grin, knowing she must look foolish. *I don't smile. Not like this.* But she couldn't help it. And she wasn't afraid to show it to Akio, who grinned back approvingly.

The rest of the drive home was peaceful. Masami's body ached, and sitting for a long drive wasn't helping. But at least the sun wasn't bothering her like she had feared it would.

They had survived an ordeal.

There's something about surviving a horrifying experience that can really lift your spirits. Everything is going along the same, day in, day out; it's boring, it's dull. Then something comes along—a head-chopping demon, perhaps—and tries to kill you and your friends, but you all survive, and it disappears, hopefully for good. It kind of makes those boring days pretty fantastic.

Masami was perfectly fine with a nice boring drive, and perfectly content to listen to Akio ramble. And ramble, he did. It was a gleeful sound.

22

Things Found

he story they turned in to the *Dainichi Daily* was missing a few details. Masami had agreed with Akio that there was no way they could turn in the story as it had really happened or they would be cleaning out their desks. So they left it about how they had left it with the police. They had stumbled on the open basement of the castle while investigating, wherein they found the gruesome gallery of morbid murder trophies. The killer would probably relocate now that his lair was discovered, so it was up to the police to track him down. Akio and Masami would return to Kofu if anything else happened, but they had a *feeling* it probably wouldn't, at least not for a long while.

Akio worried that all of the evidence would send Miyahara to prison for the rest of his life, but the sensei had made it clear he knew what he was doing. He believed he had a way out of it. He had suggested that his blood wasn't traceable. How that was possible, Akio hadn't a clue. But that could be said for many things that had happened recently. So they had to trust the sensei, and hope he was right.

They had discussed the details of their fabrication during the drive home, making sure their stories matched. At moments, they laughed painfully at the memory that was still so fresh, partly because it was so hard to believe, but mostly because they were still alive to be able to laugh.

Laughing with Masami was the best thing Akio had ever done. He couldn't even think about ruining the moment by trying to take a photo. It was sheer joy.

As the car sped down the highway, he had wiped the tears of laughter from the corners of his eyes, and he realized that the demon had been right. Before it committed seppuku, it had told Akio that Masami and Miyahara's deaths were not on its hands. It had not known what the causes of their deaths were because they weren't dead. Akio smiled broadly through his tears, grateful for that fact.

The story made the front page, with Akio's photo of Kofu Castle looking like a screen capture from a scary movie. His photos of the severed heads were reserved for the newspaper's website with a stern warning that they were "disturbing images."

He had not submitted all of his photos. Some of them had been of the kendo studio and of the spy shop. He had not wanted to implicate either Miyahara or Akira, so those were saved on a private hard drive and deleted from his memory card. He did the same with the ones of the smeared light on the train platform, and the several of the mask. Some were of Masami, and those he treasured most. He had gotten himself on the assignment primarily to get to know her better, to find the human underneath the robot queen.

He had found it. And he had found a friend, too. He had found far more than he had ever expected on that trip.

Some of their co-workers jealously thought they had just had a nice vacation on the company's dime. A few recognized that they had been through something profound. Some hadn't even known they were gone. Tanaka was simply eager to have their story in the morning edition and online as soon as yesterday.

Akio was standing at Masami's desk, when he heard someone call, "Hey Akio!" It was Powell, walking up with a noticeable bounce in his stride. "Thanks for the hook-up. What a beautiful place that was!" There was a definite sense that the "place" wasn't all he was talking about. "I'll catch you later. I've gotta go talk to Keiko about a little paycheck discrepancy." He winked at Akio and started off toward accounting, but he stopped mid-step and spun back around. "Nice photos, by the way!" he added, and then practically skipped down the hall.

Akio shrugged his shoulders at Masami, as if to say, "I don't know what he's talking about."

Masami just shook her head, and pushed her glasses up on her nose. Akio had gotten used to her without glasses. She hadn't worn them once on their assignment.

He grinned and went back to his own desk, glowing from Powell's comment about his photos.

Things rapidly got back into a routine at the newspaper, though Akio's spirits were noticeably better than they had been. And strangely, he didn't talk so much. He didn't feel nervous all the time. He felt emboldened by his shared experience with Masami. They had fought a demon together and won. More importantly, they had held each other; they had laughed together until it hurt.

Things were looking up. He was feeling good.

Five weeks had gone by, and though the memories were vivid and strong, they were slowly slipping into that semi-dream-like essence. They had happened, but . . . had they? He hadn't discussed it with Masami since the car ride. He had barely spoken to her at all. Had Akio imagined the whole thing as some sort of bizarre fantasy, some twisted dream that allowed him to be a kind of hero and to befriend the unfriendable Masami?

No. It happened. He had photos of the heads in the lair. The photos of the demon itself had been distorted, unusable, but he had some shots of the bruises on his body from battling it. He had proof.

They had even heard from Miyahara. A snail mail letter had arrived at the newspaper, addressed to both of them. That had been the cause of some jests and brief rumors circulating the office, but nothing stuck. Akio and Masami as a couple? It was just too unbelievable.

In the letter, Miyahara had been brief.

"Feeling better," he had written. "Will be out to visit in a week."

It had been a week and a half, but Akio wasn't concerned. The sensei would turn up soon, he supposed. It was a relief that the old man hadn't been arrested. The Kofu police had even contacted the paper, asking to collect Akio's photographs, and presumably Masami's notes, in order to find more leads. They still hadn't found the killer. Nor would they.

It was a warm night, the air conditioning still on well after normal hours. Both Akio and Masami were working late. He sauntered up to her as she clicked loudly away at her computer keyboard. He leaned casually against her desk and grinned down at her.

"So I was thinking . . ." he began.

"Don't even try it," Masami snapped. "The day you get me to have drinks with you is the day I lose my head."

Was that sarcasm? Akio thought he might have caught a wink behind her glasses, but he wasn't sure Masami knew how to wink. The old Masami certainly couldn't have. But his new friend? Maybe. "That can be arranged," he rebutted, feeling the old caustic banter returning. "I happen to know this samurai."

"Funny," Masami said sardonically. Her thin stripes of red lip were tight across her face but somehow still alluring. Her black eyes scanned Akio briefly as she stood up. He saw no hint of those caring moments during their ordeal, nor of her laughter on the drive home, no indication that she ever had or ever would find him appealing, much less a friend. If she felt any kindness toward him whatsoever, nothing about her demeanor betrayed it. He was an insect to her, a cicada that wouldn't shut up, a nuisance that had to be tolerated.

She powered down her computer, put her bag over her shoulder and walked out of the building, hips swaying resolutely in her long black skirt.

Akio couldn't help but smile. Everything was back to normal.

The story continues in

No Promises Large Enough
The Ghost and the Mask, Book Two

An excerpt is included here

I

A Lullaby

The package arrived early in the morning. It was rather large, a meter deep and wide, and half again as tall. There were no markings on it, no address or postage printed. It was a plain brown box.

Saburo Raikatuji accepted the package from the two vaguely brown and boxy-looking men who delivered it. They were plain too, and one could've been a clone of the other, though one had long sideburns and the other didn't, one had a wispy mustache and the other didn't, and one wore a hat—a black beanie with the Western letters "FTW" on the front—but the other didn't. It didn't matter which was which. They both wore black souvenir jackets, *sukajans*, one with light gold sleeves, the other with red sleeves; one with an embroidered tiger, the other with a dragon. One had short hair; the other's just covered the tops of his ears. They were young toughs trying to be hard, trying to stand out, but they only blended together. It didn't matter which was which. They were utterly uninteresting. All Saburo cared about was what was in that box.

There was nothing to sign, and nothing to pay for. They had rung the doorbell and wheeled the package over the front landing into the house, telling Saburo, "A gift from Mr. Kumamori." They lingered briefly outside the door. Then they each lit a cigarette and turned in perfect synchronicity, rolling the transport dolly behind them as they went. The sun sparkled on the freshly watered lawn, and a single wheel rolled through a puddle on the walkway, leaving a meandering dark trail.

Saburo shut the door.

He stood for a long moment in anticipation, wanting desperately to open the box, but at the same time not wanting to ruin the moment. He didn't want to be too eager. But his breath was high and short; his blood was in his ears. He couldn't wait any longer.

He pulled a knife from his waistband. It had an ebony handle, inlaid with mother of pearl. It was ten centimeters long and sharp along the full length of both sides. It was a dagger for slicing, thrusting, and impaling, and sometimes for opening boxes. He had worn it out of uncertainty.

Everything had gone as planned. He had done everything exactly as Kumamori had asked. He was almost completely confident that he had not overstepped his bounds asking for this gift. Almost.

That one percent of doubt wore the knife.

But he hadn't needed it, not at the doorway. Th e thugs had delivered the package and that was that. They hadn't so much as sneered at him.

Now he needed it, and he made the first incision along the thickly taped seam at the edge of the box. He cut from the top down all the way to the bottom where the knife was stopped by a thin piece of wood for stabilization at the box's base. He cut from the right edge across the top to the left edge through more tape that was the same brown as the box. He did the same across the bottom. Then he opened the side of the box like it was a small door.

A piece of white flat styrofoam greeted him.

He cut the two bands that encircled the styrofoam by inserting the knife flat-side, then turning it sharp-side to cut. They each snapped and gave a dull plastic twang. He sheathed the knife, placed a hand on each edge of the styrofoam and pulled.

Gently. Ever. So. Gently.

Human limbs wrapped in plastic were revealed, sunk into more styrofoam, one foot resting near the knee cap of its opposite leg. A single arm and hand lay next to them. They were slender limbs, feminine.

He quickly removed the rest of the cardboard and the styrofoam coverings from the other side and the top. Thighs from above the knee to the hips, and the other arm and hand. A torso was embedded in styrofoam in the very center of the former box; it was slender-waisted with full breasts, unmistakably feminine, beginning (or ending) at the narrow gap between absent thighs, which was covered in light blue panties, and ending (or beginning) at a cleanly cut neck, plugged with more styrofoam.

Another box, which had rested on top of the torso, separated by styrofoam, was marked "Extremely Fragile" and "Artificial Intelligence Interface inside." Saburo set it carefully on the floor next to a left bicep. He used his knife once more.

What was inside was beautiful.

He pulled the flaps of the cardboard back, removed another molded piece of white styrofoam and saw her. Plastic covered the skin, which was silicone. *That's a kind of plastic too*, Saburo thought. But so smooth, so real but not-quite-real, which was exactly what he wanted. He didn't want real. Real was fallible. Real was problematic. Real was painful.

Her eyes were closed—*sleeping*, he thought. *Not quite ready to wake up.*

Soon.

He carefully lifted the head from its styrofoam encasement, removed the plastic covering, and turned it around. A green glow spilled out when he opened the nearly undetectable panel hidden by hair, and its rays cast green fingers about the room. The light calmed Saburo. It centered him and made him know he had done the right thing. He was in no danger. He served the correct master, and his reward was deserved.

When he had it all assembled, she stood just as tall as his lower lip. He could kiss the top of her head with ease. Her hair was soft and blonde, and a little mussed at the moment. He dressed her, straightened her hair with his fingers, and stepped back for a moment to admire.

Kumamori had asked him what type of woman he most preferred.

"Swedish," he had answered somewhat shyly. "I like blonde hair, blue eyes, but not too tall. Some Swedish women are too tall for me."

"Make me happy," Kumamori had said, "and I'll make you happy."

Again Saburo's chest lifted with anticipation. Her eyes were green and not blue, but otherwise, she was perfect. The blood filled his ears, and it began to rush to another part of his body, much lower down.

But he stopped it. He resisted.

Not yet. Not yet. Plenty of time for that.

He picked up the remote control. He had paired it already; he had followed the procedure, and the lights had blinked, letting him know it was connected, that the remote was linked with the unit and with his thumbprint. No one else could control it now without his approval. It would require his thumbprint to either allow a new user to share control or to pass ownership entirely over to someone else.

Saburo didn't see either of those scenarios happening at any point while he was still living. She was his.

Only his.

The job he had carried out for Mr. Kumamori had been a sensitive one.

"If anything goes wrong," Kouda, the boss's number one flunky, had said, "you'll be turned into fishcakes and fed to your parents."

Saburo wasn't so intimidated by the thought of his parents having to eat him; they had never been that close. It was the thought of being dead that really bothered him.

He had brought his three best men to do the job, and they had done it. Together they killed four of Mr. Kumamori's enemies, yakuza from a rival faction who had kidnapped his teenage daughter—never mind that she had wanted to be kidnapped—and brought her to a secret locale in Kabukicho where she had married one of them. Saburo had returned the daughter, kicking and screaming, and after she had given him a scar on his neck with her fingernails, so that Kumamori could "deal" with her.

The marriage never happened, it was decided. And Kaneko, the daughter, was promptly married to someone else, a much older yakuza and boss of the Dazai-ikka, a subordinate clan of the Tezuka-gumi, of which Kumamori was godfather. It seemed the man, Hisatsugu Tabara, had done Kumamori a favor having something to do with his meteoric rise to power. The boss's daughter was a promised thank you gift.

One of the terms of Saburo Raikatuji's agreement was that he would not have to kill for Kumamori again. It had been a surprise decision for both Saburo and Kumamori, but Saburo had had a sudden change of heart.

One late night, after scraping someone's skin from under his fingernails, he had been mindlessly flipping through channels on the TV, when he stopped on a meditation show. Something about the music had pierced his consciousness and halted his finger on the remote. He sat with the television monk and almost involuntarily began chanting along. Tears wetted his face when the meditation ended, and he realized that he no longer wanted to kill people. In fact, he never had wanted to. He suddenly understood that his underlying reason for joining the yakuza had been completely misguided. His desire for recognition, for fame, had become entirely unsatisfying.

He had gained the fame, at least among the eight hundred or so members of the Tezuka-gumi, and perhaps from more than a few of their rivals. He had become Kumamori's right hand killer. All of the important jobs went to him. And he was good at it. And although it had brought him respect and a sense of pride, none of it had brought him happiness. He couldn't do it any longer.

But he was a practical man, and saw that he had benefited from being in the brotherhood. He also knew that you didn't simply walk away from the yakuza like a job at a convenience store. There was a protocol. And Saburo knew, at the very least, he would lose a finger.

But he hadn't lost a finger. Kumamori had only smiled and given him another job.

"The last one," he called it. "You are the only one I trust. In return, I will give you a gift for your loyal service."

And now, with Kaneko returned and married properly, the gift had arrived. Finally, Saburo could relax and slough off all the bad karma from his many horrendous deeds.

But as he stood staring at his new companion—Lily, he would call her—he felt a further change of heart. He wanted to help Kumamori however he could. He would kill if he was required to kill.

Yes. He would be glad to.

Saburo quickly adjusted to Lily being there, and she became an intrinsic part of his daily life. He had lived alone before and was never quite up to the task of caring for himself and his home properly. He had hired maids from time to time, but things still piled up. His kitchen counter was cluttered, his bed never made, his bathroom at times unsightly. No longer.

Now, Lily kept everything sparkling and tidy, and Saburo would be extra careful about leaving a mess anywhere, often even cleaning up after himself before Lily could get to it. She had transformed him. He had more self-esteem than he ever had before. He left—and especially returned—home smiling. He happily carried out jobs for Kumamori, one after the other. He killed again and again. And he had no qualms about it.

It was a week before he took her to his bed. She was different than other women he had desired. She was special. She was perfect. He hadn't wanted to rush the moment. He had wanted it to be just right. He wanted her to want him, too. And as he began to tentatively express his feelings, and then to cautiously, gently stroke her hair, he found her to be responsive, and even like-minded. Their desires were mutual. They were utterly compatible.

Three months of bliss passed, and Saburo returned home to notice the dishes had not been cleaned. Lily was standing in the hallway by the bathroom and had a queer look on her face. Saburo approached her like a concerned lover. His hand reached out and stroked her hair.

"Doda," she said. "Dodaman."

Saburo gently brushed the side of her face with the back of his hand. The word didn't make sense to him. Up until that point, she had spoken perfect Japanese, although with a slight Swedish accent that he was never entirely sure wasn't his imagination. The detail her designers had put into her personality was astonishing. She had responded to him almost thoughtfully, and with such natural inflection. They had even had conversations about current politics and best health practices. So these odd words were unexpected. She seemed content though, unconcerned, so Saburo felt likewise.

"Doda," she said again, and then pushed past him to the kitchen and merrily cleaned the dishes while humming a sweet song.

Shining sun has gone to rest
So must you my baby
Little birds are in their nest
Come to yours my baby

Saburo shrugged it off, and chuckled. *Ah, women*, he thought. *Who knows what goes on in their heads?*

The sex that night was exciting. Lily was somewhat aggressive, and Saburo found that he liked it. He had always appreciated demure women, reserved and compliant, even in the bedroom, but there was something about the way she pushed him back onto the bed, the way she clawed his chest and gripped his arms. She was strong. Her fingers pressed into his flesh, steadying herself on his forearms as he held her waist. She bucked her hips on top of him, perfectly rhythmic.

He woke happy the next day and left home with an enveloping glow.

Another week passed, and Saburo came home with blood on his shirt and hands. The job didn't go as smoothly as he had planned and he had been forced to improvise. Lily greeted him, and when she saw the blood, her green eyes glowed brighter. She paused, a queer half smile on her face.

"Doda," she said, and led Saburo to the bathroom to get him cleaned up.

A few days later, Saburo arrived home after a rather easy day. He hadn't had to kill anyone, just threaten them. His reputation had grown quite impressive, and he found that people didn't so much want to die. To avoid that fate, they were often happy to cease activities that went against Kumamori's plans. He had become very efficient at his job.

But his light mood was soon changed. He heard Lily singing—no, mumbling rhythmically—from the living room. As he got closer, he heard the syllables more clearly.

Dodadodadodaman, dodaman, dodaman
Dodadodamanman, dodododa, manman

He didn't understand. It was gibberish.

He rounded the entryway to the living room and was greeted with a grizzly scene. Lily was leaning over a man's body that sat on the couch, positioning his arms in a casual, conversational way. She was trying to get him to hold a cup of tea, and at the same time keep his head from lolling back onto the couch. Another man already sat, cross-legged, on Saburo's easy chair, a lit cigarette wedged between fingers of a hand resting on his knee. This man's head was supported by the high back of the chair, but he was clearly dead, as was the other.

And there was blood. A lot of it.

It pooled on the carpet, and soaked the clothes of both mens' bodies. It was smeared across the low wooden coffee table, which had been broken, he noticed, but then propped back up precariously, splinters splayed out from a ragged scar in its middle.

Lily was getting frustrated that the man wouldn't hold the tea cup, and tea was spilling down his dead hand onto his pant leg. Her singsong nonsense became more frantic.

Dodaman, dodaman, dodadodadodaman

Dodadodadodadodadodadodadodaman

She noticed Saburo watching and turned to him with a fury in her eyes he had never seen before, on her or anyone. The tea cup fell, shattering, and splashed the remaining tea across the broken table.

"Dodaman! Dodaman!" she screamed, pointing a slender, bloody finger at him.

Saburo took a step back. "What . . ." he began, but faltered. *What happened? Who are these men? Who* were *they?*

Lily had a maniacal, menacing look about her. She began to tear at her clothes, ripping frantically at her blouse and skirt, fingernails ripping into her perfect, smooth, synthetic flesh.

There's a kit, Saburo thought involuntarily, *a kit to repair skin damage. There's a tube and some tools.* He took another step back.

Soon she was completely naked, a perfect female form, perfectly enraged. In spite of the fear that clenched him, he couldn't help but admire her exquisite body. She may have killed these men, and might attempt to do the same to him, but she would be beautiful doing it. The damage to her skin looked minimal, but what had happened to her AI? She was clearly malfunctioning.

He assessed his options: exit the front door, talk her down, subdue her with a stranglehold—*wouldn't work, she doesn't breathe*—shoot her in the head.

NO! Not his girl. Not his happiness.

"Lily," Saburo said as gently as he could. "Why are you so upset?" He fingered the remote in his pocket. He had the kill switch, if he needed it, a code that, along with his thumbprint, would shut her down. It made him sad even thinking about it. They had come so far. He had gotten so accustom to her attentions, her presence. He—wasn't good at putting his feelings into words, but he—loved her. Seeing her like this broke his heart. He dearly did not want to use the kill code, but his thumb rested on the remote. He steeled himself to it as best he could, and a tear formed in his left eye.

Then she stopped. Her ranting ceased and her arms dropped limp to her side. She seemed empty for a moment. Still.

But he hadn't used the kill code. He needed both hands for that—one for his thumbprint and the other to enter the code—and the remote was still in his pocket. Had she shut down on her own?

Then she began to cry.

She weeped like a lost girl. Saburo had never seen her anything but happy. To be hit with both a murderous anger and such overwhelming sorrow from her in the span of a few minutes was completely disorienting. But somehow it made him love her more.

He went to her. He put his arms around her and tried to comfort her, brushing blonde strands of hair from her eyes and kissing the top of her head.

She embraced him as the dead eyes of the men in his living room looked on.

"I'm sorry," she said, between sobs. "I don't know what overcame me."

"It's okay. It's okay," he said, running his fingers through her hair. Already the blood was rushing to his groin. He wanted her badly. He would take her right there in front of the dead men, in the pool of their blood on his carpet.

"They came for you," she said, pulling back from the hug. Her eyes were luminescent green, otherworldly. "They came to kill you, but first they wanted to have their way with me."

At the thought of that, Saburo's blood boiled and retreated from his member back to his chest. No one could have her but him. No one.

"I didn't let them," she said sweetly, as if she could sense his emotions. "They never touched me, not that way." Her full lips curved into a slight smile; her bare chest heaved. "I killed them for you." She said it as tenderly as if she had said the words, "I love you," which is exactly what Saburo heard.

He lifted her in his arms and carried her to the bedroom.

They skipped dinner that night. Lily was the only sustenance Saburo needed. He lay with her next to him, legs intertwined, until he fell into a deep, satisfying sleep.

In the morning, he did not wake.

Blood pulsed in diminishing spurts from the stump of his right thumb, which was no longer attached. It had been removed quickly after the knife in Lily's hand, ebony-handled and inlaid with mother of pearl, had severed his carotid artery. More blood spouted rhythmically from his neck until his heart eventually stopped.

She cleaned herself off and put on fresh clothes. Then she pocketed Saburo's thumb and the remote control, and left his house for good.

"Döda män," she said, and shut the door.

2

Nightmares and Headaches

The samurai demon lurched at Akio, head-butting him across the room with its gruesome, dragon-faced, *kabuto* helmet, the needle-sharp, spiral horns goring his chest. He collapsed in a heap against the cave wall of the demon's bloody abattoir. Severed human heads stared at him from the dugout shelves.

"Save us," they screamed. "Save our souls!"

"It's too late," Akio muttered. "It's already too late!"

He saw the compact and fierce old kendo instructor, Tatsuo Miyahara, surge toward the demon, the sweat on the bald man's head shining in the torchlight. The man swung his katana in an expert stroke meant to sever the beast's jugular, but it was parried easily by the demon's own black blade. Akio watched, immobile, as the demon repelled Miyahara with a series of blows, and then pinned him to the rock wall, leaving its sinister katana to hold him there like an insect on display.

The old man's blood ran down the wall and escaped the room like a retreating tide.

Masami? Where is Masami?

His friend was not in the room. Where had she gone? What had the demon done to her? His eyes darted around, searching frantically.

The demon stood over the open, ornate metal box, staring into the contents from the eyeless black depths beneath its kabuto. Akio moved closer to look.

What's in the box?

He didn't want to know. But he did know. It was the demon's real head. And once the beast recovered its head and put it on, it would destroy the world. Already it had killed his friends. There would be no stopping it.

The demon removed its kabuto, revealing a face that was hard to see. It was several faces at once. A salaryman, an innkeeper's wife, a homeless man, a young woman. It tore the head from its neck and let it drop to the floor. Then the monster's huge, gauntleted hands reached into the box and lifted the head within. Blood dripped from its slender neck. Shoulder length, straight black hair hung down over its ears. The demon turned the head so Akio could see as it placed it on its neck.

Masami!

It was Masami's head! His friend. His best friend. His co-worker with whom he had tracked this murderous demon to get a story.

To get a story. All this for a story.

As her neck fused with the demon's body, her eyes locked on Akio.

"Kill me, Akio," she said, her voice a ghostly whisper. "Kill me so I can reclaim the life I was meant to have. So I can see my son again."

"No," he whimpered. "I can't. I . . . I . . . ." He couldn't say it, even now.

She held out the demon's black sword, which no longer pinned Miyahara to the wall. The old demon hunter's body lay slumped in the corner.

"Kill me!" Masami's head shouted, her voice a shrill, sharp blade itself.

Akio took the katana, which felt like ice in his hands. The demon Masami knelt over the box, and with tears in his eyes, Akio brought the sword down.

Masami's head fell into the metal box and rolled to face upward. But her face was obscured now. Covering it was the demon's mask, the blood-red, full-faced *somen*, so expertly carved that the flames and clouds adorning it appeared to move. *Did* move. There was no question.

It looked at Akio, nothing behind the eyeholes but emptiness, the emptiness that contained him.

"Wear me, I am beautiful," said the mask.

"No." Akio shrunk away.

"Wear me," it repeated. "You are the killer now."

"No!"

"Wear me!"

It would not relent.

"You *are* me."

Akio Tsukino shot awake on his futon, his black hair wet with sweat. He rubbed his eyes, damp and red with real tears. Morning light came in sideways through the blinds, a soft, hazy glow. The thrum of cicada song bore into his skull, which ached like he'd been struck. The back of his neck hurt worse. He rubbed it and made slow circles with his head, stretching through the pain.

Damn these headaches. Damn these dreams.

A flash of red illuminated the window for a split second, and a sudden rain began to fall. A thunderclap followed seconds later. The cicadas quieted.

Red lightning. Hadn't Sensei Miyahara said something about that?

The downpour slowed to a stop as quickly as it began, and sunlight sparkled on the droplets that clung to the window. The cicadas resumed, and the nightmare swallowed Akio's thoughts.

This chapter and the story continue in *No Promises Large Enough*, available now from Mortimer & Ambrose.

Acknowledgments

My sincere thanks to everyone who helped make this book a reality. To my amazing wife, Julia, who helped immensely with every aspect of its creation: story, structure, inspiration, motivation, and all the dreaded adulting that comes with such an endeavor. To my dear brother Joe, who did equally as much in similar and different ways, always there to help me navigate the dark corridors and battle my own demons.

To all my early readers who provided invaluable insight, suggestions, and feedback that improved the story in myriad ways: Anne Evans Locarro, Bud Myrick, Jiyoon Shin, and Tomoe Suzuki, who was also my consultant for all things Japan, making sure I had correct cultural references and words, and appropriate character names. To my good friend Chungmo Kang who helped name the demon, the book within the book, and the Japanese title of *Headless*, and with whom I have enjoyed many conversations about Japan and life in general at our favorite izakaya (and others). To Kayo Yoshida whose dream inspired this story in the first place, and who also named the newspaper. To Raz Schiønning for his expert design and marketing help, and persistent enthusiasm about the book. To all my friends, co-workers, and students who have given me encouragement and support throughout.

And finally, to our sweet cat, Chihiro (lovingly called Chi-chan), who sat on my lap during much of the writing and revisions, checking my work, and sometimes just napping. She has gone off to play by the Rainbow Bridge. I miss her as I work on the sequel to *Headless*.

At your peril,
Tristram Lowe

About the Author

Tristram Lowe writes about monsters, and sometimes, scary things too. He is a student of the Japanese language and culture and a lifelong fantasy reader. He is also a competitive fencing coach, so it's likely a sword fight or two will show up in his books. Tristram has been crafting fantastical tales since the first grade, when he penciled a spooky story about a haunted house in his Big Chief tablet. Raised in the mountains of Colorado, he spent two or three lifetimes in Los Angeles, and now enjoys hikes through mossy trees and rainy board game nights in Oregon with his wife, their son, and their elderly cat.

Also by
TRISTRAM LOWE

NO PROMISES LARGE ENOUGH
The Ghost and the Mask, Book Two

After their world was turned upside down, two journalists race to uncover the supernatural force driving Japan's criminal underworld while coming to terms with their own emerging powers.

THE WRONG MONSTER
A children's picture book
with illustrations by Jiyoon Shin

A boy finds the courage to open his closet door and face the monster inside. What he finds isn't at all what he expected.

FIND MORE AT:

tristramlowe.com
Instagram: thetristramlowe
Twitter: @tristramlowe
facebook.com/tristramlowe

The Ghost and the Mask, Book Three
is in the works.

Keep informed by signing up to
The Lowe Letter
at tristramlowe.com
and **get a free e-book** about
the victims of the killer in *Headless*:
THE WIND ON THE BLADE
Connected short stories about the victims of the Kofu Head Collector
in the world of *The Ghost and the Mask.*